PRAISE FOR JENNA VORIS'S
EVERY TIME YOU HEAR THAT SONG

"A must-read for anyone who loves layered characters, true-to-life personalities, and country music!"
—Jason June, *New York Times* bestselling author

"If you've ever tried to make yourself smaller for a world that was never meant to contain you, this book will be a balm to your soul."
—Dahlia Adler, author of *Home Field Advantage*

"A powerful, moving anthem for anyone who's dared to dream big and grow new roots while discovering the meaning of home."
—Brian D. Kennedy, author of *A Little Bit Country* and *My Fair Brady*

"*Every Time You Hear That Song* is a love letter to the strong hold music has on all of us and the magic that comes with sharing it."
—Jenna Miller, author of *Out of Character*

"With the fast-paced storytelling and lyrical prose of the best country songs, this book made me a Decklee Cassel and Jenna Voris fan for life!"

—Kaitlyn Hill, author of *Love from Scratch* and *Not Here to Stay Friends*

★ "Discoveries of love, legacy, and self take center stage in this musical tapestry of a novel."

—*Kirkus Reviews*, **starred review**

★ "Voris teases out tension between a longing for privacy and a desire to live and love out loud in this messy, complicated search for community."

—*Publishers Weekly*, **starred review**

★ "Though readers can't hear it, 'Whiskey Red,' the fictional ballad at the novel's heart, hits all the right notes—longing, excitement, the anticipation of inevitable heartbreak—and this classic coming-of-age tale blending a puzzle mystery with country music and romance does, too."

—*Booklist*, **starred review**

Say a Little Prayer

JENNA VORIS

VIKING

VIKING

An imprint of Penguin Random House LLC
1745 Broadway, New York, New York 10019

First published in the United States of America by Viking,
an imprint of Penguin Random House LLC, 2025

Copyright © 2025 by Jenna Voris

Penguin Random House values and supports copyright. Copyright fuels creativity, encourages diverse voices, promotes free speech, and creates a vibrant culture. Thank you for buying an authorized edition of this book and for complying with copyright laws by not reproducing, scanning, or distributing any part of it in any form without permission. You are supporting writers and allowing Penguin Random House to continue to publish books for every reader. Please note that no part of this book may be used or reproduced in any manner for the purpose of training artificial intelligence technologies or systems.

Viking & colophon are registered trademarks of Penguin Random House LLC.
The Penguin colophon is a registered trademark of Penguin Books Limited.

Visit us online at PenguinRandomHouse.com.

Library of Congress Cataloging-in-Publication Data is available.

ISBN 9780593692745

1st Printing

Printed in the United States of America

LSCC

Edited by Maggie Rosenthal

Design by Lucia Baez | Text set in Birka LT Pro

This book is a work of fiction. Any references to historical events, real people, or real places are used fictitiously. Other names, characters, places, and events are products of the author's imagination, and any resemblance to actual events or places or persons, living or dead, is entirely coincidental.

The publisher does not have any control over and does not assume any responsibility for author or third-party websites or their content.

ALSO BY JENNA VORIS

Made of Stars
Every Time You Hear That Song

To anyone who's ever been hurt by
those who pretended to embrace you.
There are so many people who
will love you as you are.

Dear Reader,

The first time I heard someone say that being gay was a choice—and a bad one at that—was in church. I was twelve. Even back then, I remember thinking the whole thing was pretty ironic. After all, we'd just spent half an hour talking about how Jesus loves everyone, and here was a strange, one-off caveat thrown in at the end.

The original idea for *Say a Little Prayer* started as a one-sentence pitch—what if someone purposefully set out to commit all seven deadly sins at a Christian church camp? What kind of funny, subversive situations would those characters find themselves in if they openly treated their administration with the same derision I used to feel in secret? I ended up with seventeen-year-old Riley, a bisexual girl who's already made the choice to leave her congregation for good. She's angry at the church, resentful of everyone in town who maintains the status quo, and grappling with her growing feelings for her best friend, who is also the pastor's daughter. In short, she's mad and not afraid to let everyone know it. Her quest to commit the seven deadly sins isn't born of some selfless desire to unpack years of manipulative teachings but rather a need to enact revenge on the very people who cast her out.

However, just like in real life, things are hardly ever that simple. Even though Riley's relationship with religion has been fundamentally damaged, there are other characters who still find comfort in their faith and everything it's supposed to represent. I wanted to explore a wide variety of teenage experiences in the pages of this book, and I wanted them all connected by the same overarching truth—that each experience is valid and real.

It took me a long time to unlearn the hateful things I was taught growing up. Now I know that saying the Lord's Prayer won't "cure" anyone's gay thoughts. I know that some churches are safe and welcoming and kind, but that wasn't my experience, and it's not Riley's, either. Because of that, *Say a Little Prayer* includes elements of religious trauma and homophobia, but it also includes hope. My wish is for everyone who picks up this book to carry a little of that hope back into the world with them.

Happy reading!
Jenna

So when the woman saw that the tree was good for
food, and that it was a delight to the eyes,
and that the tree was to be desired to make
one wise, she took of its fruit and ate.
—Genesis 3:6

I

Everything That Happens Next Is Because of *Shrek the Musical*

I've been sent to Principal Rider's office exactly twice in my life—once last year, when he'd personally handed me a trophy for winning the state geography bowl, and again today, for slapping Amanda Clarke across the face.

I don't think there's a prize for this one, unfortunately.

Instead, I'm sitting empty-handed in front of his desk, Mom and Dad looming stiffly behind me as Mr. Rider surveys us over the tops of his steepled fingers. He's uncharacteristically quiet, but for once, I don't mind the scrutiny. I have absolutely nothing to hide.

Despite the cramped room and low ceiling, Mr. Rider has managed to stuff an impressive amount of decor into his windowless office. Over his shoulder, an oversized piece of Hobby Lobby wall art tells me to CHOOSE KINDNESS in bright red script. A wilting fern sits on top of a filing cabinet covered in children's finger paintings, and the bookshelf along the opposite wall looks dangerously close to collapsing. My gaze skims over a collection of dusty Civil War memoirs and three different copies of the Bible before stopping on a faded photo of Mr. Rider wearing an Ohio State football uniform.

That's not surprising now that I think about it. The Madison High School football players hardly ever get sent to the office, and when they do, Mr. Rider always lets them off with a warning. Maybe if he tries to give me detention, I can pretend to be their new kicker or something.

"Okay, you two." Mr. Rider's voice drags my attention back to the center of the room. He's still reclining in his chair, one ankle resting casually across the opposite knee as his gaze slides from me to Amanda. "Would either of you care to explain what happened?"

Before either of us can answer, Mrs. Clarke lets out a dismissive snort. "What *happened*?" she asks, both hands planted firmly on her hips. "That girl *slapped* my daughter. What else is there to talk about?"

It takes every ounce of my rapidly waning self-control not to point out that her daughter totally deserved it.

Mrs. Clarke was Miss Teen Ohio 1998. I know this because the first time I met her back in sixth grade, she'd introduced herself with the title, and also because the custom Chanel purse swinging from her arm now has MISS TEEN OHIO 1998 stitched across the front in gold letters. She and Amanda have the same blond hair and pale, heart-shaped faces, but I've always thought Mrs. Clarke's blue eyeshadow and glittery body spray make her look more like a poorly animated cartoon villain than a beauty queen.

I'm suddenly very grateful for my own parents, who, despite their unflinching ability to insert themselves into every aspect of my life, have never once monogrammed a decades-old accomplishment on a purse.

To his credit, Mr. Rider doesn't acknowledge Mrs. Clarke's outburst. He just tilts his head in Amanda's direction and asks, with surprising gentleness, "Is that true?"

Amanda's gaze drops to her lap. She's clutching a comically large ice pack to her cheek, but it doesn't fully hide the blush creeping up the side of her throat. *Good*, I think. She should feel bad. She should feel embarrassed at the thought of telling everyone what happened.

"I was just standing in the hall," Amanda says, eyes fixed stubbornly on the cuffed ends of her designer jeans. "We were all about to head into econ when Riley walked over and hit me."

Mrs. Clarke throws up her hands like *See?* and I whip around in my seat. "Really?" I snap. "That's what you're going with?"

Amanda's shoulders bob, a tiny, infuriating shrug. "It's what happened."

"No, it's not! Don't you want to tell everyone what you said? You seemed really proud of it before—"

"Enough!" Mr. Rider pushes himself to his feet, both hands braced flat against the desk. "I don't care what was said, Riley. Violence is never the answer. You know better."

Mom's hand closes over my shoulder, but I barely feel it over the anger burning its way up my throat. For a second, I wonder if she already knows exactly what Amanda said to make me snap. I wonder if she would have done the same thing.

Mrs. Clarke lifts her chin. "He's right, you know," she says. "You're lucky we aren't pressing charges."

"Okay." Dad holds up a hand. "They're seventeen, Mallory; let's take a breath. You're right—no matter what, Riley shouldn't have hit her. It was completely out of line, and we're sorry you had to come all the way down here because of it."

He nudges the back of my chair with a foot, and it takes me a second to realize he's waiting for me to apologize, too. Everyone is. Honestly, my only regret is not hitting Amanda harder, but I don't think I can leave this office until I say something acceptably remorseful. I close my eyes, think about the dress rehearsal I'm going to miss if this isn't resolved by the end of the day, and exhale through clenched teeth.

"I'm sorry, Amanda. I shouldn't have hit you. It was wrong, and I regret my actions."

The words burn on the way out, each more difficult than the last, but at least it sounds genuine. This is where three years of drama club and community theater pay off, I guess—acting my way through an apology I decidedly do not mean.

The CHOOSE KINDNESS sign over Mr. Rider's shoulder is starting to feel a little personal.

Amanda slides down in her seat, gaze still fixed on the graying carpet, but Mrs. Clarke shakes her head. "No," she says. "Not good enough. Where's the punishment? Where's the accountability? How is anyone supposed to feel safe with her wandering the halls?"

SAY A LITTLE PRAYER

"Funny," I mutter. "That's what everyone says about Amanda."

"Quiet, Riley." Mr. Rider shoots me a pointed glare before extending a placating hand in Mrs. Clarke's direction. "Believe me, we take allegations of physical violence very seriously here, and I assure you, this will be dealt with. But if it's all right, I'd like to get Amanda back to class. No need for her to miss any more instructional time while we handle the situation."

He stands, motioning for Amanda and Mrs. Clarke to follow him into the hall, and I realize too late that the "situation" he's referring to is me. My punishment. My consequences. The phrase "allegations of physical violence" sounds so much worse when he says it out loud, and my hands curl into fists as I run through the list of possibilities.

Surely I'm not getting expelled. Surely he wouldn't do that right before spring break, so close to the end of the year. We're opening a musical in two weeks. I have finals to study for and a driver's test to pass and summer jobs to apply for. I've never, in my three years at Madison High School, gotten so much as a warning, so *surely* I didn't mess up that badly.

But when Mr. Rider settles himself back into his creaky leather chair, gaze fixed on me across the expanse of his desk, I realize I have absolutely no idea what he would or wouldn't do. This is unfamiliar territory. He takes his time fiddling with the papers on his desk, letting the space between us tighten with each passing second. I wonder if it's supposed to be intimidating, if he's imagining himself as some grizzled FBI detective instead of a fortysomething high school principal with a receding hairline.

Eventually he looks up, clasped hands resting on his desk.

"I'm disappointed in you, Riley." He says my name like we're friends, like he's not about to dole out a punishment that could impact the rest of my high school career and probably my life. "You're smart. You're an excellent student, and you have more potential than half the kids who walk through my doors. I understand it's been a difficult semester for you, but this kind of behavior is unacceptable."

"It's been a great semester, thanks."

The words are out before I can stop them. Mom's fingernails dig into my collarbone in silent warning, but I ignore her. Mr. Rider can punish me for hitting Amanda, sure, but he doesn't get to pretend to know me.

"Fine," he concedes, flipping over a new form in the center of his desk. "Here's what we'll do, then. Since this is a first-time infraction and since you're such an active member of our community, I'm not going to expel you."

The relief is instant, a giddy, dizzying wave. "You're not?"

"No. I don't think it would be particularly helpful given the circumstances, but I also can't let you off with a warning. So I'm assigning you a week of in-school suspension instead. You'll sit back here, complete all your assignments, and perform office aide duties as needed. And, of course, you'll be banned from all school-sponsored sports and activities. We're out for spring break tomorrow, so the suspension would happen the week we get back. Sound good?"

SAY A LITTLE PRAYER

"The week—?" I shoot forward in my seat, a fresh bolt of panic searing through me. "No, Mr. Rider. The week after spring break is tech rehearsal for *Shrek*."

Mr. Rider pinches the bridge of his nose. "No offense, Riley, but I don't think the school musical should be your biggest concern right now. You started a fight in the middle of the school day. You're lucky Amanda wasn't seriously hurt, and you're lucky the Clarkes aren't pursuing legal action. I have sympathy for your situation, of course, but my hands are tied."

"That's not fair!"

I hear how I sound, how backward my priorities seem, but this can't be the solution. The Madison High School theater department has been my one constant all year, my haven in a sea of uncertainty. I don't hear the whispered rumors when I'm laughing my way through our preshow handshake rituals or slurping down Steak 'n Shake after tech. I don't see the raised eyebrows or pointed looks when I'm running lines in the rafters with Leena or Kev. Realistically, I know people like Amanda and Mrs. Clarke are talking about me no matter what, but when I'm onstage, sweating beneath the lights and the costumes and the pounds of makeup, I don't think I care.

We've been working on *Shrek* for months. I finally have my first lead role after two years of playing Townswoman Number Four, and I won't let Amanda's inability to face her own consequences derail it now.

"Taking me out of tech would hurt the entire department," I

7

blurt, searching wildly for an excuse Mr. Rider might buy. "The rest of the cast did nothing wrong. Please, we've been working on that show since November."

I meet his eye across the desk and try to channel my inner football player, anything to help me understand how they always seem to walk away from these confrontations unscathed. I try to remember how Amanda acted earlier, how she'd bowed her head and played the victim, but nothing helps. I've never gotten detention before. I've never even seen a tardy slip, but here we are.

Because Amanda Clarke couldn't keep her mouth shut for five seconds.

Mr. Rider shakes his head. "I'm sorry. I understand where you're coming from, but I already told you—I can't just give you a warning."

"You gave Jake Pullman a warning for smoking weed in the bathroom," I point out.

"That was a very different situation."

"Why? Because he had a playoff game that night?"

Behind me, Dad clears his throat. I barely register the sound, too focused on the way Mr. Rider's face is slowly turning the same crimson as his decorative wall art.

"Jake Pullman got a warning," he says, carefully, "because he signed up for a volunteer program instead. That was his choice."

"I'll do a volunteer program!"

I hate how desperate I sound, but it's true. If Mr. Rider looked me in the eye right now and told me to mow his lawn, or retake geometry, or run laps around the track in our school's moth-eaten

Corny the Corncob mascot uniform, I would.

I brace myself for another rejection, but to my surprise, Mr. Rider looks genuinely thoughtful. "You would?"

I nod vigorously. "Of course."

I'd do anything, really.

He hesitates a second longer before leaning over and tugging a blue pamphlet from the bottom drawer of his desk. I lean forward, hands deliberately tucked under my thighs. No matter what it is, no matter what program Mr. Rider is considering, I will act like it's the most wonderful opportunity in the world. Because it will be. But when he flips it over to reveal the words PLEASANT HILLS SPRING YOUTH CAMP stamped across the front, my resolve vanishes.

Because if a suspension during tech week is the absolute worst thing that could happen to me, then attending Pleasant Hills Baptist Church youth camp is a pretty close second.

"As you know, Pleasant Hills is a real cornerstone of our community," Mr. Rider says, seemingly oblivious to the way I'm sinking back in my seat. "The congregation has always worked closely with our student volunteers, and I know you're already familiar with their programming. Were you planning to attend camp next week?"

My chair creaks as I dig my nails into the soft leather. I feel Mom shift behind me, arms crossing over her chest, even as Dad remains uncomfortably still. "No," I say. "Wasn't planning on it."

I haven't been to church in over a year. Mr. Rider knows this, of course. Everyone in town knows it, because apparently the fact that I don't want to sit in a musty chapel and listen to Pastor Young talk about all the different ways I'm going to hell is the most interesting thing that's ever happened around here.

Mr. Rider's mouth turns down in the corners. "That's a shame. I can't tell you how to live your life, Riley, but I can offer you guidance. If you're serious about doing a volunteer program, I'll allow it. You could join the Pleasant Hills youth congregation next week, spend time reflecting on your actions, and when you return, write me an essay about what you've learned. Hand it in the Monday after spring break, and I'll consider your slate clean."

It says a lot about how much I hate Pleasant Hills that this is even a remotely difficult decision. It shouldn't be. I'd practically begged Mr. Rider for an alternative and here it is. He's handing me a way out, but I've never been good at letting things go. Mom says it's because I think too much. My sister, Hannah, says it's because I'm a Scorpio. Either way, I don't think I have much of a choice now.

"Why does it have to be camp?" I ask, arms crossed tightly over my chest. "Can't I, like, volunteer at the nursing home or something?"

I don't miss the way Mr. Rider's gaze flicks toward Mom and Dad. He must know they also haven't attended a service since Christmas, and I wonder if this is some weird ploy to save all of our collective souls. Maybe Pastor Young put him up to this.

"Shifts like that require more preparation, more paperwork." Mr. Rider slides the pamphlet toward me. "Long story short, I'm your principal, Riley. I want you to succeed. I want your time at Madison to be an exciting learning experience, both in and out of the classroom, and studies show that students are happier when they're involved in their communities. I can't make you go anywhere, but if you truly don't want a suspension, I think this would be a great opportunity for you."

He's watching me with a mixture of pity and wary concern, like he's afraid I'm going to burst into flames at the mere mention of the Lord. Maybe I will. Maybe I'll set myself on fire to prove a point.

I glance over my shoulder to where Mom and Dad are silently watching our exchange. Dad's expression is stubbornly neutral, but I can tell Mom is angry by the way her left eyebrow arches slightly higher than her right. It's a small comfort, but I take it. She might lecture me later tonight. She might ground me for the rest of the year, but right now, within the confines of this office, she is stubbornly and unshakably on my side.

"It's your choice," she says, and I know she means it.

In the end, it's not much of a choice at all. I can't lose this show. I can't disappoint my cast. I might feel messy and tangled and *wrong* most days, but onstage, I'm untouchable. And that's not something I'm willing to give away.

"Fine." I reach across the desk and slide the pamphlet toward me a fraction of an inch. "I'll go. I'll write your essay."

Mr. Rider's face splits into a wide grin. "Excellent! That's wonderful, Riley."

He turns to say something to Mom and Dad, but I'm no longer listening. I grab my backpack, and when I stand to leave, pamphlet crumpled between my fingers, I think it's almost a pity I don't believe in God anymore.

I think this would probably be a good time to pray.

My Lord and Savior Daddy Christ

"*I* can't believe they're sending me to *Kentucky*." I toss a wadded-up T-shirt in the vague direction of my overflowing suitcase. "It's not even a real state!"

Hannah catches the shirt in midair from where she sits on the corner of my unmade bed. "I don't think you're allowed to slander the Midwest when you live in Ohio," she says, smoothing the wrinkles from the fabric before tucking it next to my other clothes. "But I suppose you can always tell Mom and Dad you changed your mind."

"Absolutely not. Ms. Tina would kill me if she had to find another Donkey a week before tech."

"Right." The corner of Hannah's mouth lifts in an exasperated smile. "I forgot Donkey is the real star of *Shrek the Musical*."

"I don't know why you're saying that like it isn't true."

I turn back to my closet, trying not to think about how disappointed Ms. Tina had looked when I told her I wouldn't be able to make this weekend's rehearsal. Next week's hours are optional—just a casual get-together for anyone still in town over spring break—but I'm the drama club vice president. I'm one of the only students who actually wants to study theater when I graduate, and I'm supposed to be someone she can count on. I'm definitely *not* supposed to spend the week before tech rehearsal in rural Kentucky with no way to practice our new blocking, but that's not entirely my fault.

Personally, I blame Amanda Clarke and Madison High School's borderline-unconstitutional obsession with producing students with "good Christian values."

Across the room, Hannah holds up a well-worn T-shirt with the words LIVE, LAUGH, LOBOTOMY stamped over the front. "Was this a yes or a no?"

I sigh. "That's a maybe. Put it in the pile."

"There's a pile?"

There's supposed to be. I glare at the mountain of clothes. I've spent the last three years watching Hannah pack for this very camp, tucking dusty pink compression cubes into an equally pastel suitcase and zipping it shut without protest. She made it look easy, simple, but I must have torn through half my closet in the hour I've been home, and I still have no idea what to pack.

The Pleasant Hills camp pamphlet suggested bringing "hiking shoes, a Bible, and a spirit ready to receive the Lord," which was entirely unhelpful considering I currently have none of the above.

"It's fine," I say, nudging a pair of discarded gym shorts aside with my foot. "I probably won't need those, right? It's just a week. And Mr. Rider didn't say I had to turn in a *good* essay, so theoretically, I could write about how Amanda Clarke is a judgmental, hypocritical bitch who totally deserves to get slapped and call it a day."

Hannah shakes her head and tosses the lobotomy shirt onto the floor. When she straightens, arms folded across her chest, I already know exactly what she's going to say. She's only a year older than me, but thanks to Mom's love of matching overalls, most people thought we were twins until we started school. We have the same green eyes, thick eyebrows, and straight brown hair, but Hannah keeps hers long while I get annoyed if mine grows below my shoulders. The similarities end there, though. Hannah's like this living, breathing fairy princess who was born to float through life on a gossamer pastel cloud. She's taller than most of the senior class with long, graceful limbs toned by years of ballet, and she's kind in ways I can't begin to understand. I grew up hearing, "Oh, you're Hannah's little sister? How lucky!" so many times that I would have completely resented it if I didn't love her so much.

I would slap a thousand Amanda Clarkes for her without a single hesitation.

"I know," I say before she can speak. "I should have ignored her."

Hannah's jaw tenses. "Yes, you should have. I know Mom and Dad already gave you the lecture, but she's not worth it."

My fingers tighten around an empty hanger. Of course Mom and Dad had spent our car ride home lecturing me on everything from the importance of conflict resolution to the extent of their collective disappointment, but I still don't regret what I did. "She's horrible, Hannah," I say. "They all are. Amanda said—"

"I *know* what she said. It's the same thing everyone's been saying since Christmas."

"That doesn't make it okay!"

It's not hard to remember the sound of Amanda's voice this afternoon, lilting and snide and just quiet enough for Mr. Johnson standing nearby to remain blissfully unaware. I'd been cutting through the senior hallway on my way to Spanish when I passed her standing with Greer Wilson and Jorgia Rose, three identical copies of the same lacy tank top and Rare Beauty–sponsored skin-care routine.

"Hey, Riley," she said, throwing a too-wide smile in Greer's direction. "We missed Hannah in homeroom this morning. Where is she?"

Four months ago, it wouldn't have been a weird question. I would have answered without a second thought and kept walking because four months ago, Hannah would have been standing with them, too. She would have motioned me straight into their little group so we could all laugh at something Mr. Kahn said during the seniors-only assembly or plan our after-school boba run. I would have sat next to Greer in the back seat of Hannah's car on the way home with Amanda assembling the perfect playlist in the passenger seat, and absolutely nothing about it would have felt wrong.

A lot can change in four months.

This afternoon, for example, I'd just shrugged and said, "She's

SAY A LITTLE PRAYER

at home. Wasn't feeling well this morning," before continuing down the hall. But Amanda's freshly glossed lips had parted in an unconvincing display of faux concern.

"Oh? Did she get herself knocked up again?"

I'd been fully prepared to ignore her and keep fighting my way to class when Amanda turned to Jorgia Rose and whispered, loud enough for half the hallway to hear, "You know that's where she went over Christmas break, right? Her parents drove her all the way to Cleveland to get an *abortion*. That's why she stopped going to church with us, too. Pastor Young says all we can do is pray for her."

I don't remember turning around. All I know is that one second, my entire body flashed white hot as the anger coiled under my skin finally snapped, and the next, Amanda was stumbling into the lockers, hand pressed to her cheek, while Mr. Johnson charged down the hall to pull us apart.

Remnants of that heat still thrum through me as I sink onto the edge of my mattress. "I hate her," I say. "I know for a fact she used to hook up with Terron Parker after your pointe class. And Greer had sex with that Model UN guy last fall, remember? The one with the ferret? It would be one thing if they owned it, but they're going to spend next week acting like God's personal messengers when they don't even *try* to follow their own rules. I mean, they're all still friends with Collin."

Hannah flinches, and I immediately wish I could take it back. She doesn't need me to remind her that her ex-boyfriend had been welcomed back into the social fabric of Madison High

School without a second thought while she's still clawing her way through senior year.

"I know," she says. "I see them every day. I just don't care what they think."

"How?"

"You'd be surprised how many problems can be fixed by moving to California."

She knocks her shoulder against mine, and some of my frustration fades. The fact that Hannah hasn't asked me to drop out of school and come with her to Stanford next year is kind of insulting, especially since I keep having vivid, borderline-horny dreams about waking up in a town with a real sushi restaurant and a Trader Joe's. In my magical dream land, there's always reliable public transportation, a beach around every corner, and no sign of the HELL IS REAL billboard that haunts the Madison County highway exit. It's also blessedly free of Amanda Clarke, a perk that not even Pleasant Hills church camp can offer.

I groan and bury my face in my hands as the full weight of what I'm doing crashes over me. "I can't believe I'm spending spring break with them."

"I know." Hannah nods sagely. "Someone's going to *Parent Trap* your bunk for sure."

"Hannah!"

"I'm kidding! Once the counselors put you in groups, you'll barely see anyone else. Besides, you'll have Ben and Julia to protect you."

I decide not to mention the time Ben broke his foot leaping

off our back porch because he "thought there was a bee." He's probably the last person I'd call in a crisis, but the thought of spending next week with him and Julia is the only thing keeping me from throwing my suitcase out the window.

Ben and Julia Young have attended every Pleasant Hills retreat, youth camp, and mission trip since they've been able to walk, partially because their dad is the pastor and partially because I think the worship band would fall apart if Julia wasn't around to transpose their sheet music. They're two of my best friends in the world, and if I have to spend my spring break listening to Pastor Young proselytize about how God cured his friend's brother's uncle's depression or something, at least I won't be alone.

I stand and pick my way across the room as Hannah goes back to folding my clothes. When I yank open my curtains, I can see right across the narrow stretch of yard and straight into Julia's room next door. Most afternoons her own curtains are pulled tight, room quiet and dark as it waits for her to return from softball practice or student government or her latest volunteer project, but today her window is thrown wide. She's sitting at her desk, typing away at her laptop with a stack of textbooks perched precariously in the corner. I unlock my own window and cup my hands around my mouth.

"Jules!"

She looks up, face shifting from concentration to relief when she spots me. "Hey! Are you packed yet?"

"Not even close!"

I had texted her and Ben about my new spring break plans the second I got home, trying desperately to find some silver lining to my week of mandated holy reflection.

You signed up?? Julia had asked. For real? Blink twice if you're being held against your will.

I mean, it's definitely against my will, but it's happening, I texted back. It's the only way Mr. Rider will still let me do the musical.

Ben's reply had come a few minutes later, accompanied by a line of smiling devil face emoji. Don't be so modest, Riley. I think Daddy Christ is thrilled you're ready to welcome him back into your heart.

Personally, I think Daddy Christ has bigger things to worry about.

"Come over," I say, motioning Julia toward my room. "Help me pack."

Julia hesitates. "Aren't you grounded?"

"You're *grounded*?" Ben's head pops into view over Julia's shoulder, glasses sliding down the bridge of his nose. "I didn't think your parents knew how to do that."

Honestly, I didn't either. Before today, the most trouble I'd ever been in was last year when I ditched school and let one of the senior drama club kids drive me downtown for a protest march against gun violence. Even then, my lecture had basically boiled down to *If you're going to skip class for a cause you believe in, that's fine, but for the love of God, please tell us where you're going so we don't spend the afternoon thinking you're dead in a ditch.*

"Please?" I try again. "I have no idea what I'm doing."

Julia pretends to consider for a second longer before closing her laptop. "Hold on. We're coming."

SAY A LITTLE PRAYER

She snaps her curtains closed, and less than a minute later, I hear our doorbell ring. I open my bedroom door and promptly trip over three different pairs of sneakers on my way into the hall. I can't see much from up here, but if I lean over the banister, I can hear Mom's voice loud and clear as she opens the front door.

"You know Riley's grounded, right?"

"Hi, Mrs. Ackerman." Julia's voice is sugary sweet. I picture her and Ben standing shoulder to shoulder on the porch, flashing Mom their best Oscar-winning smiles. "Yeah, that's a bummer, but we're here to see Hannah, actually."

Mom hesitates, appropriately wary. "You're *both* here to see Hannah?"

"Yup!" Ben chimes in. "I don't even know who Riley is."

The silence stretches a few seconds longer before Mom seems to decide turning them away is more trouble than they're worth. She heaves a sigh, and the front door creaks as she tugs it the rest of the way open. "You have fifteen minutes."

Hannah slips off my bed as two pairs of footsteps pound up the stairs, leaving a pile of neatly folded socks in her place. "I'll let you three finish," she says. "Don't overpack."

She steps into the hallway right as Ben and Julia round the corner. Ben promptly trips over the rug, then catches himself on the banister just in time to avoid tumbling back down the stairs. "Hi, Hannah." He leans one elbow against the wall in what I think is supposed to be casual nonchalance. "You look nice."

Hannah considers him for exactly half a second before slipping under his outstretched arm. "Thanks, Ben."

21

I bite my lip as the three of us watch her retreat downstairs. "Wow," I say. "That was your worst performance yet, I think."

"You weren't there yesterday," Julia says. "He asked her if she liked food. No intro or anything."

Ben closes his eyes. "That's not what I meant. I was asking what *kind* of food she likes."

"Still a weird thing to ask someone you've known since the third grade, but okay." Julia nudges him into my room, then freezes as she takes in the mess. "Whoa. What's all this?"

I wince. Until now, I hadn't realized it looked this bad. Without Hannah's help, I have no idea what the different piles on my bed are for or where we left off. "It's not my fault," I say. "I've never packed for church camp before."

"Hannah has," Julia points out. "Multiple times."

"She doesn't count. Her suitcase is, like, two inches wide. I don't know how she does it."

"Well, she doesn't bring this many shoes, for starters." Julia reaches inside my suitcase and pulls out a lone sandal. "Why are you packing three pairs of Birkenstocks?"

I hesitate. "Options?"

Ben peers over my shoulder. "Why do you *own* three pairs of Birkenstocks?"

"I'm bisexual, Ben. It's basically a requirement."

He laughs and plops into my perpetually deflating beanbag chair as Julia starts rummaging through my suitcase. The two of them actually are twins, but it's hard to tell by looking at them. Ben's solid and tall, built like a linebacker, despite his distinct lack of athletic ability, and Julia is almost shorter than me. They both have their mother's auburn hair, but Julia's is smooth and wavy while Ben's tight curls add a few extra inches to his height. The first day we met, I told them they didn't look anything alike, and seven-year-old Julia had launched into a very thorough explanation of fraternal twins where she used the word "dizygotic" no less than five times. She's always been like that—precocious, talkative, smart. I think she'd make an excellent addition to our drama department if her parents sent her to Madison instead of the Christian prep school across town.

"You don't need five sweatshirts," Julia says, dumping an armful of clothes onto the bed. "It's not even supposed to be cold."

"It could be!" I cry. "We can't control the weather, Julia."

"We're not sleeping outside. You'll be fine."

I scowl as she drops another sweatshirt to the floor. I've never once felt like Julia judges me—not when I came out last year, not when I stopped going to church, not when Hannah told her and Ben about her abortion. It is, however, hard not to take her disregard for my graphic T-shirt collection personally.

"I just want to be prepared," I say. "The pamphlet says to 'expect anything.'"

Ben snorts. "The pamphlet also says we have a full working kitchen, and that's optimistic at best."

Oh. My stomach sinks. I hadn't even thought about food. Will there be enough? Should I bring snacks? Could I Uber Eats a veggie burger in a pinch? I glance around my room, taking in everything from the clothes dripping out of my dresser to the toiletries piled at the foot of the bed. My pulse hammers against my throat the way it always does when I feel underprepared, but I don't think it's the packing list I'm worried about. Not really. It's more the thought of returning to Pleasant Hills when everyone has already made it abundantly clear that my family doesn't belong.

It's the memory of Hannah going to church the week she got back from Cleveland and coming home in tears because someone told Pastor Young she went to get an abortion. He'd singled her out in front of the entire congregation, told her to repent right there in front of everyone, and he's spent the last several months leaving graphic pro-life brochures on our porch.

"Riley." Julia's hand lands on my arm, and I realize I've gone silent, glaring at my suitcase with a rejected sweater clutched in my fist. "It's fine," she says. "No one's going to, like, make you memorize the book of Psalms."

"Mostly because they made us memorize Psalms last year," Ben offers. "It'll probably be Corinthians this time."

Julia shoots him a glare. "Not helpful."

"What? It's true!" He sinks further into the beanbag, arms folded behind his head. "But she's right, Riley. We'll have sermons, of course, but most people go to camp because they like seeing their friends. It's chill. Except for capture the flag," he adds. "That gets *really* intense."

I hesitate. "How intense?"

"Last year, Mary Ann Thorton tripped and knocked out a tooth?"

I laugh. When I left Pleasant Hills, Mary Ann Thorton told everyone it was because I was "doing weed," then cried in the bathroom when I said that gossip wasn't very Christian.

"See?" Julia gives my arm another squeeze. "It's fun. Dad will get super preachy, of course, but no one's going to force you back to church."

She flashes me a quick, furtive grin, and I don't have the heart to say that I think her father would love nothing more than to permanently glue me to a pew. I never told him why I left. I didn't have a choice, really. I just remember sitting in church the week after I came out, listening to Pastor Young preach about the dangers of homosexuality, and realizing with a sudden, terrible clarity that he was talking about me. I told Mom and Dad when we got home, and that was it. They let me stay behind while they occasionally attended church with Hannah, and when Pastor Young turned on her, too, we started spending Sundays together, making brunch and watching bad Hallmark movies.

The crumpled camp pamphlet sitting on top of my suitcase proudly proclaims that "everyone has a place at Pleasant Hills." If I could, I'd add "as long as Pastor Young lets you stay."

I straighten and force myself to return Julia's grin. "I know," I say. "I can survive anything for a week."

"That's the spirit!"

Julia slings an arm around my neck, and I laugh as I stumble toward her across the floor. The three of us used to spend most afternoons sprawled in each other's rooms like this, but without the extracurricular church activities binding us together, it's become harder and harder to find the time. Now, however, Julia's face hovers inches from mine. I'm close enough to smell her signature vanilla perfume, and for a brief, wild second, I imagine her dabbing it across her collarbone in the early morning glow of her bedroom.

"Yeah." Ben stands, yanking my attention away from Julia's throat as he wraps us both in a crushing embrace. "And you'll have *me*, which is arguably more important."

"Okay, okay!" I pull out of their collective embrace. "I get it. Maybe it's not the end of the world."

Julia inclines her head toward my suitcase. "It might be if you pack those Crocs."

I groan and turn back to the closet. The thought of pulling into the Pleasant Hills parking lot on Sunday and boarding a bus to Kentucky still makes me want to suffocate myself in my pile of graphic T-shirts, but I don't think there's another way out of this.

Write about what you learn, Mr. Rider said when I'd left his office this afternoon. *This is a great opportunity for you, Riley, and I expect that essay on my desk first thing when you get back.*

I don't know what, exactly, he thinks I'll learn from a Midwest Baptist church, but I'll go if I have to. I'll spent time with Ben and Julia, make up a few teary stories about how God appeared to me through the trees, and spend the rest of the time praying for Amanda Clarke to fall on her face during capture the flag. I'll keep my head down, grin and bear it through Pastor Young's sermons, and leave knowing I have a community of people who

SAY A LITTLE PRAYER

actually care about me waiting back home, ready to put on a show.

And then, when I'm done, I'm going to put an entire year of AP lit classes to use and write Mr. Rider the best, most nuanced essay he's ever seen about how I will simply never be returning to the state of Kentucky.

It's Not Gossip If It's in a Prayer Request

*T*he thing about Pleasant Hills Baptist Church is that it has the worst parking lot in the state of Ohio. I don't think that can be scientifically proven, but it takes Mom a full ten minutes to find an empty spot amid the potholes when she and Dad drop me off on Sunday morning.

It's still dark when I climb out of the car, sky the same chalky gray as the asphalt under my feet, but the parking lot is already bustling. All around us, campers pull brightly colored sleeping bags from their trunks and hug their parents goodbye. A faded yellow school bus idles in the narrow alley alongside the church, and I can just make out the sharp outline of Pastor Young's profile as he talks to the driver up front.

Good, I think, turning to retrieve my backpack from the floor of the car. That means Ben and Julia are already here.

"Whoa." Dad groans as he helps me drag my suitcase from the trunk. "What on earth did you put in here?"

I glower down at the bag. "A spirit ready to receive the Lord. It was required."

"Well, your spirit is throwing out my back."

I let him pull me into a tight, one-armed hug as Mom tucks another breakfast bar into the front pocket of my backpack. I know they're both still disappointed in me, but I also know how easy it would have been for them to stick me in the Youngs' car this morning and call it a day. Instead, they're here, standing shoulder to shoulder in the Pleasant Hills parking lot for the first time in months, and when Mom gives me one last rib-crushing squeeze, I feel my throat tighten, just a bit.

"Have fun," she says, breath clouding in the cool early-April air. "And stay out of trouble."

I grin. "Always do."

Then I pull back, give them both one final wave, and join the crowd gathered in front of the church.

Pleasant Hills doesn't have a particularly large congregation, but what it lacks in numbers, it makes up for with a healthy dose of righteous outrage. The church itself is a plain two-story building set against a flat backdrop of Ohio cornfields. The marquee out front is blank today—probably because someone took a picture of the time it said YOU CAN'T ENTER HEAVEN UNLESS JESUS ENTERS YOU and now Pastor Young is afraid of accidentally implying that we should canonically fuck the Lord—and the top of the Madison County highway cross is just visible over the line of trees out back.

I remain on the outskirts of the crowd, trying not to draw attention to myself as I scan the parking lot for Julia. I recognize about half the kids milling around me now, including Amanda and Greer, but I'm surprised by how many are strangers. Madison is the only public high school in the county, but there are a few private academies nearby whose students also pop into Pleasant Hills from time to time. Some families even drive in from the surrounding towns specifically to attend service here, either because they don't have a home church or because they think Pastor Young is particularly fiery, so the youth group is always this weird collection of anyone who lives within a thirty-minute radius. There had never really been a difference between the Madison kids and everyone else, but now, standing between groups of people who all seem to know each other, I think the divide is clear.

Them on one side, me standing alone on the other.

When I finally spot Julia, she's talking animatedly with a group of girls by the bus. Her hair is piled in a messy bun on top of her head, and when she sees me, she throws her arms in the air and cries, "Good morning!" with so much enthusiasm that my sleep-addled brain momentarily short-circuits.

Julia's always been a morning person. I think it's genetic. I spent exactly one Thanksgiving with the Youngs back in sixth grade before realizing they're the kind of people who wake up at dawn to run half marathons, and I haven't been back since. Now it takes every ounce of my stage training to return Julia's grin without looking like I want to die.

"Good morning," I say. "Happy to be here for this completely normal call time."

Julia waves a hand. "It's not that bad. Come on. I want you to meet everyone."

SAY A LITTLE PRAYER

She tugs me across the lawn, weaving effortlessly through the crowd as the sky lightens overhead. It's been a year since we've walked the Pleasant Hills parking lot together, but I fall into step beside her, my feet hopping over the sidewalk cracks with familiar ease. I'd still rather be curled up in bed, but when Julia's fingers slide through mine, I feel myself steady. Sometimes I wish I knew how much I'd be giving up when I left this place. Last year, I saw Julia at least three times a week—at church, at youth group, and at Bible study. Now I'm lucky if we can sneak in a movie night or two between our equally packed schedules. We're still friends, of course. She still feels like my other half, but there's a strange distance between us now that we don't have this thing in common. A crack in our foundation that's never been there before.

Maybe that's part of why I agreed to come this week. Because even if I don't believe in church or camp or organized religion, I can still spend this time with her and Ben. I can still pretend nothing has changed.

"Over here." Julia releases my hand, gesturing toward where a tall Black girl stands on the other end of the sidewalk. "Riley, this is Delaney."

I haven't officially met Delaney Adebayo, but I know she's one of Julia's school friends. Another East Christian Academy girl, who still attends Pleasant Hills camps even though her family goes to another church across town.

"Hey." I stifle a yawn with the back of my hand. "Sorry, I think I'm still waking up."

Delaney nods knowingly. "It's way too early for this, isn't it?"

31

She rolls her eyes in Pastor Young's direction, an expression that's equal parts joke and condemnation, and I decide I like her. Despite the early hour, Delaney's wearing a dark-green Academy crewneck over a perfectly ironed collared shirt. Her black hair is braided tightly down her back, and there's even a hint of golden highlighter brushed across the tops of her cheeks. She looks more like the star of a CW show where the teenage cheerleaders also happen to be vampires, for some reason, than someone who's about to spend a week in the woods.

I've just glanced down at my own baggy jeans when Pastor Young's voice cuts through the hum of the crowd. "Can everyone circle up, please?"

The crowd in the parking lot has thinned; there's finally room for us to shuffle reluctantly into a circle as Pastor Young does a quick head count. He's wearing a faded gray T-shirt and a pair of acid-washed jeans, which I think is part of a very misguided attempt to appear Cool and Hip with the Teens. On Sundays, he always wears white—long flowing robes with a bright red stole hanging around his neck—and when I see him around the neighborhood during the week, he's strictly business casual. So this morning, he's clearly trying to curate a *vibe*.

"There we go," he says, spreading his hands to acknowledge the entire circle. "Thank you all for coming out so early and for dedicating your spring break to this week of spiritual growth. Whether it's your first time here or you've been a regular throughout your high school career, I'm thrilled to welcome everyone to this year's spring retreat. Why don't we join hands and say a quick prayer before we head out?"

There's a brief awkward moment where we all hesitantly reach for each other in the dark. Delaney takes one of my hands, her collection of rings pressing cold lines into my skin, and Julia grabs the other. I keep my gaze deliberately fixed on my shoes as Pastor Young leads us in a prayer for safe travel. It's mostly a lot of talk about "blessing the youth" and "opening our eyes to the glory of God's holy word," and after everyone has mumbled an appropriately humble *Amen*, he raises his voice to acknowledge the circle again.

"Are there any prayer requests before we hit the road? Anyone to keep in our thoughts this week?" Pastor Young's gaze slides from person to person before landing very pointedly on me. "Riley," he says, and every cell in my body turns to stone. "It's so good to have you back. Is there anyone in your life you'd like us to pray for?"

My hand instinctively tightens around Julia's. Pastor Young's gaze is curious as he watches me across the circle, almost kind, but I know better. I know exactly what he's implying, and the worst part is everyone else does, too. He's made sure of that. Heat creeps up the back of my neck, fingers trembling in silent rage, but Julia doesn't flinch. She just squeezes my hand and holds me steady as the pavement tips ever so slightly under my feet.

"No," I say.

Pastor Young lifts a brow. "Are you sure?"

I've just opened my mouth to tell him exactly where he can shove his prayer requests when Ben's hand flies into the air.

"I have one," he says, eyes darting nervously between me and his father. "I would personally like to pray that the ice cream shop in downtown Rhyville is open this year. I really miss their rocky road."

I don't get the reference, but the tension around the circle eases as a few people exhale breathy laughs. Even Pastor Young cracks a smile, attention turning toward Ben instead. Someone else throws out a new request, the conversation moves on, and still, I can't make myself move.

This, I think. This is why I don't want to come back. This is why Hannah will never set foot in Pleasant Hills again. Not just because Pastor Young wants her to repent for some made-up crime, but because he'd rather get his daily dose of hot gossip prayer requests than offer support to the people who need it.

"You okay?"

Julia's voice is soft in my ear, pulling my gaze away from the dirty patch of grass at my feet. I blink and realize the circle around us has dissolved, everyone crowding toward the bus in search of a good seat. We're the only two left on the sidewalk, and it takes me another second to realize she's still holding my hand. I release her immediately.

"Yeah," I mutter, shaking out my numb fingers. "Let's go."

The Pleasant Hills parking lot might be the worst place on earth, but Rhyville, Kentucky, is really giving it a run for its money.

According to Ben, the downtown area is "super cute once you get there," but I see nothing but gas stations, yellow-green fields,

SAY A LITTLE PRAYER

and billboards for six different adult films stores on the drive south. By the time we pull into the camp parking lot, my neck aches from leaning against the seat and there's a red indentation of the windowsill pressed into my cheek. I rub it away as I follow Julia down the aisle. We join the crowd of people outside, and when I finally find my suitcase, I have to concede that packing the extra shoes was a truly terrible idea. It takes most of my strength to haul my bag across the parking lot, gravel spraying beneath the wheels as I try to keep up with Ben and Julia.

Pleasant Hills doesn't actually own these campgrounds. I know that much from the brochure. Instead, they rent it a few times a year from some church in the area, but I wouldn't be able to tell at first glance. Everything from the parking lot to the winding paths to the peeling buildings has the signature Pastor Young touch, like some part of this camp is permanently stuck in 1995. It's warmer than it was back home, air thick with the slightest touch of humidity, and by the time the others come to a stop in front of what looks like a chapel, I'm covered in a thin layer of sweat.

"Cell phones! Drop your cell phones here!"

A counselor in a bright blue T-shirt stands in the middle of the path, shaking a wicker basket in our direction. She looks to be in her early twenties with a short brown bob, almost translucent skin, and an overly toothy grin that immediately makes me suspicious. My hand flies to my back pocket, where my phone is tucked securely next to the folded camp brochure.

"They take our phones?" I hiss.

35

Ben nods. "Don't worry—we get them back during the free day. And if there's an emergency, you can always ask my dad for the camp phone."

I would literally rather die than ask Pastor Young for anything. "What if my emergency is being here?"

"Then we're all going down together." Ben drops his phone into the basket and flashes the counselor a quick grin. "Hi, Cindy. Glad to see you're back."

"Benji!" She reaches up to ruffle his hair. "Don't you look dashing!"

I choke back a laugh. Ben looks, as always, like someone who grew up watching a little too much Disney Channel. He's never met a layer he doesn't like, patterns are always in, and there's a very high chance at least half his clothes are thrifted. He's tried to explain the difference between vintage brands to me multiple times, but there's a reason he's the one attending some fancy art camp this summer and I'm the girl who was politely asked to leave a scenery workshop when Ms. Tina saw me hold a paintbrush. There are some things the human brain isn't meant to comprehend.

Cindy's gaze slides to me and most of her softness fades. She shoves the basket under my nose. "Cell phone," she repeats.

I hesitate. Before I left, I made Leena and Kev promise to send me a thorough recap of every missed rehearsal note. It's not the same as being there in person, but I figured I'd at least be able to review any new videos. Without my phone, there's nothing tying me to the outside world. I glance over my shoulder, momentarily considering making a run for it, but something about the way Cindy's watching me makes me think she isn't above hunting me down. She gives the basket another pointed shake, and I sigh before dropping my phone inside.

"See?" Ben says as we continue down the path. "That wasn't so bad."

I glare at his retreating back. "Sure, *Benji*. Whatever you say."

We continue past the chapel and hike through a sparse stretch of trees, following the gravel path until it opens into a wide field of freshly mowed grass. Twelve cabins sit in a perfect semicircle on the far edge of the field, six on one side, six on the other. I swat through a cloud of gnats as we approach, already out of breath from tugging my suitcase through the parking lot. Ben turns left, toward what I assume are the boys' cabins, but I keep following Julia. Delaney is a few paces ahead of us, deep in conversation with a girl I recognize from school. She's a sophomore, I think, a volleyball player named Robin, but everyone calls her Torres on account of how there are somehow three different girls named Robin on the team. One of them even spells it with a *y*.

"We're still going to the lake after dinner, right?" Delaney asks, glancing back at Julia.

"I'm in," Torres says. "Do you think your bra is still under the pier?"

"You tell me! You're the one who put it there!"

Something in my chest contracts as I watch the three of them dissolve into giggles. Even when I attended church regularly, I never felt bad about skipping camp. I always had rehearsal, or

37

a preplanned family vacation, or an overwhelming desire to *not* be one with nature, but there's a strange ache settling under my ribs now. Not for Pleasant Hills itself, but for the bond everyone already seems to share. These girls have attended camp together twice a year since ninth grade. Most of the other attendees have, too. It makes me realize that no matter how close Julia and I are, there will always be a part of her I don't quite understand.

I wonder if she feels the same way about me, if she thinks about Hannah's choices or my queerness with this same careful distance. I wonder if she'd tell me if she did.

"We're in here, Riley."

I glance up to find Julia waving me toward one of the cabins. I shake away my lingering unease and drag my suitcase onto the porch. The first thing I notice is that it's remarkably cooler inside. Brightly colored curtains are pulled tight over the windows, keeping most of the light at bay, and uneven floorboards creak under my feet as I turn to take in my home for the week. It's not much, just three sets of bunk beds lining the walls, a fan creaking steadily overhead, and a narrow hallway leading toward what I assume is the bathroom. Delaney and Torres have already claimed the bed near the window, and Julia turns in a circle before tilting her head in my direction.

"Top or bottom?" she asks.

"That's a personal question, actually."

She lifts an eyebrow, and it takes a minute for me to remember we're not alone. I'm probably not allowed to joke like that here, and she's probably not allowed to think it's funny. I bite my lip,

SAY A LITTLE PRAYER

but before I can apologize, Delaney lets out a choked laugh.

"Nice," she says. "Riley, right?"

I nod, and Torres's face lights with recognition. "Oh yeah!" she says. "I thought I recognized you. I know your sister." Something must shift in my expression because she immediately adds, "She's in my precalc class. It's mostly seniors, and she was the only one who bothered to learn my name."

The tension releases with a rubber band snap. I exhale, grin tugging unbidden at the corner of my mouth. "Yeah, that sounds like her. Nice to meet you." I glance over my shoulder toward the bunk Julia pointed out and add, "I'll take the bottom. Don't know if I trust the infrastructure in this place."

I slide my suitcase under the bed, doing my best to maximize what little floor space we have. Torres is just in the middle of throwing open the curtains for light when the screen door bangs open again and a gratingly familiar voice chirps, "Good morning!"

I freeze. Usually, when two students at Madison get into a fight, the administration does everything they can to keep them apart. According to the handbook, it's to make sure everyone "feels as comfortable as possible" and "can still engage in a healthy learning environment without fear of retaliation." It doesn't apply to everyone, of course. When Joseph Bates assaulted his girlfriend at last year's homecoming game, Mr. Rider was just like "boys will be boys" until she transferred schools, but I still can't believe he let me attend the same camp as Amanda Clarke. I also can't believe she's standing in the doorway to our cabin now, shoulder to shoulder with Greer Wilson.

39

JENNA VORIS

The others exchange a brief, bewildered look before Julia turns to face them. "Good morning," she says, voice surprisingly pleasant for someone who's listened to every aspect of my *How to Dethrone Amanda Clarke and Possibly Frame Her for Murder* revenge plan. "Can we help you with something?"

Amanda's smile is a shade too bright to be genuine. "Yes, actually. Brooke's cousin is here this year, and Nicole wants to room with her sister."

"That means the numbers are off in cabin two," Greer interjects, like we're all not fully capable of doing basic math. "We need to take those bunks."

They're halfway across the cabin before I fully process the development. Last time I'd seen Amanda, she'd been slouched in Mr. Rider's office, a timid contrast to my own raw nerves. Now she turns the full force of that infuriatingly genial expression in my direction.

"Hey, Riley," she says. "I didn't know you were coming."

I barely resist the urge to roll my eyes. Bold of her to pretend we're cool when she's the only reason I'm here in the first place. "I didn't know I needed to ask your permission."

"Of course you don't. I'm just surprised. I think we were all under the impression you wanted nothing to do with this place."

"Yes, well, the Lord works in mysterious ways."

The silence that follows lasts a beat too long. I've known Amanda for years. She and Hannah have danced together as long as I can remember, and nowhere in that time have I ever seen her angry. Greer's the one with bite, always ready with a sharp retort

40

or cutting glare, but Amanda is famously above it all. Madison High School's resident ice queen. Even last week, when I slapped her in the middle of the senior hallway, all she'd done was flush a delicate shade of pink and sit demurely in Mr. Rider's office. She didn't cry out. She didn't hit me back. But looking at her now, with her pale green eyes ever so slightly narrowed, I think she might want to.

Then she blinks, expression softening into cool nonchalance. "Yes," she says, voice just loud enough for the two of us to hear. "He sure does."

She brushes past me without another word. When I look up, Delaney and Torres are watching me, wide-eyed and open-mouthed. Of course they are. Amanda's probably been nothing but kind to them. They probably *like* her, and here I am, glaring across our very small, very intimate cabin with open disdain. I exhale through my teeth and turn back to my suitcase.

The six of us unpack in strained, awkward silence, Amanda and Greer occasionally stopping to whisper to each other in the corner. I can't make out exactly what they're saying, but every sentence is punctuated by a pointed glance in my direction, which means either they're the worst gossipers of all time or they want everyone to know they're talking about me. Right as it's starting to hit me that I really am trapped here, two hours from home with no way to call for help, a loud chime sounds from outside.

"Orientation," Julia says before I can ask. She tosses the rest of her things onto her neatly made bunk. "We're supposed to meet in the chapel for opening sermon and schedules."

Sermon. Right. In the chaos of this morning, I'd almost forgotten about the "church" part of this week's camp. Amanda and Greer are out the door before the last chime finishes echoing across the field, Torres and Delaney trailing close behind. Cabin doors bang open on either side of us, excited chatter filling the air, and again, I feel that dark twist in my gut.

Pastor Young is going to give a speech about how Satan invented gay sex or something, and we'll all be expected to listen. I'm expected to learn something impactful enough to write in an essay when all I want to do is take a match to this entire congregation.

"You coming?"

Julia has one hand braced against the doorframe, head casually tipped to one side. Sunlight dapples across her feet, painting her hair with fiery strands of gold, and for a second, a word echoes through the back of my mind. It's tentative and soft, almost dusty from disuse.

Holy.

I shake the thought away and flash her a grin. "Of course. Wouldn't want to keep Daddy Christ waiting."

IV

Through Christ, All Sins Are Possible

The camp chapel has exactly one door, zero windows, and no less than two dozen homemade crosses hanging from the walls.

It was clearly a basketball gym in another life, and the evidence still lingers in the high vaulted ceilings and exposed rafters. The hoops are gone, and someone has covered the hardwood in a weird beige carpet that looks a little too much like human skin, but the bleachers remain, pushed haphazardly against the far wall like some half-finished construction site. Staggered rows face the stage in the center of the room where a few kids already sit, plucking away at instruments as the rest of us file inside. Above it all, an enormous projector hangs from the ceiling, flipping through a series of poorly designed informational slides. One reads JESUS TAKE THE WI-FI: NO PHONES ALLOWED. The next is just a picture of Pastor Young's face.

"Do you know the theme this year, Jules?" Delaney asks as the four of us file into the bleachers.

Julia shakes her head. "Dad doesn't usually tell us. The only reason we knew last year was because he left his laptop open in the kitchen."

"There's a theme?" I ask.

"Oh, there's *always* a theme," Delaney says. "Last year was Fearless Faith, which was just a lot of monologuing about how you should be able to say whatever you want in the name of the Lord."

Torres nods, taking the bleacher steps two at a time. "Right. And the year before that was Rooted in Grace. I must have planted, like, fifty prayer tomatoes."

I hesitate. "And a prayer tomato is . . ."

"Oh, it's basically a regular tomato, but you have to pray for someone each time you plant one. It's a whole thing."

Right. Why didn't I think of that?

The bleachers fill up one row at a time, the band underscoring the entire process with a collection of soft, vaguely out-of-tune guitar chords. I couldn't get a good head count on the bus, but there are probably around fifty of us total, ranging from hesitant clusters of first-time campers to the rowdy group of senior boys in the front row. *This used to be me*, I think as the voices swell around us. I used to be happy at Pleasant Hills, too.

"Welcome, welcome!"

I look up to find Cindy, the counselor who'd kidnapped my phone earlier, standing at the end of our row. As I watch, she starts passing stacks of identical notebooks from camper to camper. "These are your schedules, lesson plans, and prayer books," she says. "Make sure to keep them on you at all times and write your name in the front so you don't forget."

Her face is still frozen in that same too-wide grin, but she manages to slide me a pointed look, like she can already tell I'm planning to "forget" mine in the woods later. I take both notebooks before heaving the stack into Julia's lap. They're heavier than I expected, the first one practically the size of the unopened SAT workbook on my desk back home. The next is a small blue notebook the size of my palm. The phrase TODAY I'M PRAYING FOR is printed across the top of each blank page, and when I spot the cartoon doves sketched in every other corner, I can't entirely suppress my groan.

Julia glances up from her own notebook, her brow furrowed in gentle concern. "You okay?"

I straighten, just now realizing how far I've slid down in my seat, and flash what I hope is a casual grin. "Of course. Just tired."

I can hear the lie lifting the end of each word into a question, but I don't care. It feels wrong to complain about the lessons of Christ when we're being watched by a dozen different versions of crucified Jesus. Especially since I shouldn't even be *thinking* about complaining in the first place. I shouldn't want to. The only thing I should be doing is keeping my mouth shut and my head down, focusing on writing my essay, and making it through this week in time for tech rehearsal.

Julia's still watching me, lips parted like she wants to ask a follow-up question, but I purposefully flip open my workbook instead. The words LIVING WITH VIRTUE glare up at me from the cover page, and I lift it higher, angling it so the others can't see my face. The inside looks exactly like the algebra workbook Mr. Johnson gave us on the first day of class, but instead of math equations and homework problems, this one appears to have one goal: curing the world—and our apparently very susceptible teenage hearts—of sin with the seven heavenly virtues.

Diligence, charity, temperance, patience, chastity, gratitude, humility.

Each virtue gets its own chapter, complete with sermons, suggested group activities, and prayer templates, all designed to counteract the seven deadly sins—sloth, greed, gluttony, wrath, lust, jealousy, pride. The words STAMP OUT THE DISEASE OF SIN, LIVE VIRTUOUSLY IN THE IMAGE OF THE LORD are printed across the bottom of every page, right next to a strangely graphic cartoon of someone being set on fire.

I close my eyes and slide back down in my seat. This is going to be a very long week.

I'm just debating whether I can excuse myself to the bathroom and never return when the overhead lights dim. The bleachers creak as everyone shoots to their feet and I instinctively follow, tossing my notebooks behind me as the band starts playing their way through a few poorly rehearsed worship songs. I'm nodding my way through the second verse, trying very hard to pretend I don't still remember every word, when Julia grabs my arm.

"Look," she whispers. "Is that Amanda?"

I follow her gaze toward the back of the chapel and sure

SAY A LITTLE PRAYER

enough, there's God's perfect angel sneaking in the side door. No one seems to notice her in the dark, but I watch as she carefully slides into the pew next to Greer. *Interesting*. I don't think Amanda's ever been late for anything in her life. She and Greer had been the first ones to leave our cabin, yet here she is, slipping back into the chapel alone. Maybe she's not as perfect as she wants everyone to believe.

I make a mental note to write this down later.

> Things Riley has learned at church camp:
> 1. Amanda Clarke still gets to do whatever she wants.
> 2. Everyone else still lets her get away with it.
> 3. People who are this moved by worship music clearly didn't drive four hours to see the Eras Tour last year. Talk about a spiritual experience.

Eventually, the song comes to a crashing end, and the band files back into the bleachers. There's a minute of awkward silence where we all sink back into our seats before Pastor Young jogs onto the stage. He's still wearing his casual outfit, wireless mic clutched in one hand, and he waves to the crowd as a single spotlight illuminates his path.

"Good afternoon, campers!" he calls into the mic. "How's everyone doing?" Most of us clap, but he waves a hand as if that completely normal reaction isn't good enough. "Oh, come on. You can do better than that. I said, *how's everyone doing?*"

This time, the answering cheer echoes off the rafters. "That's more like it," he says. "It's such a joy to see all of you gathered here, ready to embark on another incredible journey at Camp Pleasant Hills. We have a ton of fun surprises in store for you this week, but as always, I'm most excited for you to use this opportunity to accept Jesus into your hearts."

I shudder. The thing about attending church as long as I have is that you get intimately familiar with the process of being Saved. During the first week of seventh grade, I'd sat in the dark, windowless Pleasant Hills basement with half a dozen other girls and cried when Pastor Young told us we were going to hell unless we all believed, with absolute certainty, that Jesus had died for our sins. That day, I sent up half a dozen increasingly anxious prayers to whoever might be listening, confirming that *yes*, I *did* think Jesus was our one true savior and *yes*, of *course* I'd show my devotion to the church through weekly offerings as soon as I was able. I whispered the same prayer to myself that night and again every few weeks after that, just to be sure. Pastor Young had made it sound so final, like eternal damnation was the default and he was the only thing keeping us tethered to the light. I believed him. We all did, and even though it's been over a year since I prayed about anything, I still feel the low pangs of guilt as everyone around me bows their heads.

Pastor Young points back at the screen as it flicks to another slide that reads LIVING VIRTUOUSLY.

"I don't know about you," he says, "but I've spent the last few years thinking about plagues and pandemics and all the terrible, deadly diseases that exist in our world. It's strange, right?" He locks eyes with the first row of bleachers and the group of senior boys finally quiets. "That our entire society can shut down because of something that small? That it can change lives and alter history? Stranger still that the real disease eating away at us today, the deadly hidden virus that the Bible warns us about, doesn't appear to be a concern for our lawmakers."

"Let me guess," I say to no one in particular. "It's the virus of sin."

"I'm talking, of course, about the virus of sin," Pastor Young continues solemnly.

Julia snorts into her hand. I make the mistake of glancing at her out of the corner of my eye, and the two of us descend into silent giggles as the image on-screen changes to a very dejected-looking cartoon Eve holding an apple in the middle of a garden. The fact that she has to wear a full leaf turtleneck while Adam stands bare chested next to her only makes us laugh harder.

"Sin, much like a virus, infects our hearts and minds," Pastor Young continues, oblivious to our inability to keep it together. "It also starts small, so insignificant you might not think to care, but if left untreated, it spreads into our spiritual immune system, weakening us and distancing us from God's love."

He launches into a theatrical synopsis of the seven deadly sins, the same ones laid out in our camp workbooks. The week's theme couldn't be clearer, even if Pastor Young's analogy is problematic in more ways than I can count. I flip open my workbook and run a finger down the list of sins printed in the table of contents. *Sloth, greed, gluttony, wrath, lust, jealousy, pride.* When Pastor Young turns to pace the opposite side of the stage, microphone in hand like some kind of radio DJ, I lean over to Julia and whisper, "Is this what it's like all week? Just a bunch of reasons why we're going to hell?"

She keeps her eyes locked up front even as the corner of her mouth curls up. "Of course. Why else would we come all the way out here?"

"Damn." I sigh. "Figures." Then I straighten. "Oh, shit. Am I allowed to say that?"

"No. You're going to hell, remember?"

Something about her perfect posture and completely straight face cracks my composure. I let out a choked laugh, then freeze, hand flying up to cover my mouth, but it's too late. Pastor Young stops midsentence. He raises a hand to shield his eyes from the spotlight, and despite the sea of faces between us, his gaze still lands on me.

"Riley." His voice echoes through the gym, somehow louder than it had been before. "Is there something you feel called to share with the group?"

Every head turns in my direction, faces backlit in the harsh glare of the spotlight. *So much for keeping your head down.* I force a grin, cheeks burning from the sudden attention. "Nope."

"Are you sure? Seems like you two have a lot to say."

SAY A LITTLE PRAYER

His gaze lands on Julia next, and I feel her shoulders stiffen as she slides down in her seat.

"It just feels a little extreme, right?" I blurt, suddenly desperate to pull his focus back to me. "Some of those sins seem kind of unavoidable. Like pride. It's listed as a sin, but isn't that a good thing? Aren't you supposed to be proud of who you are?"

The focus is back on me, all right. Throughout the chapel, people shift uncomfortably in their seats, whispering to each other behind cupped hands. I catch a brief flash of Amanda in the front row, eyebrows lifted as she shares a knowing glance with Greer, but Pastor Young's face is a portrait of grave concern. A disappointment so deep it momentarily pins me to the bleachers.

"Giving in to sin is never unavoidable," he says. "The road to faith is not without challenges, of course, but the strength to resist earthly temptation is a direct result of our Heavenly Father's grace and protection. It doesn't matter if it's accidental. If someone were to commit one of those seven deadly sins, for example, without accepting the Lord's virtues, they'd be doomed to a life of misery on earth and eternal suffering in the afterlife. There's no such thing as a *good* sin."

And just like that, the whispers around me vanish, like they've been sucked out of the room along with the air. I don't like how the other campers are looking at each other. I don't like the way Torres grips the edge of her seat, like she thinks we're all about to spontaneously combust, but the longer I sit with the weight of Pastor Young's stare, the more I think we just might. Maybe it's the windowless room. Maybe it's the dim lighting or the crosses or his general conviction, but I almost believe him again. I'm almost afraid.

For a second, I wonder if this is how Hannah felt the moment before he kicked her out of church. A strange, disconnected sense of unease as an entire room of people averted their eyes and pretended she didn't exist.

I force a tight smile past my aching jaw. "Cool," I say. "Good to know."

Pastor Young switches his microphone to his other hand, but I don't relax until he turns away, striding toward the other side of the stage to continue his monologue. Only then do Julia and I finally exhale.

"Told you," she mutters, bracing her elbows against her knees. "It's always hell."

But I can't bring myself to respond. Instead, I glare down at my camp workbook, and the list of virtues seems to glare back, taunting me in stark black and white.

Diligence, charity, temperance, patience, chastity, gratitude, humility.

This is what Pastor Young wants me to learn. This is what I'm supposed to write about, but the only thing I've learned so far is how smart I'd been to leave Pleasant Hills when I did. Hannah isn't the first person Pastor Young drove out. I don't think she'll be the last either, and looking around the chapel now, I think this is how it starts. This is how he creates congregations who are willing to sit back and watch a girl get tossed onto the street without batting an eye. Because they're all too afraid of accidentally committing some hypothetical, irredeemable sin to notice the ones happening in front of them.

There's no such thing as a good sin.

But how does he know that? Did God descend from the heavens and tell him the only way to be truly holy is to shame teenage girls into repenting their imaginary sins? Why does Pastor Young get to decide who's worthy—and why, in the entire time I'd attended church, did no one think to question his authority?

My fingers curl around the edge of the page, crinkling the paper and the list of sins printed at the top. *Sloth, greed, gluttony, wrath, lust, jealousy, pride.*

Seven virtues. Seven sins. Seven days at camp.

Oh.

Last week, I'd accidentally touched a live wire in science class, just grabbed it in my fist when I meant to pick up a battery instead. The shock lingered under my skin long after I pulled my hand away, and that's how I feel now as an idea shoots its way down my spine.

Mr. Rider is expecting an essay on his desk next Monday, a clear, concise write-up of everything I learned at camp. He wants something humble. He wants an apologetic, reflective take on my past actions, and until right now, that's what I intended to give him. But what if I learned something else? What if there was a way to prove Pastor Young isn't as powerful as everyone believes him to be?

If I could find a way to commit each of these supposedly

"deadly" sins, spin them into something positive and useful, it would completely negate his entire sermon. This week's theme would cease to exist, and everyone sitting in this chapel would realize what I've known for a year now—nothing Pastor Young says is true. He's not our salvation, he's not the light holding the darkness at bay, and he's definitely not the definitive voice of moral purity. In fact, he's usually wrong.

And if he's wrong about this, I think, watching him move from one side of the stage to the other, *I could prove he's wrong about everything else, too.*

Like how he runs his congregation. Like how he treated Hannah.

I wouldn't even have to stop at Mr. Rider. I could send my findings to the entire congregation, just file my name off the top and let everyone draw their own conclusions. I could slip it to the local paper, post it on every social media platform, or plaster Main Street with copies until it became impossible to ignore. People would notice. People would complain, and the message at the core of every grievance would be the same—we're better off without him.

Onstage, Pastor Young tips his face toward the ceiling. "Let us pray."

The bleachers groan as everyone bows their heads, but I keep my gaze fixed on the open workbook in my lap.

"Dear Heavenly Father, thank you for bringing us together in this beautiful place, surrounded by your creation. As we embark on our journey this week, we ask for your guidance, your wisdom, and your presence to be with us. May we return from this retreat with a renewed sense of purpose and faith. In your name we pray. Amen."

I grin down at the list of sins in my lap and bite back a vicious grin. "Amen."

That night, I settle onto my lumpy mattress and fish a pen from the bottom of my backpack. I hadn't thought to bring a notebook to camp, so I flip open my prayer journal instead, hastily scrawl my name across the front, then write the date at the top of the first page. I leave the "I'm praying for . . ." prompt blank for now, since the only thing I'm actively manifesting is Pastor Young's downfall, and start writing down everything I remember—the opening sermon, Pastor Young's condemnation of sin, the nervous hesitation of the people around me.

It's not much, but by the time Cindy comes around for lights-out, I feel settled. More in control. I tuck the notebook under my mattress and try to punch my pillow into a more comfortable shape.

"Don't bother," Julia mumbles from above me. "That only makes it worse."

She is, unfortunately, correct. The pillow seems to harden under my fists until I finally give up and flop onto my back. Across the room, I watch Torres lean forward to peel back the edge of the curtain.

"She's gone!" she whispers.

Delaney heaves a sigh. "Finally."

The floorboards creak as she slides out of bed, and I sit up, watching her double-check the window before reaching under her mattress. "What's going on?"

"Just a little opening night tradition. It's always a toss-up if one of the other churches will find it or not, but—there!"

When Delaney straightens, she's holding a dented *Footloose* DVD in one hand. It's not until she drags an ancient-looking TV from the closet and dumps it in the center of the floor that I realize what's happening.

"Pastor Young accidentally ordered it for the rec room a few years ago," she explains, reaching over to plug the TV into the only available outlet. "And then he immediately tried to throw it away after figuring out the plot."

Torres snorts into her pillow. "That's why we don't have movie nights anymore."

"It's tragic." Delaney sighs. "Anyway, Julia dug it out of the trash, and now it lives under that mattress. It's old, so the quality isn't great, but we always watch it the first night."

I lean forward as she inserts the DVD, staticky glow illuminating the dusty lines of the cabin. When the grainy opening image fades into view, Delaney flashes us a thumbs-up and starts climbing back into bed.

"Wait." Greer sits up. "You do this *every* year? After lights-out?"

SAY A LITTLE PRAYER

Delaney's eyes narrow. "Yeah."

"How come no one ever talks about it?"

"Because it's a secret, Greer. What happens after lights-out stays in the cabin. If you have a problem with that, you're more than welcome to sleep in the woods."

"Oh my god, chill." Greer's nose wrinkles in disgust. "I was just asking."

She settles back against her pillow, arms still crossed in silent protest, but I can see her watching the screen from across the room. I half expect Amanda to chime in, to point out all the different ways this is against the rules, but she doesn't move either. Instead, she remains facing the opposite wall, so I can't quite tell if she's awake. I flip onto my side right as Julia's mattress creaks overhead.

"Hey," she whispers, leaning down to peer at me through the dark. Her hair tumbles around her face, still frizzy from today's humidity. I bite back a grin.

"Hey."

"I'm really glad you're here. Have I told you that?"

"Yes, many times."

"Shh!"

Delaney tosses a pillow in our direction. Her aim is terrible; it falls harmlessly to the floor, but our bedframe still shudders as Julia topples back into bed. I let out a muffled snort, immediately smothering it with a hand when Delaney rounds on me with a fresh pillow held aloft.

Music swells faintly from the TV. As the first lines of dialogue

57

work their way through the speakers, Julia's hand drops back over the side of the bunk. "Goodnight," she whispers.

I reach up without thinking, weaving my fingers through hers. "Goodnight."

And when she squeezes my hand, purposeful and quick, I don't want to let go.

V

God Gives His Toughest Battles (Surviving Church Camp) to His Gayest Soldiers (Me)

I wake to the piercing wail of police sirens rattling the springs of my mattress.

My heart slams against my rib cage as I scramble up in bed, feet tangled in the sheets, and for a terrifying second, I can't remember where I am or what I'm doing here. I almost think the sirens are real, that someone knows I've just been wrenched from a very vivid dream about running Pastor Young over with the camp bus and they're coming to take me away.

"Not again!"

Torres's bunk creaks as she rolls over, one arm flung across her face. Below her, Delaney groans and buries her head under her pillow. "Turn it off!" she snaps. "Julia, I'm going to *kill* your brother."

Only then do I realize the sound is coming from the alarm clock in the corner, a shrill crescendo of the worst club music I've ever heard. I'm about to launch myself out of bed and throw the entire thing against the wall when the ladder at the foot of my bunk creaks. Julia crosses the room in two quick strides and slams her fist against the top of the alarm. The song cuts off mid-chorus, sweet, blessed silence falling across the cabin at last, and she exhales a low sigh of relief.

"Don't worry, Delaney. I'm going to kill him, too."

I shake my head, still trying to clear the echo of phantom sirens. "What the hell was that?"

"That's Ben." Julia drags a hand down her face. "He got this random CD stuck in our alarm a few years ago, and now it won't come out. We've woken up to"—she picks up the abandoned CD case and reads from the back—"'Flexin' on That Gram' by YouTube sensation Mike Fratt for the last two years and will, apparently, continue to wake up to it every day for the rest of our natural lives."

"Oh my god." I yank my comforter over my face, blocking out the sun spilling cheerily across the cabin. "Does that man not terrorize the internet enough?"

Even within my cocoon of blankets, I can hear birds chirping outside our open windows and the occasional slam of screen doors as the other cabins start to come alive. Everyone is stirring, climbing out of bed, and getting ready for our first real day of camp. I should be joining them, but something about being yanked from sleep by a poorly made SoundCloud party remix is really making me contemplate my life choices.

"Come on, Riley." Julia's hand lands on my shoulder. "You'll miss breakfast."

The lines of her pillow are still imprinted across her cheek, but her eyes are bright despite our abrupt awakening. I scowl and bury myself deeper into the mattress. "It's too early."

"It's seven thirty."

"Exactly."

Amusement flickers across Julia's face. "Suit yourself. But if you want a shower before breakfast, I'd go now. The hot water only lasts, like, two seconds."

As if on cue, Torres snatches her shower caddy from the floor and dashes onto the porch with Delaney and Greer in close pursuit.

"You should go," I say, waving Julia toward the door. "I'll meet you at breakfast."

"Promise?"

I slip my pinkie out from under the blanket. "Promise."

Julia's finger is cool around mine, steady and reassuring as always. She gives it one firm shake before dropping my hand and following the others. I watch her go, ignoring the way her absence makes my chest ache. I've learned to adapt this year without her constantly at my side, and now that I have her back, I don't want to let go. It's like that time in eighth grade when I knocked out my front tooth over Thanksgiving break. It took two days to get into an emergency dentist, and I'd spent the entire wait prodding at the empty space with my tongue, still expecting to find a tooth. It was like my brain couldn't process the loss, and that's how I feel about Julia now. Like she's a part of me. Like no matter what happens between us, there's not a world where I can conceivably comprehend her absence.

By the time I throw the blankets aside, the cabin is empty, quiet except for the faint hum of static still emanating from the alarm clock. Even though I'd packed and repacked more times than I can remember, the array of clothing piled before me now feels impossibly overwhelming. Yesterday, we'd all been in our bus clothes—a casual collection of jeans and sneakers, but what about today? Is there an unofficial camp dress code? Am I going to get lectured for wearing a *Legally Blonde* the musical shirt to breakfast because Elle Woods uses the Lord's name in vain?

I sit back on my heels, knees aching where they press into the dusty floor. I used to think about clothes a lot—what I wore, how I wore it, how other people might perceive me. There was always this little judgmental voice in the back of my mind each time I pulled on a pair of shorts or reached for a cropped shirt at the mall, and it wasn't until I left Pleasant Hills that I realized it sounded an awful lot like Pastor Young. It's better now. Most days I can push aside those insecurities completely, but something about being here makes me feel fifteen again. Like I'm being handed a lost and found cardigan by a smiling church elder in front of the entire congregation for daring to show my collarbones on Easter Sunday.

Strange how I didn't see anything wrong with that at the time. Strange how I assumed it was my fault.

"Are you ever going to tell us why you're here?"

I freeze, faded T-shirt still clutched in one hand, and when I glance over my shoulder, I realize the cabin isn't empty after all. Amanda's sitting up in bed, legs dangling over the side of her bunk. Even now, when it's just us, her expression remains frustratingly nonchalant. Like this is a perfectly normal conversation. Like we're still friends.

I shrug. "I don't know. Are you going to tell us why you were late for yesterday's sermon?"

A muscle feathers in Amanda's jaw so quickly I almost miss it. *Because there's something here*, I think. Some weakness tucked behind her layers of curated compassion, and the longer I watch her, the more I want to dig it out.

I stand with my clothes draped over one arm and start walking across the cabin. Amanda's throat bobs as I approach, a quick up and down that completely betrays the indifferent curl of her lips. I hear her breath catch, watch her eyes widen ever so slightly, like she's suddenly remembering our last violent interaction, and then, just as she starts to scoot back across the mattress, I turn and walk right out the door, leaving the screen swinging wildly in my wake.

The thing about Ben Young is that when he's not trying to talk to my sister, he's actually pretty cool. He has this charming, unironically effortless vibe that's impossible to ignore. Maybe it's related to his vintage sneaker collection or his ability to make the world's greatest latte despite never having consumed a sip of coffee. Maybe it's from the time his painting won first prize at the state fair and the mayor invited him to a special brunch for "future city leaders." Maybe it's because he's the only person I know who's spending two weeks of his summer at some fancy

Manhattan art school and I'm convinced he's going to return with the ability to finally eat somewhere spicier than Taco Bell. That's just how he's always been—Ben is cool, he's my friend, and I've never really thought about it further.

But when I find him in the cafeteria during breakfast, talking animatedly with his group of friends, it becomes immediately clear that he's already sitting at the camp's designated Cool Table. And that none of the other occupants seem to want me there at all.

Most of them go to Madison—Patrick Davies with his buzzed football player haircut and crooked nose, Levi Huxley wearing the same silver cross necklace he's had since the fifth grade, and Adam Yarrow, the only person I know whose parents let him get a tattoo. They all look up when I stop in front of their table, like they're not quite sure it's allowed. Ben, however, nearly upends his tray as he reaches for me.

"Riley!" he cries. "Happy first day! How was—?"

I knock his hand away, ignoring the way Patrick's mouth falls open in surprise, and snap, " 'Flexin' on That Gram,' Ben? Really?"

"What—?" Ben's eyes widen as realization slowly dawns across his face. "Oh my god. Is that still stuck in there?"

"Yeah, it is. And it's awful."

"To be fair, I don't think it's meant to be listened to this early in the morning."

"I don't think it's meant to be listened to ever."

Ben laughs, then claps a hand over his mouth as the buzz of lunchroom conversation falters. I look up to find Pastor Young

SAY A LITTLE PRAYER

making his way down the cafeteria's main aisle, one hand raised as the other tugs a mic from his back pocket. "Good morning. Can everyone take a seat, please? Riley?"

His eyes lock on mine, and I realize, too late, that I'm the only one standing. I hurriedly drop onto the bench between Ben and Patrick.

"Thank you." Pastor Young flashes me a too-wide smile before turning to face the room. "I hope you're all feeling settled in after last night. We have quite the journey ahead of us—seven virtues in seven days—but I have a feeling you're up for the challenge. Before we jump into today's lesson, though, there are a few housekeeping notes I need to run through. If you open your workbook, you'll find a group number, meeting location, and the name of your head counselor printed at the top of the first page."

There's a shuffle of movement as everyone flips through their book. Sure enough, there's a large number three printed at the beginning of mine, telling me I should meet Counselor Gabe in the picnic area after breakfast. I crane my neck, trying to catch Julia's eye across the cafeteria, but she's too busy with her own book to notice. I nudge Ben with my elbow instead. "What group are you?"

"Two," he whispers. "You?"

My heart sinks. "Three."

"For the next week, your group will be like your family," Pastor Young continues. "You'll work together, pray together, and most importantly, grow together. That's what this is about at the end of the day, right? Pleasant Hills is a community and everyone in

65

this room—from the counselors to the campers beside you—is here to support you on your spiritual journey."

I sink further into my seat so Pastor Young can't see me roll my eyes. I haven't spoken to some of these people in a year. Our friendships conveniently ceased to exist around the same time I stopped going to church, and I'm not trying to rekindle them now. No, I'm here with a plan—seven sins in seven days. A week to prove Pastor Young wrong.

I lean over and fish my prayer book out of my bag. Last night's notes stare up at me from the first page, but I flip past them and start a new paragraph instead. *Who, exactly, is Pleasant Hills here to support? Who gets to make those decisions?*

"What are you doing?"

Patrick leans over my shoulder, so close I can smell the syrup on his breath. I snap the book closed and tuck it under my thigh. "Praying."

"Already?"

"It's never too early to speak to the Lord."

He blinks, like he can't figure out if I'm serious, and Pastor Young chooses that moment to lead the cafeteria in a very long, very self-indulgent group prayer. I flash Patrick my most innocent smile as I bow my head.

The fewer people who know what I'm doing, the better.

My initial confidence fades, however, when we're finally dismissed and everyone starts separating themselves into groups. I'd kind of hoped I could stick with Julia all week, but as I watch her make her way toward the chapel, arm in arm with a younger girl I don't recognize, that small bubble of hope bursts. Instead, I turn and hike toward the picnic area alone, trying my best not to look back.

Until this week, I've been able to pack all my strange, complicated feelings about leaving Pleasant Hills into neat little boxes. I missed it quietly, I ignored the ache of watching my old friends post pictures from the ice cream shop near the church, and if I tried hard enough, I found I could make everyone believe that I was really, truly okay. I could almost make myself believe it, too. Now I think it's easier to pretend those feelings don't exist.

If I acknowledge them, it means admitting the real reasons I hate watching Julia walk off without me. It means wondering how much of our own relationship had been built on common interests and convenience, if there would be a day where she decides that being my friend is more trouble than it's worth. I know it's possible. Amanda and Greer chose Pastor Young over their friendship with Hannah, and he's not even their dad.

I shake the thought away, purposefully sealing it back where it belongs. I've spent a year ignoring that particularly painful reminder, and I'm not about to let it out now. Instead, I focus on the path ahead of me, gravel crunching under my feet as I walk toward the picnic area.

Three long tables sit at the edge of the forest, each stacked with a different haphazard pile of supplies—nails, rolls of packing tape, bottles of glue. A counselor who I assume is Gabe sits on top of the nearest table, feet resting on the bench below as he scrolls through something on his phone. He has the same smooth, shiny look as Cindy, like they've both been run through a religious rock tumbler on the way here. Three first-year boys stand off to the side, and I'm just bracing myself for a week of pretending to relate to them when a familiar face appears over the hill.

"Oh, thank god." Delaney pauses to catch her breath, both hands braced on the knees of her pink cargo pants. Her braids are tied back with an identically bright bandana, and when she meets my eye, she looks as relieved as I do to not be standing here alone. "I thought I was going to have to deal with *that* by myself."

Delaney jabs a thumb over her shoulder, and the relief I felt at her arrival abruptly vanishes when I spot Greer on the path behind her. She gives me a dismissive once over, eyes flicking from my still damp hair to my paint-splattered sneakers before brushing past us without a word.

It takes every ounce of my self-control not to groan. "Are you serious?"

"Unfortunately." Delaney slings one arm over my shoulder. "Come on. We're in this together, I guess."

Her words echo in my mind as we continue down the path. *We're in this together.* I had assumed most of the campers this week would be like Amanda or Greer—righteous and arrogant and eager to throw each other under the bus if Pastor Young willed it, but Delaney feels like someone I could be friends with.

We come to a stop in front of the picnic table, finally joining the rest of the group. There are six of us total—me, Delaney, Greer, and the three boys from before. It's not until Greer purposefully clears her throat that Gabe finally looks up.

"Oh!" He jumps, phone clattering to the table like he's just now remembering he has a job. "Hey, fam. I'm Gabe, and I'll be your group leader this week. Before we get started, I just want to let you know that this is a safe space, so if you have any questions or concerns during your time here, you can totally bring them to me."

I think the fact that Gabe's phone is currently open to a page advertising "hot singles in your area" kind of undercuts his message, but sure.

"Why don't we go around the circle and introduce ourselves?" Gabe continues. "Tell me your name, grade, and your favorite Bible verse."

I close my eyes. "You've *got* to be kidding me."

Delaney snorts. "Just say you like John 3:16 or something. Everyone likes John 3:16."

"Quiet, please." Gabe waves a hand in our direction before motioning for Greer to start.

Her eyes narrow on us across the circle, like the fact we're talking during her introduction is a personal affront. "Hi, I'm Greer, I'm a senior at Madison, and my favorite Bible verse is John 3:16."

Of course it is. Gabe turns toward me and I hurriedly rack my brain for another verse. Surely I have one. Surely I didn't sit through sixteen years of Sunday school for nothing. Eventually, I give in and mutter, "I'm Riley, I'm a junior at Madison, and my favorite is . . . that one, too."

The silence that follows lasts a beat too long. Gabe cracks a hesitant smile. "What a coincidence."

I stare down at my shoes as he continues around the circle. I know this isn't a test, but I still feel like the entire school just watched me drop a line on opening night. Like my inability to recall basic Bible verses is another example of how much I've changed.

After the last introduction, Gabe picks up his workbook and flips to the first page. "Great," he says. "Now, can we all take a look at chapter one? We don't have a lot of time this morning, and I'd like to get started." He clears his throat, then starts reading in a halting, stilted monotone. "Diligence—a Commitment to God. In the journey to cultivate a virtuous life, diligence is the radiant beacon of youth. It guides us through the labyrinth of worldly distractions and calls us to reject the insidious lure of sloth—a deadly sin that seeks only to numb our spirits."

I skip ahead as Gabe continues, letting his voice fade into the background. I couldn't care less about the *radiant beacon of youth*, but I'm very much interested in the deadly sin numbing our spirits. There's a definition printed halfway through the first chapter, a warning inked in stark black and white. I pause.

Sloth. Noun. A habitual disinclination to exertion. Lazy, careless.

I see where this is going before Gabe finishes reading. He's probably going to send us into the woods to perform some pointed, physically exhausting task, and if any of us even *think* about taking a break, he's going to smack us over the head with a Bible or something because sloth is *bad*. It's a sin, and according to Pastor Young, that's all it takes to earn a one-way ticket to hell.

But I'm not Pastor Young. And I don't think there's anything wrong with being lazy once in a while.

Gabe slams his book shut, the sound jolting me back to reality. "Okay," he says. "I know this one isn't super fun to read about. Personally, I think the only way to truly understand the virtue of diligence is to implement it in our lives through action. Which is why today's activity actually takes place outside the pages of this book."

There it is.

Greer thrusts a manicured hand into the air. "So what are we doing, exactly?"

"Excellent question. Through the virtue of diligence and self-control, we're going to build"—Gabe drums his hands on his knees—"an outdoor shelter!"

No one moves. Even the branches rustling overhead fall momentarily silent. "A shelter?" I ask. "Like . . . a tent?"

"Uh, no. It doesn't have to be a tent."

"But you want us to build a shelter? For humans?"

"That's right!"

There's a single second of confused silence before everyone turns in unison toward the items scattered across the top of the picnic tables. I suppose there's a world where someone might find themselves in the middle of the woods with nothing but a roll of packing tape, a bottle of Elmer's glue, and several dozen thumbtacks, but I'm under no delusions that it'll help us now. Hesitantly, I reach for a pair of scissors.

"Not so fast!" Gabe snatches them out of reach. "It's tempting to give in to instant gratification, isn't it? To make your task easier by outsourcing work or using tools? These supplies might seem helpful now, but diligence is the only thing that will get you over the finish line. Just like it says in Proverbs 13:4, 'the soul of the diligent is richly supplied.' So, Riley, do you still want these?"

"Yes," I say without hesitation.

"No, you—" Gabe closes his eyes. "That's not the point. You're supposed to work hard for meaningful rewards."

"Okay, but what are the rules?" Delaney asks. "Do we have to build something that fits the whole group? What supplies *are* we allowed to use? No one knows how to build a shelter."

"Sure you do." Gabe sweeps an arm toward the forest behind him. "Everything you need is right here, provided by God for this very task. You have until lunch to build a suitable shelter for one person, then you'll be judged by a panel of counselors." When no one moves, he blows out a long exasperated breath and adds, "The winning group gets an extra hour of free time tonight, okay? Just . . . do the assignment."

I run a finger over the spine of my prayer book as we all turn toward the trees. Time to be . . . slothful, I guess. Of all the sins facing me this week, this feels like a good place to start. Sloth doesn't have to be bad. It could be self-care or relaxation. It could be *not* building a shelter in the middle of the woods because, honestly, who came up with that idea in the first place? I take a deep breath, sneak a glance at Delaney out of the corner of my eye, then take a hesitant step toward the trees.

Part one of my seven-step plan is officially in motion.

VI

Jesus Might Have Been a Carpenter, But I Most Certainly Am Not

"Okay, this *has* to be illegal." I duck under another low-hanging branch, swatting it aside right before it smacks me in the face. "They can't just, like, make us do manual labor."

We've spent the last half hour wandering through the sparse wooded area across from the picnic tables, and the only thing our group has managed to build is a small pile of misshapen twigs. Not that I care. I have no delusions of success when it comes to this competition, but I also haven't figured out how to embody sloth without literally collapsing to the ground and becoming one with the earth. I like my clothes. I don't want to sacrifice them to the rough Kentucky dirt.

Behind me, Delaney swipes her way through a swarm of gnats. "This is what I get for quitting Girl Scouts. Maybe we could use those leaves over there for a roof? Or something?"

"Definitely not."

I jump as Greer appears on the other side of a nearby tree, one hand lifted so she can examine her perfectly buffed nails. "You can't use the leaves," she adds, like she didn't just materialize out of nowhere. "You need something sturdier. And preferably waterproof."

I roll my eyes and keep walking. "Like what?"

"I don't know. Like a tarp. Or a bunch of tightly woven vines."

"Sure. Let me pull a bunch of tightly woven vines out of my ass, Greer."

Delaney chokes back a laugh, and to my surprise, the corner of Greer's glossy mouth twitches, too. Then she blinks and the expression dissolves. "It's not supposed to be easy. We're supposed to be diligent."

"In this economy?" I shake my head. "You're not going to hell for using scissors."

"Sloth is a *sin*, Riley. That's literally the whole point!"

The fact that someone as rich and beautiful as Greer can also be this outrageously annoying feels like proof enough that prayers don't work. She's glaring at me like I've just kicked her puppy or something, and for the first time, I wonder if this plan might be harder than I thought. Greer "I Got a Thirty-Five on the ACTs and Also Run the Madison High School Student Government Association like It's the Marine Corps" Wilson has never relaxed a day in her life. She's not going to start now when she obviously still thinks Gabe can give her an A in diligence.

I glance over my shoulder to where the edge of one picnic table is half visible through the trees. The supplies Gabe brought to tempt us are still sitting unattended, slowly baking in the midmorning sun, and I think I *could* probably grab a pair of scissors

SAY A LITTLE PRAYER

if I wanted to. It might not prove my point exactly, but it would definitely make Greer's head explode, and that feels like a start.

Sure enough, her shoulders stiffen the instant I turn toward the clearing. "Where are you going?"

"None of your business."

If there's one thing I know about Greer, it's that she believes everything, to some extent, is her business. I keep my gaze locked on the path ahead, but it's only a second before I hear the sound of her footsteps hurrying after me.

"You can't," she hisses. "That's cheating, Riley. We're supposed to figure this out ourselves."

"I thought we're supposed to have fun."

"I mean, *yes*, but—"

"Then what's the problem, Greer? Isn't that the whole point?"

"How would you know what the point is? You don't even go here—"

Greer breaks off, almost plowing me over as I come to an abrupt stop at the edge of the clearing. The supplies are still there all right, gleaming up at us from the picnic tables, but that's not what I'm looking at now. Instead, I'm staring past the tables altogether, back down the hill and over the tops of the buildings below.

I knew the picnic area sat at the eastern edge of camp, across from the chapel and directly behind the parking lot, but I hadn't realized how far we'd walked this morning or how high we'd climbed. The Dayton suburbs are mind-numbingly flat, but northern Kentucky is full of these soft rolling hills that stretch toward the sky. From where I stand at the edge of the clearing, I can see across the entire camp—the twisting paths, the patched roofs of the cabins, the other groups wandering through the central field. A handful of puffy white clouds dot an otherwise clear sky, and everything smells vaguely of pine.

I'm not an outdoorsy person. I've been on exactly one hike in my life and most of my biggest fears can be categorized as "finding outside creatures where they don't belong," but something about the view up here feels steadying. Distant. I release a shaky breath, and for the first time since getting on that bus yesterday, I feel the tension lining my shoulders release.

"It's a great view, isn't it?"

I glance over my shoulder to find Delaney following my gaze over the hill. She has her face tilted toward the sun, arms slightly outstretched like she wants to physically soak it all in, but before I can answer, Greer lets out a low scoff.

"It's fine," she says. "It's great. Now can we *please* get back to work before Gabe sees us? We can't have much time left."

Unfortunately, I think she's right. The sun is creeping toward the center of the sky, the morning is almost over, but I have absolutely no desire to return to the woods or finish our project. Instead, when a breeze ruffles the hair hastily knotted at the back of my neck, the first brush of a new idea slips through my mind.

"Come here." I step into the clearing and motion for the others to follow. "I have a better idea."

Delaney falls into step beside me, but Greer hangs back,

SAY A LITTLE PRAYER

shooting nervous glances over her shoulder as I circle around the far edge of the picnic area. It's not until I drop to my hands and knees and crawl under one of the tables that she takes a hesitant step forward.

"What are you doing?"

"Finding shelter." I turn so I can sit cross-legged on the grass, then smack a palm against the bench to my left. "Looks sturdy to me."

Delaney sinks into a crouch, one hand braced against the table. "Oh my god," she says, grin slowly spreading across her face. "You're a genius, Riley."

She crawls in next to me, slouching to avoid hitting her head against the underside of the table, and I very purposefully avoid eye contact with the cobweb lurking in the corner. Greer wavers, bottom lip caught between her teeth.

"This isn't . . ." she starts. "The rules . . ."

"I don't think *Gabe* knows the rules," I say. "If you want to keep picking up sticks, be my guest, but I'm taking a break."

"Same." Delaney pats the ground next to her. "Chill, Greer. There's room."

Part of me wants Greer to give up, to head back into the woods and leave us alone, but another wistful, disgustingly nostalgic part still remembers what it's like to exist in her orbit. I used to come home from rehearsal to find her and Hannah on our couch downstairs, utterly engrossed in some mediocre reality show with their homework forgotten between them. They'd

77

call me over, give me a recap I absolutely didn't ask for, and then Greer would absentmindedly hand me a coffee she'd picked up on the way—a medium iced with oat milk, a shot of espresso, two pumps of mocha, and no sugar.

I never asked her to get me one. I don't think I ever told her what I liked, she just heard me order one day and tucked the drink away in that color-coded memory bank of hers. She always remembered my birthday, she knew Hannah and Amanda's dance schedule by heart, and even though we haven't really spoken since January, I'm pretty sure she still remembers my locker combination.

I hope she does, anyway. I hope there's a Riley-shaped file rattling around her skull at all times, and I hope it reminds her of all the things she's no longer a part of.

I keep my gaze fixed on the grass curling around my ankles and purposefully ignore the hesitant glance Greer shoots my way. Then she lowers herself to the ground and crawls under the table to join us.

"There," Delaney says, scooting over as Greer tentatively tucks her legs beneath her. "Was that so bad?"

Before she can answer, a twig snaps on the other side of the clearing, and we all whip around to find Gabe emerging from the trees. His eyes immediately narrow on our hiding spot. "Hey!" he calls. "What are you doing?"

I feel Greer stiffen beside me, like every ounce of her rule-following, type A personality has found its way into her spine. I lean over to peer at Gabe across the bench. "Finding shelter. Nice, isn't it?"

"That's not what we meant. You're supposed to build something."

Greer shoots me a look that clearly says, *I told you*, but I force myself to shrug. "I thought we could use the materials God provided."

"You can."

"And didn't God provide these tables?"

"I . . ." Gabe's mouth opens, closes, and opens again before he shakes his head. "No, that's not . . . You need to finish the assignment."

Delaney leans back on her elbows. "Why?" she asks. "Do you get paid based on our ability to build a wilderness shelter or something?"

From the look of unease flickering across Gabe's face, I think he genuinely might. I grin and stretch my legs out in front of me. "Well, you're doing an excellent job, Gabriel. Really. I feel super sheltered."

For a minute, Gabe looks like he's about to physically drag me into the clearing. He turns in a frustrated circle, then storms back into the woods, probably to make sure the rest of our group, at least, is still working.

Delaney snorts, teeth sinking into her bottom lip as she tries to hide her grin. "I think you broke him."

To my surprise, Greer also cracks a smile. She watches Gabe until he disappears between the trees, then slowly reclines against the edge of the table. "This *is* kind of nice, I guess," she says. "That project was stressing me out."

"Really?" Delaney's brows lift in mock surprise. "But you hid it so well."

I snort out a laugh and pull my prayer book from my waistband. Part of me is still waiting for the moment to sour, for this temporary win to curl in on itself like a charred scrap of paper and leave me with nothing to write about. Because sloth is supposed to be a sin. Because I'm avoiding our task, being lazy on purpose, but the only thing I feel is an overwhelming sense of relief.

Greer rolls her eyes in Delaney's direction. "Whatever. Did you really want to spend your last week of camp doing manual labor?"

"Last week?" I pause, looking up at them both. "Are you a senior?"

I try to remember if Julia had mentioned that before. Surely she did. Surely Delaney said it during this morning's introductions, but I don't remember anything besides my own personal frustration with Greer's choice of Bible verse.

"Yeah," Delaney says. "Finally, right? Come visit me in Columbus next year."

"Ohio State?"

She nods and Greer's eyes light up. "Wait, really?" she asks. "I didn't know you committed! Who are you living with?"

"No idea. My mom made me choose random roommates 'for the experience' so I told her she has to pay my therapy bills if they try to murder me in the night or something. Are you still thinking about rooming with Amanda?"

SAY A LITTLE PRAYER

Greer shakes her head. "No, she's doing the dance program at Indiana, but I met a few girls at orientation who seem nice."

"You're doing social work, right?" Delaney asks. "My sister would probably talk to you if you had any questions about the program. She really loved it."

I can't help it. I choke back a laugh. Greer has always been the smartest person in the room. I have no doubt she'll excel in whatever program she picks, but the idea of her purposefully choosing one that's supposed to help people is laughable. She's done nothing but make Hannah's life miserable since the new year, and I don't think that kind of cruelty is something they train out of you in Columbus, Ohio.

I try to stifle the sound as Greer's head whips toward me, but it's too late. "What?" she snaps. "Do you think that's funny?"

I shrug. "I mean, yeah. A little."

"Why? It's a good program. I worked hard."

"I never said you didn't."

"Then what's your problem?"

Gone is the easy smile and casual posture. Greer's shoulders cut a stiff line in the sunlight leaking through the slats of the picnic table. Her jaw is set, a poisoned retort clearly waiting on the tip of her tongue, so before I can think better of it, I throw my hands up and say, "I don't know, Greer. It's just that you're kind of a bitch."

Delaney sucks a surprised breath through her teeth. I watch Greer's cheeks flare a delicate shade of pink before her expression twists into something that feels suspiciously like disgust. "What-

81

ever, Riley," she mutters. "Takes one to know one, I guess."

I round on her as best I can in the cramped space. "I'm not—"

"Do you know the name of anyone else in our group?"

One of Greer's eyebrows quirks in an infuriating angle. I open my mouth to tell her, *Yes, of course I do,* but something stops me. I'd listened to the boys introduce themselves earlier. We just spent the morning in the woods together, but now that she brings it up, I realize I have no idea what their names are.

"Jack," I decide, with more confidence than I feel.

"It's Jace."

"Okay, well, Jace is a dumb name. That's not my fault."

Greer's answering laugh is entirely devoid of humor. "There you go," she says. "You think you're so much better than everyone because you left. I know you don't believe in God anymore, but that doesn't give you the right to hate everyone who stayed."

"I don't hate you because you still go to church, Greer," I snap. "And I never said I don't believe in God."

"Oh?" Her gaze rakes across my face, and for a chilling second, I think she can see right through me. "Well, you could have fooled me."

The air beneath the picnic table thickens. Delaney has gone quiet, twisting a chunk of grass around her finger as she waits for me to respond, but it's like the words are physically stuck in my chest. I bite the inside of my cheek, nails digging into the dirt as Greer's smile widens ever so slightly.

Got you, it says. *Nice try.*

There's a rustle of fabric to our left. I tear my gaze away from

Greer right as Gabe drops to his knees beside us, looking utterly defeated as he runs a hand through his newly tousled hair. "Okay," he pants, completely oblivious to the tension under the table. "Is this really what you're going with? Because I need to go drag the boys out of the river, so I really don't have time to help you make something new."

Greer folds her arms over her chest. "You should ask Riley," she says. "She's the one who knows everything."

Gabe turns on me, expression half imploring, half expectant as my cheeks heat. I sigh and lean my head against the cool wood of the picnic table. "Yeah, Gabe. This is what we're going with."

We lose the competition so spectacularly I'm surprised Gabe doesn't quit on the spot. To be fair, the other groups aren't much better. By the time the judges declare a tentative winner and we all break for lunch, the most anyone's managed to create is a haphazard pile of foliage and a newfound hatred for the word *diligence*.

The sun has parked itself directly overhead as we climb out from under the table, baking the soft dirt of the clearing into dust. Greer emerges from our makeshift shelter without so much as a speck on her white top, but I take my time brushing off my legs. Her words still echo in the back of my mind, hanging off my shoulders like a razor-clawed shadow.

You think you're so much better than everyone because you left.

I wish I could deny it. I wish I could tell her she's wrong.

"You coming to lunch?"

Delaney watches me from the top of the hill, one hand raised to block the sun. I glance over my shoulder and realize the rest of our group has already left, heading toward the cafeteria with the other campers. I haven't eaten all day, but I don't think the hollow feeling in the pit of my stomach is entirely due to hunger.

"You go ahead," I say. "I want to change first."

I gesture down at my dirty shorts, and Delaney cracks a smile. "I'll save you a seat."

I watch the back of her head until she disappears down the hill, pink bandana fluttering in the breeze. Then I turn in the opposite direction and start walking toward the cabins instead. I do want to change my clothes. I'm not lying about that, but I also need a minute alone, somewhere I don't have to force a smile and pretend Greer didn't unintentionally crack the armor I'd spent the last year reinforcing.

I thumb through my prayer book as I walk. The only reason I'd crawled under that table in the first place was to prove my point. And I *had*. For a brief second, Delaney, Greer, and I had sat in the shade and taken a single collective breath. I hadn't thought about my essay or the days ahead or the way my chest tightened at the thought of Julia's hand in mine. It was the opposite of diligence. According to Pastor Young, taking a break like that should be unforgivable, but we were fine. It felt good, actually, until Greer started coming after me.

Or maybe I'd gone after her. I don't really remember who started it.

I'm so focused that I don't notice the other person heading

SAY A LITTLE PRAYER

toward me until it's too late. I slam directly into their shoulder and my prayer book tumbles to the ground.

"Sorry!" I drop to my knees, snapping the book shut before anyone else can see my hastily scribbled notes. "Sorry, I wasn't—"

I look up, and the rest of my apology dies in my throat. Pastor Young stands a few feet away, absentmindedly rubbing his shoulder as he grins down at me. "Where are you going in such a hurry?"

He's changed into one of the blue counselor T-shirts, the same thing he sometimes wears to mow his lawn back home. That's the strangest thing about this whole situation, I think. The fact that I've known the Youngs almost as long as I can remember. That I know *him*. I know Pastor Young is an excellent cook, that he used to run marathons until he dislocated his knee a few years ago, and that he throws a killer Fourth of July party. I know he spends his Saturdays golfing in Dayton, that he's allergic to dogs, and I know, without a shadow of a doubt, that he'd personally throw me into the fiery pits of hell if he knew how much I think about kissing girls.

I scramble to my feet and tuck my prayer book casually behind my back. "Sorry," I say again. "I was just going to change before lunch."

Pastor Young's smile is still infuriatingly warm. "Of course. It's hot out today, isn't it?"

"Sure is."

I try to step around him, but he shifts to the side, subtly blocking my path. "I'm glad we ran into each other," he says.

85

"I've actually been meaning to talk to you."

Several dozen alarm bells explode inside my head at once. "About what?"

"Don't look at me like that." Pastor Young waves a hand, but the dismissive gesture does nothing to steady the sudden thrum of my pulse. "You're not in trouble. I just wanted to check in. You've been away from us for a while, and I know the circumstances of this trip are . . . less than ideal. But I really do think you're going to learn a lot."

His smile doesn't waver. It's the picture-perfect portrait of concern, but my fingers tighten instinctively around my prayer book. Of course Mr. Rider told him about our deal. Of course Pastor Young knows I'm not here of my own free will. He gets community service kids from the high school all the time—he's probably supposed to report on my progress or something.

I force myself to smile through the tight set of my jaw. "It's nice to be back," I lie. "Thanks again for letting me join so last minute."

"Well, we're always happy to have you. And we really do miss you at Pleasant Hills. I know I speak for the entire congregation when I say we'd love to see you at church."

I have to bite the inside of my cheek to keep my pleasant expression from slipping. "Would you be happy to see Hannah, too?"

Pastor Young's grin is as unwavering as mine, but the warmth of it doesn't quite reach his eyes. They're the same color as Julia's, a rich brown that feels soft and inviting on her. On him, however, it feels dangerous. Bottomless. "Well," he says. "That remains to be seen."

"Of course." It takes everything in my power not to roll my eyes. "Good talk."

I start walking again, not bothering to hide my frustration. This time, I make it all the way to the fork in the path before Pastor Young calls my name.

"Riley?"

There's an edge to his voice now, a warning that slides across my rapidly fraying nerves. Every muscle in my body coils tight. "Yes?"

Pastor Young's hands slide casually into his pockets. "I am glad you're here," he says. "I want you to know that. This week is a wonderful opportunity for you, and I don't want to tell your principal that you're wasting it by sitting under tables and encouraging bad behavior in your fellow campers. Understand?"

So I have a chaperone now, a personal attendant tracking my every move. Heat pulses under my skin, but my smile doesn't slip. "Sure."

"Good." Pastor Young's gaze doesn't leave my face. "I know you mean well, Riley. I'm here to guide you on your journey, but I also have to look out for my family. I have to protect my children from the perils of the world, and I'd hate for you to become a bad influence."

Despite the warm, cloudless sky, a chill whispers down my spine. I don't know when the shift happened, exactly—when I stopped seeing Pastor Young as my best friends' dad and started seeing him as a threat. Maybe it was when he told an entire congregation that Satan created homosexuality to keep people out of Heaven. Maybe it started the day with the sweater in church, long before I thought to question why so many people allowed something like that to happen.

I've spent months telling myself that if he tried coming after me the way he came for Hannah, I wouldn't let him get away with it. I'd created scenario after scenario where I finally stood up to him, where I threw those accusations back in his face, where the people watching would believe me, but no one is watching now. I'm alone, faced with the full force of Pastor Young's stare, and the only thing I can do is nod.

"Excellent." He smiles then, a quick flash that does nothing to warm the space between us. "I'll see you at lunch, Riley."

And then he's gone, heading toward the cafeteria with his arms swinging casually at his sides.

I'd hate for you to become a bad influence.

The warning is clear—sit down and be quiet. Don't cause problems, don't ask questions, and maybe, just maybe, you can keep your best friends. Watching him walk down the path now, tall and confident in a place that's his to command, I think I understand why so many people have let him go unchallenged for this long.

I can almost believe that kind of power is preordained.

I don't move until Pastor Young rounds the corner and disappears into the line of trees. Only then do I stumble toward the safety of my cabin, mind racing the entire way. I always thought

SAY A LITTLE PRAYER

Pastor Young's interest in me was administrative—he didn't know why I'd left his congregation and the thought probably haunted his otherwise impeccable record. I know he hates Hannah. I know he resents my whole family for leaving, but now I think he might hate me the most. The girl who left before he could kick her out. The girl who's been brushing him off and ignoring his Bible study invitations all year.

The girl who, despite his best efforts, is still best friends with his perfect, God-fearing children.

VII

Hey, Macklemore, Can We Go Thrift Shopping?

"*A*nd then he said, 'I'd hate for you to become a bad influence.' Like, what the hell am I supposed to do with that?"

I press my phone to my ear and lean against the rough bark of a nearby pine tree as I watch the line of campers file onto the bus a few yards away. It's Field Trip Day—a.k.a. the morning where Pastor Young ships us all into downtown Rhyville so the senior counselors can have their own day of training and worship. It also means we get our phones back, a concession that's supposed to exemplify today's virtue of generosity.

I personally think returning my own property is less generous and more an act of psychological warfare, but whatever. At least I'd been able to scroll through the list of notes Kev sent me from yesterday's rehearsal and at least I'm able to talk to Hannah now.

"That's a weird thing to say, right?" I press when she doesn't answer. "That's, like, a threat?"

Hannah makes a noncommittal noise in the back of her

throat. "I don't know, Riley. Everything that man says sounds like a threat. Have you talked to Julia about it?"

"You know we don't talk about him."

"I know *you* don't talk about him. But she's your best friend. She probably wants to know how you feel."

I hesitate, digging the toe of my sneaker into the ground. She's right, of course. Julia knows me better than anyone, but we've never explicitly talked about the role her father played in ruining Hannah's life. At the time, it hadn't felt necessary. We both knew what happened even if no one said it out loud, and now, after months of talking around it, it doesn't feel like there's a way to bring it up.

It's not like I'm required to tell Julia everything. I'm not telling her about my new and improved essay, for example. I'm not telling her about the conversation I'd had with her father or about how this entire thing feels personal now, like if I can't prove how wrong Pastor Young's sermons are, then I might lose her, too. And I'm absolutely not telling her about how I fell asleep last night desperately wishing she would reach down and squeeze my hand again.

Some things are better left unsaid. There's not a way to take them back.

"Yeah." I tip my head up toward the cloudless sky. "We'll see. How are you?" I add before Hannah can press me further. "Do you still have rehearsal this week?"

If she notices the sudden change in subject, she doesn't

comment. Fabric rustles on the other end of the line, like she's falling back against her pillow. "Sure do. I have, like, three private lessons tomorrow for that adagio. The turn sequence at the end is still a bit shaky."

I grin, momentarily forgetting my own problems. I would bet anything that Hannah's adagio is flawless. Her Snow Queen solo in last year's *Nutcracker* was so good I momentarily considered signing up for ballet classes myself.

"I'm sure it's fine," I say. "Didn't Bruno say you looked 'angelic' last week?"

"Sure, but he also said he didn't cast me as Aurora to have a subpar adagio."

"Did he really?"

"No," Hannah admits. "But he might as well have."

I picture Hannah in her room back home, sprawled across her bed with the sun spilling over her lavender duvet. She always gets like this before a big show—quiet, withdrawn, intense—but today it feels different. Heavier. Eventually, she heaves a sigh.

"I don't know. It's probably fine, but it's my last show. Most of the girls in my class are dancing somewhere after graduation, but I'm not. I went through a lot to make sure I could still have this, and I want it to be perfect."

My throat tightens instinctively. "I know," I say. "I want that, too. I'm so proud of you, Hannah."

"Thanks." I hear her smile through the phone as some of the tension finally leaves her voice. "But enough about me. Are you

SAY A LITTLE PRAYER

having fun out there? Making memories? Making friends?"

"Absolutely not."

"Oh, come on. It's not *that* bad. I used to love camp."

"You used to love the Communion bread, too. No one's accusing you of having good taste."

Hannah laughs. "Well, try to have fun today at least. I know you're still mad, but maybe you could let it go? Just for this week?"

I drag my toe back and forth until a small trench opens in the dirt before me. She knows as well as I do that I've never let anything go in my life. Liam Robertson stole my lunch money in third grade, and I still think about it every time I pass him in the hallway.

"I don't know," I say. "That's pretty unrealistic."

Another laugh floats down the line, and I relax, ever so slightly. "Fine," Hannah says. "But don't let it get to you. Don't let them win."

I glance down to where my tote bag still sits against the base of the pine tree, the creased corner of my prayer book just peeking out over the top. "Don't worry," I say. "I won't."

And I mean it. Pastor Young can threaten me all he wants. He can corner me alone and smile until his face aches, but I'm not going to stop. It was one thing to plan his downfall with my reputation on the line, but if this is how I keep Julia, I'll do whatever it takes. Because why would she believe I'm a bad influence if I show her evidence of the dozens of things her father has lied about? Why wouldn't she trust me instead? I might have to be careful now, more subtle with my plan now that Pastor Young noticed my little stunt with the picnic table, but it's still doable. I can still win.

"Riley!"

I look up to find Torres waving at me from the parking lot. In the time I've been talking, everyone else has boarded the bus, leaving me alone on the sidewalk. I grab my tote from the ground and push myself off the tree.

"Sorry, Hannah, I have to go. See you this weekend."

"Of course," she says. "Good luck!"

I hang up and half walk, half jog onto the bus. Amanda is sitting in the front row, headphones on, face determinedly turned toward the window. Her fingers tap a staccato rhythm against her thigh, and for a minute, I wonder if she's reviewing the same choreography as Hannah. She doesn't look up when I pass, but Greer's gaze lingers on me a second longer than usual. The two of us haven't spoken since yesterday's diligence activity, not even when our entire cabin tried in vain to pry Mike Fratt's criminally offensive CD from our alarm last night. We aren't friends anymore. I don't really want to be, but I have the strangest urge to justify myself to her now. To prove I'm not the terrible person she somehow believes me to be.

Instead, I drop into the open seat next to Julia and let my head fall back against the cracked leather. "Hi."

She raises an eyebrow in my direction. "Cutting it a little close, aren't we?"

SAY A LITTLE PRAYER

"If your dad wanted everyone to be on time, he shouldn't have let me come this week."

Ben lets out a rough snort from the row in front of us. "Oh, he was always going to let you come," he says. "The elusive Riley Ackerman returning to Pleasant Hills after a year of living in sin? No one could resist that. I'm pretty sure he still thinks Jules and I can *Save you* or something."

He says it like it's a joke, the words accompanied by a single eye roll and a wave of his hand, but an uneasy thrill crawls down my spine. Back home, I might have laughed it off, but here, surrounded by people who probably view me the same way, I have to wonder how much truth lives in the core of that statement. If maybe Pastor Young explicitly told Ben and Julia to watch out for me in the same warm, vaguely threatening tone he'd used when he told me to be careful.

If maybe part of the reason Julia still wants to be my friend is because she thinks she has some cosmic duty to a higher power.

I shake the thought away and glare up at the ceiling, counting the cracks in the plaster until Ben reaches back and nudges my shoulder.

"Don't look so glum," he says. "Today's supposed to be fun."

I glance at him out of the corner of my eye. "You think getting dropped off at a Walmart in Rhyville, Kentucky, is fun?"

He nods eagerly. "It's always nice to get out of camp for a bit. Plus, I really need new clothes for New York."

"And you're going to buy them from Walmart."

"Don't be elitist, Riley. There's nothing wrong with a good department store."

Julia laughs as the bus turns out of the parking lot. "Just tell her, Ben. She'll find out eventually."

I straighten, gaze flicking between the two of them. "Tell me what?"

Ben glances over both shoulders, but everyone's too absorbed in their own conversations to care about ours. "Okay," he says. "The truth is, we don't actually go to Walmart. It's a ruse."

"A ruse." I lift an eyebrow. "Who's 'we'?"

"Us," he clarifies. "Me and Jules."

"So where do you go?"

Ben's gaze darts across the aisle again as he lowers his voice and whispers, "We found this really cool thrift store a few years ago. It's right across the street from where the buses drop us off. That's where we usually spend our free morning."

Now that sounds more like Ben. The person it doesn't sound like, however, is Julia. I turn to face her as best I can in the cramped seat. "*You* sneak away?"

Julia holds up both hands, face flushing ever so slightly. "They have really good deals, okay? Where did you think Hannah got her homecoming dress?"

"She told me she found it at Goodwill!"

Ben rolls his eyes. "Well, yeah. We can't have just anybody finding this place."

SAY A LITTLE PRAYER

"Not that you're just anybody," Julia cuts in. "But it's kind of a camp thing. I think you'll really like it, though!"

I know she doesn't mean anything by it, but the words still lodge themselves in my chest like tiny shards of glass. *It's kind of a camp thing.*

Something else I'm not a part of, another crack in the space between us.

"Fine," I say, smoothing over the bitter edge in my voice. "I get it. Still annoyed Hannah didn't mention it on the phone just now, but I'll live."

"Just now?" Ben twists in his seat, voice shooting back up to its normal volume. "Is that who you were talking to? How is she?"

There's a sharp squeak of static as one of the counselors taps the mic at the front of the bus. "Sit down, Benjamin."

Several people giggle as Ben plops back in his seat. He waits until the counselor turns around before pressing his face into the crack next to our window. "How is she?" he asks again.

I bite back a grin. "Good. Busy. She has a bunch of private lessons this week."

"Oh yeah." Ben nods. "She was talking about that before we left. I don't know why she's so worried about the adagio."

"Me either. I think she just wants her last show to be perfect so she can leave for California with a clean slate."

Ben's face falls, and I realize too late how final that sounds, how close we all are to the end of the year. The four of us have

97

always known what's coming. Ben's spending the summer at his art camp in New York, Julia's softball team starts practice at the end of May, and I want to find a job before senior year. The era of spending lazy, casual summers sprawled in each other's backyards is already over, but the thought of Hannah moving to the opposite side of the country still doesn't feel real.

Julia's the one who breaks the silence, voice purposefully light as she looks between us. "Well, she's not leaving yet," she says. "We still have prom."

Ben immediately perks up. "Right! Did you get your mom's dress, Riley?"

I hesitate, rubbing my palms against the outside of my shorts. East Christian Academy doesn't technically have a prom, just a highly supervised spring banquet where seniors are allowed exactly two songs to dance with the opposite-sex date of their choice. Hannah and I decided a while ago that Ben and Julia would come to our prom instead, but those original plans had also included Collin and Hannah's group of senior friends. Greer was going to hire a professional photographer. Amanda's mom had already booked the limo. I don't think we're welcome at either activity now.

I force the thought away. "I got the dress. I have to get it altered when we're back home, but if I'm honest, I don't think Hannah wants to come."

"What?" Julia looks up. "Why not?"

"Have you seen *Carrie the Musical*?"

"I've seen *Carrie* the movie, like a normal person?"

SAY A LITTLE PRAYER

"And I've seen the *Carrie* episode of *Riverdale*," Ben says. "Which is basically the same thing."

"First of all, it's not," I say. "But I don't think she wants to watch her friends have the time of their lives without her."

Ben shakes his head. "That's bullshit. *We're* her friends. *We* want her there. She shouldn't have to miss her senior prom."

"I know. She shouldn't have to do a lot of things."

The words come out sharper than I intend. I feel Julia stiffen next to me and realize we're straying dangerously close to the thing we don't talk about. I swallow the anger crawling its way up the back of my throat and scramble for another topic. Something safe. Something normal. Something that hides my growing urge to stick my head out the window and scream.

I'm saved by the squeal of feedback through the bus speakers as someone taps on the microphone again. We all flinch, and when I peer over the rows of heads in front of me, I see Cindy standing at the front of the aisle.

"Good morning, campers!" she chirps, one hand braced on the seat next to her as we bump over another pothole. "Who's ready for field trip day?"

Her voice is so sweet it makes my teeth hurt, but most of the people around us cheer, like they think this bright-eyed, slightly manic persona is completely believable.

"We're all going to have *sooo* much fun," Cindy continues, dragging out the ends of her words until they start to run together. "But, before we begin, let's take a minute to preview today's lesson. Like your schedule says, today's focus is the virtue of generosity. You'll still get your free time in town, don't worry," she adds, when a few of us exchange nervous glances. "But I encourage you to use this time to reflect on how you can spread God's word to the larger community. Can anyone tell me why generosity is so important?"

The first few rows of campers look down, purposefully avoiding eye contact as Cindy peers at us over the mic. Julia tips her head in my direction, lips curling in a soft, secret smile, and whispers, "You'll never guess what she's about to say."

Her breath ruffles the hair tucked behind my ear, and for a minute, my brain goes wonderfully, blissfully blank. "Does it have to do with going to hell?" I ask.

Up front, Cindy seems to give up on waiting for an answer. She tightens her grip on the mic and says, "Generosity is important because God doesn't want you to end up in hell. He wants you to experience eternal salvation, and Proverbs 14:21 says, 'blessed is he who is generous to the poor.'"

"Yup." I nod. "There it is."

Julia bites her lip to keep from laughing, and I'm suddenly very glad Pastor Young isn't here to lecture us again. I like watching her laugh. I've seen her do it thousands of times, but as I watch the dimples deepen on either side of her mouth, a single thought clangs through the back of my mind.

You can't lose this.

I don't care how many sins I have to commit this week. I don't care if Pastor Young thinks I'm a bad influence. I can't lose Julia, and if the only way to keep her is by proving her father

SAY A LITTLE PRAYER

wrong, I'll tear his congregation apart from the inside.

Cindy clears her throat, pulling everyone's attention back to the front of the bus. "Now I want to talk about something serious," she says. "Generosity can be a guiding light, but that means it also has a shadow—greed. I'm sure I don't have to tell you that greed is everywhere. It exists to drive a wedge between us and God, to lure us in with false promises of material gain. I know we're all looking forward to shopping this morning, but before you check out, take a minute and think about what you're buying. Is it something you need? Are you trying to show off to your friends? Could you be using your time and resources to help someone else instead?"

Cindy presses a dramatic hand to her chest as her gaze sweeps the length of the bus. "The best way to show God's generosity is through action. Remember that. And don't forget to fill out your workbook prompts before we get back to camp. You'll need them later tonight when you meet with your groups."

She hands the microphone back to the driver, but it takes another minute for talk to resume across the bus. The implication is clear—even though this entire field trip revolves around our short-lived ability to purchase material goods, we are not, under any circumstances, to do anything of the sort. Cindy will probably make a list of anyone who returns to the bus with a shopping bag. She'll probably make everyone pray for them on the way home.

That's fine, I think, watching the cornfields outside my window give way to gray strip mall parking lots. *This time, I won't get caught.*

101

Committing the sin of greed seems pretty straightforward, especially compared to yesterday's lesson. I just have to buy something. I just have to want something badly enough to take it without considering the consequences, and Ben and Julia's thrift store side quest has given me the perfect opportunity.

The bus turns into the parking lot, circling until it finds a spot near the back, and I'm out of my seat before we stop moving.

"Be back at noon!" Cindy calls from the front. "And don't forget your workbooks!"

Julia squeezes into the aisle behind me. There's a line forming between her eyebrows as we follow each other down the aisle, and I wonder if she's also thinking about Cindy's warning, how it would look if the pastor's daughter came back with a bag of thrift store finds. I used to joke that Hannah inherited Mom's perfectionism, but sometimes I think Julia could give them both a run for their money.

Ben keeps tossing furtive, knowing looks over his shoulder as we disembark, completely oblivious to the vibe shift happening behind him. "Wow," I say after he nearly trips down the stairs. "He's really bad at this whole secret thing."

To my relief, Julia's expression finally softens. "Terrible," she confirms. "I'm surprised the whole camp doesn't know by now."

"Maybe they've just decided to let you have this."

She snorts out a soft, delicate laugh, and when she steps onto the asphalt behind me, she almost looks like her old self. "Maybe," she says, throwing an arm around my shoulders. "Let's go find out."

VIII

When God Closes a Door, He Opens a (Thrift Store) Window

*W*hen Ben and Julia said their secret thrift store was "just across the street," I kind of assumed there'd be a sidewalk or, at the very least, a gravel path snaking from the back of the Walmart over to the strip mall. You know, the kind of thing a girl in Birkenstocks could theoretically cross without fearing for her life. I had not, however, been expecting the acre of knee-high grassy weeds stretching between us and our destination, littered with trash and humming with unseen insects.

"This better be worth it," I say, brushing dirt from my legs as we emerge into the parking lot on the other side. "Or I swear to god, Ben, you're carrying me back."

He laughs and hops onto the sidewalk. "Told you not to pack Birkenstocks."

The strip mall is relatively empty, just a few cars parked between a smoothie shop and a vet clinic, but the building on the end looks deserted. A fine layer of dust covers the door, and the only indication it's not completely abandoned comes from the handwritten sign taped inside the front window that reads THREADS SECONDHAND CLOTHES.

Ben steps around me and opens the door. "Smell that?"

I inhale, then almost choke on the thick pine-scented air. Or at least, I think it's supposed to be pine. I also detect hints of Febreze and mothballs and something that may or may not be dead. "What *is* that?"

Ben pats my shoulder as the door falls shut behind us. "Possibility."

It takes a minute for my eyes to adjust to the gloom, and when they finally do, it takes another for my brain to fully process what I'm seeing. The store is larger than I expected, rows of tightly packed garments stretching from wall to wall. There's hardly room to walk, let alone browse, and there's a different disheveled display everywhere I turn. Racks of sequined evening gowns, piles of frayed denim, dusty bookshelves stuffed with Hawaiian shirts. After years of tearing my way through frustratingly generic Midwestern Goodwills, this place feels like a gift.

"Holy shit," I whisper. "This is incredible."

Julia's lips twitch in a tepid smile. "Told you."

But when I turn to follow Ben down the first aisle, she doesn't move. Instead, she wavers in front of the door, watching his retreating back with a mixture of longing and concern. I tip my head to the side. "Are you coming?"

"I don't . . . I shouldn't."

"Why? Because Cindy might think you're a bad person?"

SAY A LITTLE PRAYER

Julia's shoulders stiffen. "You don't always have to be like that, you know."

"Like what?" I ask.

"*That*." She waves a hand in my direction. "Scornful and dismissive. You don't know everything, Riley."

I bite back another instinctive, snappy retort. Julia has the end of her braid twisted around a finger, knuckles whitening with each anxious tug. Maybe I don't know everything, but I know her. I know when I've hit a nerve.

"I'm sorry," I say, stepping back into the aisle. "That's not what I meant."

"I know." Julia releases a breath. Her hand falls back to her side, but her fingers still scratch nervously at her jeans. "And it's not Cindy. It's . . . I'm an example, Riley. I can't just do whatever I want. People look to me here."

"For what?"

"I don't know." She gives a half-hearted shrug. "Guidance?"

A memory stirs in the back of my mind, hazy and slightly out of focus. Ten-year-old Julia standing at the pulpit during Christmas Eve service, reading from the Bible in a clear, strong voice. She barely looked at the book open before her. She didn't need to. Someone else took her place after that, another youth group girl I can't quite recall, but Julia was the one everyone talked about. *She was lovely wasn't she? Such a wonderful speaker, just like her father.*

She *was* wonderful, of course, but I also remember how she'd paced my room the week before, reciting her assigned lines over

105

and over. She'd taped the passage inside her textbooks so she could practice between classes, muttered it to herself on our walk home from school, and tried so many different inflections that the words started looping through my mind, too, a constant, anxious refrain.

And the angel said to them, "Fear not, for behold, I bring you good news of great joy that will be for all the people."

And the angel said to them, Fear not.

Fear not, fear not, fear not—

I hadn't thought anything of it at the time. Even then, I knew how particular Julia could be, especially when it came to church activities. I'd brushed it off as another one of her perfectionist tendencies, but now, when she finally meets my gaze through the dust motes swirling between us, I'm wondering if it's always been deeper than that.

Maybe this is why I'm here. Maybe this is why Pastor Young thinks I'm a bad influence.

"Do you trust me?"

I hold out a hand and watch as Julia blinks in surprise. "I . . . what?"

"Do you trust me?" I repeat.

"Of course, but—"

"But nothing." I motion her toward me, deeper into the store. "Come here and show me how this works."

Julia's expression is still guarded, but this time, when I step into the aisle, she follows. "You don't need me to show you," she says. "You've been thrifting before."

SAY A LITTLE PRAYER

"Sure, but according to you and Ben, this store is *special*. What's the secret?"

"There is no secret!"

We both jump as Ben's head pops out from behind a rack of graphic T-shirts. "Jesus Christ, Ben!" I press a hand to my chest. "Don't do that! I thought you were a ghost."

He ignores me, gliding a hand over the top of the hangers instead. "There's no secret," he repeats. Then he lowers his voice and whispers, "*The store provides*," before sinking back behind the rack. When I peer around the corner, he's gone.

"Cool," I say. "That was normal. *The store provides?*"

Julia nods. "He's right. Close your eyes."

"Excuse me?"

"Do you trust me?"

The same question I'd just asked her. The same one I'd always answer with a vigorous, emphatic *yes*. Julia's finally grinning, hand outstretched in my direction, and I think that even if I didn't, even if she wasn't one of the most important people in my life, I would absolutely lie to keep her here. I squeeze my eyes shut, and I have a single second to process the warm press of her fingers around my wrist before she tugs me into the next aisle.

"Good," she says. "Now put your hand on the rack."

I swallow, suddenly very aware of my pulse fluttering under the exact spot where Julia's touching me. "I know how to thrift."

"Do you want me to show you or not?" She places my hand deliberately over the nearest rack. "You can't look. Just stop when something feels right because the store—"

"'The store provides,' I heard. It actually gets weirder the more you say it." I shake my head, eyes still stubbornly closed. "And what do you mean by 'feels right'?"

"For me, it's kind of like a spark."

I choke back a breathy laugh. My fingertips are already buzzing with a very different kind of energy, and I flex both hands as Julia guides me down the aisle. At first, the only thing I feel is my own uneven heartbeat and the reassuring press of Julia's palm between my shoulder blades. Then, just when I'm wondering how long I have to pretend to do this, something soft snags between my fingers.

"Wait!"

We both stop, and I tug a long mustard-yellow skirt from the rack. Julia's eyes widen. "Oh," she breathes. "It's beautiful."

The pleated fabric is silky between my fingers, and even though it's not something I'd usually wear, I can't seem to put it down. It feels like it belongs on an art teacher or an up-and-coming actor, someone eccentric and glamorous who knows exactly what they want. It's my size, too, and when I look up, mouth partially open in disbelief, Julia is grinning.

"Told you," she says. *The store provides.*

Maybe it does. I tuck the skirt over the crook of my arm as we continue browsing. No wonder Hannah likes this place. It gives off the same strange, vaguely disarming energy as her collection of crystals back home. Like any second I'm going to read my fortune in the row of hats dangling from the wall or find my true love lurking between the plates of tarnished jewelry.

SAY A LITTLE PRAYER

Ben is already digging through the back aisles when we catch up, occasionally tossing another garment into the haphazard pile at his side.

"Find something?" he asks without looking up.

I shrug. "Maybe. I'm not usually a skirt girly."

"The store doesn't give you what you want. It shows you what you need."

"Oh, really?" I pluck a starchy gray button-down from the top of his pile. "And you need this for what, exactly?"

Ben snatches it back, tips of his ears flaring pink. "It's for New York."

I've never been to New York, so it's entirely possible everyone dresses in the same dull, neutral palette Ben keeps pulling from the racks, but something about the lack of color makes me stop. I glance down at the blue flamingos patterned across Ben's tie-dye tank top and try to imagine him buttoning himself into a business-casual dress shirt for two whole weeks this summer. The hesitation must be clear on my face because he stops digging, arms falling dejectedly at his sides.

"Oh," he says. "You hate it."

"No!" I shake my head. "Of course not! It's just . . . a little boring, don't you think?"

"This is what they wear in New York."

"Says who?"

"A Google search for 'Manhattan street fashion'?"

"That can't possibly be right. You're going to art school, Ben. No one is this allergic to color."

109

Julia reaches down to pluck a pair of khaki trousers from his ever-growing pile. "Didn't you already figure out your packing list? Why do you suddenly need a new wardrobe?"

Ben's shoulders slump. "I don't know. It's just that most of the other students have been doing this program since they were, like, ten. They all live in the city. They probably take classes like this all the time, and I don't want them to know I don't."

"Who cares?" Julia asks. "You got into the program, too. If your classmates don't already like who you are, that's their problem."

"Weird advice from someone who tried to go blond last year."

"Hey! That was *your* idea!"

She glances at me for backup, but any words of reassurance stick in the back of my throat. Because I get it. I understand what Ben is trying to say even if Julia can't. It's one thing to measure success in test scores and college admissions. Numbers are tangible. They're real. At the end of the day, people like Julia can know for a fact that their work is better than everyone else's, but Ben and I live in the subjectivity of creative pursuits. There's no real way to know if we're ever good enough because everyone's definition of "good" is different. Ms. Tina thinks I'm good enough to cast in her show. She trusts me with the material, but I could get onstage in a few weeks and find that the entire school hates my performance. It's a different kind of vulnerability that never stops being terrifying.

I wonder how long Ben's felt the pressure of it eating him from the inside out. I wonder how long I haven't noticed, too absorbed in my own problems to think about the people around me.

110

SAY A LITTLE PRAYER

"Hey." I step forward and gently tug those hideous khaki pants from his grip. "You know I think you're brilliant, right? You're talented and smart and so fucking cool that if your new classmates don't see it, I'm honestly worried for their health."

Ben snorts out a laugh. "It's not just the students, you know. Even the faculty list is stacked. Did I tell you they got Markell Fansworth to come for week two? I literally did my final last year on the historical implications of the 1982 Fashion Week, but sure. He can just *be my professor*. What if—?"

"Ben!" I grab him by the shoulders. "I'm going to be so real with you. No one knows who that is."

Julia raises a hand. "I do."

"That doesn't count, Julia; you know everything. The point," I say, forcing Ben to look me in the eye, "is that one person's opinion will not make or break your career. You got into that program for a reason, and you're just as worthy of being taught by whatever niche, underground art celebrity they hire for the week."

"He's not—" Ben closes his eyes. "Sometimes, it physically pains me how little you know about things that aren't musical theater."

"I have to be selective, okay? There's only so much room up here."

"Yeah, and most of it is Sondheim lyrics."

I give his shoulder a playful shove, but the corner of Ben's mouth is finally lifting in a hint of his usual smile. "Go," I say. "Find something else." I drop the khakis to the floor as he disappears between the racks, then turn toward Julia. "Thank god we're here. Can you believe he wanted to dress like a Midwestern bank teller all summer?"

Julia laughs, absentmindedly tugging a dress off a nearby rack. "Tragic."

I don't know if she's actually browsing or just looking for something to do with her hands, but the minute she holds up the dress, my breath catches in the back of my throat. It's absolutely her style—knee-length and subtly vintage with the dark green fabric cinched in at the waist. I immediately picture her wearing it downtown, sunglasses perched on the end of her nose as the fabric swishes around her bare legs. People would probably stop to ask where she'd bought it. They'd probably compliment her, too, point out how the color makes her eyes look like melting pockets of amber.

"Oh my god," I breathe. "*Please* tell me you're getting that."

Julia's head snaps up, like she's suddenly remembering where we are. "Oh, no," she says, guilt clear on her face. "I'm not . . . We can't buy anything, remember?"

"Ben's buying something," I point out.

"That's different. He's Ben."

"But do you want it?"

Her gaze drops to the floor. I know she wants the dress. I know she wants to leave with *something*. It's the whole reason she and Ben dragged me out here in the first place, but the indecision is clear on her face, baked into the tense set of her shoulders. Maybe a kind, generous person would leave it at that. Maybe the fact that I don't let her go means I'm just as terrible and greedy as Cindy wants me to believe, but looking at Julia now, her face shadowed in the dim light of the store, I don't see how that's a bad thing.

"I shouldn't," she says, voice barely more than a whisper. "It would go against the whole lesson, wouldn't it? Besides, Ben might need help, and I still haven't started our assignment for the afternoon and—"

"Julia!"

She stops, fingers once again tugging at the end of her braid. I pry the dress from her grasp, then hold out my other hand. "It's okay," I say. "We're just looking. You're allowed to look."

Julia's throat bobs. She glances over her shoulder, like she's fully expecting Cindy to appear between the racks and smack her across the face with a Bible, before her gaze drops to my outstretched hand.

"Fine," she says, completely oblivious to the heat pooling in the center of my palm. "I'm just looking."

I grin and tug her into the dark embrace of the aisle. The mothball scent is worse back here, still laced with something I think has to be dead squirrel, but I shove the thought away as we move. I can't see Ben through the racks. I have no idea how far we've wandered from the door, but I don't care. We keep walking, pulling piece after piece from the shelves as we go. A vintage pair of wraparound pants. A denim jumpsuit with stars sewn on the cuffs. Floor-length gowns and matching silk gloves. Beautiful things. Impractical things. Things I want to hang in my closet, just so I can call them mine.

Last year, I'd become low-key obsessed with Oliver Henderson, the senior who played Javert in our production of *Les Misérables*. He was one of those boys who felt too pretty to be real, who looked you in the eye when you talked and always optioned up in "Stars." I used to tell Mom rehearsal started half an hour before it did just so she'd let me stay after school and watch him rehearse through the window of a practice room. I felt desperate, like I'd do anything in the world for more time with him, and even when I had it, the satisfaction never lasted long.

That's what greed is, I think. Wanting more, wanting too much. I've seen the way it warps people—how Pastor Young likes to guilt his congregation into dropping a few more dollars into the offering plate or how most of the church elders drive new cars and live in nice houses while preaching against material wealth. This morning, it seemed like an easy enough sin to commit. I was going to buy something nice, something I felt good in, then sit back and bask in the knowledge that greed didn't have to be this dark, twisted thing if I didn't let it. There's power in taking the things you want, but right now, I'm not thinking about the clothes at all. I'm just thinking about Julia. About how the only thing I truly want is more of her. I want to see her in the dresses we pull from the rack. I want to drink in every second of her beside me, and I want, more than anything, to pretend we're *fine*. That there's not a chance the universe will tear us apart the second we leave this shop.

Vaguely, I know time is passing. I know somewhere outside the dusty confines of this room, the world continues to turn. I know that someone might take this from me, too, one day, so when Julia gets stuck halfway inside a vintage Buffalo Bills

SAY A LITTLE PRAYER

sweater and laughs like she doesn't have a care in the world, I sink my claws in a little deeper. *More.* I want more vintage gowns and pinstriped blazers and ugly graphic T-shirts. I want more time in this cramped, windowless dressing room where neither of us care what consequences might be lurking outside.

"I like this," Julia says, struggling to zip the back of my very tight, very itchy velvet dress. "You look like a movie star."

I hold my breath as the fabric closes around my ribs. "I look like I'm doing a low-budget production of *Sunset Boulevard*."

"Isn't there a movie star in that show?"

"Yeah. She murders a guy at the end of the second act."

"Iconic." Julia finally gives up on the zipper and tosses a sweater in my direction. "Try this instead."

She's still wearing a dress I'd tugged off a dusty mannequin—a strapless tulle number covered in sequins. I personally think she looks great, so the fact she's handing me the single ugliest piece of fabric I've ever seen is a little insulting. It's like someone decided halfway through production that the plaid they'd committed to wasn't going to cut it. It's a mess of orange and red splotches, the words STAY GROOVY embroidered across the front in neon green thread. The unflattering combination of colors does nothing but wash out my already pale skin, but if I look at it from the side, it's almost camp.

"I don't know," I say. "I don't think it's for me."

One of Julia's eyebrows arches toward her hairline. "Really? I like it."

There's a single bulb dangling from the ceiling above us. Its

115

orange glow catches in Julia's hair, illuminating her reflection in the mirror behind me. Her gaze drops to my neck, where the front two buttons of the sweater lay open against my skin. It's just a glance, hardly more than a second, but a strange pressure closes around my ribs.

More, I think. *More, more.*

"You sure?" I ask. "It's not too much?"

I can't tell if the heat building under my skin is because I'm wearing layers of wool in seventy-five-degree heat or because of the way Julia's looking at me now. I don't know which I'd prefer. Both options feel safer here, with a heavy velvet curtain strung between us and the rest of the world. Julia blinks, lips parting on a sudden inhale, but before she can speak, the curtain surrounding the dressing room is pulled back.

"Oh my god!" I squint into the sudden burst of light. "What the hell, Ben?"

"Chill." Ben has his eyes purposefully trained toward the ceiling, one shoulder braced against the wall. "I'm not looking. Just making sure you two know how late it is."

He holds up his phone, and after I get past the screensaver of his face photoshopped onto all four *Stranger Things* kids, I notice the time: 11:52. Eight minutes before we're supposed to be back on the bus.

"Oh shit!" I yank the curtain closed, suddenly grateful for my years of backstage quick changes. It takes less than thirty seconds to kick off my dress, shimmy back into my street clothes, and grab my things. "Julia, we have to go!"

"Coming!"

Her voice is muffled, head stuck somewhere in the sleeve of her T-shirt. I help her tug it the rest of the way on before racing toward the counter, fumbling with my wallet as I go. Schedule or not, I still have a sin to commit. By the time the silver-haired woman sitting behind the register folds my purchases into a plastic bag, Ben is hovering by the door, eyes peeled on the parking lot across the street.

"They're boarding," he says, one hand pressed against the dusty glass.

I shoot him a glare as I snatch my bag from the counter. "Would it have killed you to give us a time check any sooner?"

"First it was 'How dare you interrupt me?' and now it's 'Wow, Ben, why didn't you interrupt me earlier?' There's no winning with you."

Julia skids to a stop between us. She still has that green dress slung over her arm, but I feel her hesitate when she reaches the counter. Every line in her body is tense, clearly torn between her desire for the dress and her prior obligation to God, and for the first time all morning, I hesitate, too. The plastic bag dangling from my elbow feels absurdly conspicuous now. Pastor Young would notice it immediately. He'd notice Julia's, too, and that would be all the confirmation he needed.

Bad influence. Sinner. Wrong.

"Here." I stuff my shopping bag into the bottom of my tote, making sure my workbooks cover the plastic. "Put your dress in my bag."

Julia's eyes widen. "What? No, Riley, I can't—"

"No one has to know, Julia. I promise."

Her teeth skate over her bottom lip, and I want, more than anything, to reach out and tell her it's okay. It's okay to want things, to take them when she can. It's okay to be greedy, regardless of what her father says, and it doesn't make her a bad person.

Slowly, Julia tugs her wallet from her back pocket. She runs her thumb back and forth across the faded leather until her jaw sets, and she rips it open.

Ben pumps his fists into the air, and I bite back a grin as the cashier rings her up. When she's done, I stuff her dress into my bag. Let Julia think my offer is generous. Let her think I'm being a good friend. She doesn't need to know I'm still thinking about the way Pastor Young's gaze had narrowed on me yesterday or the very particular way his lip had curled when he said the words *bad influence*.

He's looking for reasons to write me off. I won't give him this one, not before I finish what I came here to do.

"Let's go."

I pull Julia toward the door, ignoring the awkward thump of my tote bag against my back. Ben stuffs his phone back in his pocket. He has just enough time to shout, "Thank you!" over his shoulder to the cashier before the three of us spill back into the sunny afternoon.

IX

I Seriously Consider Cannibalism

I keep our purchases tucked in the bottom of my bag for the duration of the trip home, but the minute we file back into the cafeteria, it's clear that Ben, Julia, and I aren't the only ones who sinned this morning. When Torres joins us in line for food, she glances over both shoulders before surreptitiously slipping a tube of lip gloss into Delaney's palm.

"Here," she whispers. "I could only grab the one."

Delaney nods and tucks it safely into her back pocket. "Thanks. Remind me to show you the eyeshadow palette tonight."

I hate how guilty Torres looks when she turns back to the front, like she thinks Jesus is going to rip himself off the wooden cross on the wall and call a plague upon her house or something. Even Cindy—God's favorite counselor and Heaven's chosen mouthpiece—is sporting a shiny silver charm bracelet I know she wasn't wearing this morning. She keeps tucking her hair behind her ears, flashing it in Gabe's direction like she wants nothing more than for him to tell her it looks nice.

So much for ignoring the false promise of material gain.

Pastor Young stands at the end of the kitchen assembly line, wearing an oversized apron with the words GRILL, PRAY, LOVE stitched across the front. It's his Sunday Game Day Outfit, the same one he's worn every weekend for as long as I can remember, and the sight of it sends an unexpected pang through me now. Hannah and I hadn't been invited to this year's Super Bowl party. It used to be a tradition. We used to huddle together on the Young's patio, pretending not to feel the biting February chill as Pastor Young flipped burgers in this very apron. He'd felt like a second father back then, someone we could trust, and it wasn't until last year that I realized how impossibly naive I'd been.

When I came out, my own father bought a shirt that said GAY DAD in rainbow letters and only dropped it at Goodwill because I told him wearing it would probably send the wrong message. When Mom brought Hannah back from Cleveland, he'd sat in her room for hours, pointing at the different birds outside her window and reading stories from the local paper so she wouldn't have to be alone. Mom might have taught me how to throw a punch, but Dad's the one who told me it was okay to cry about it. I can't imagine Pastor Young crying over anything except the majesty of the Lord, and I'm fairly certain he's never worn a rainbow in his life. That's not someone I want to miss, and I hate how even now, when I'm fully planning to destroy his life, part of me still feels a little bad about it.

Pastor Young looks up when Julia and I step forward. "Welcome back," he says, his gaze sweeping from my face to

SAY A LITTLE PRAYER

my mud-flecked sandals. "Glad to see you took today's lesson to heart."

I know the compliment is supposed to be genuine. I know he can't see the clothes tucked in the bottom of my bag, but I still feel the warning laced beneath every word. "Of course." I nod toward the sizzling tray of casserole behind the counter, eager to change the subject. "Did you make that?"

Pastor Young shakes his head. "Not this time."

"Bummer. Yours is always the best."

I flash Pastor Young my most charming grin as he hands me a plate, ignoring the way the corners of his mouth pinch. Julia's watching me, too, expression locked somewhere between concern and alarm, and it's not until we're out of earshot that she leans in and whispers, "What are you doing?"

Being a good influence. I force the thought away. "Just being polite."

"Well, stop it. It's freaking me out."

But that's the thing, I think as we drop into two empty seats toward the back of the cafeteria. I *can't* stop. Pastor Young might want me back. He might genuinely believe he's saving my wayward soul, but he's still waiting for me to slip. I can't give him or Mr. Rider any reason to discredit me, not before I've blasted my essay to anyone who will read it.

Most of the people around us are still waiting for food, but the ones who've already found seats are poring over their workbooks. Greer's sitting at the other end of our table, one foot propped against her chair as she frantically circles a line at the bottom of

121

the page. Something about the image feels off, and it's not until I look again that I realize the seat beside her is empty. Amanda is nowhere to be seen. I avert my gaze and pull out my own workbook. Vaguely, I remember Cindy telling us to finish our assignments before we returned, but I haven't opened my book since yesterday. I don't think generosity is something you can study for, but even Ben pauses by our table on his way to the kitchen.

"Did either of you finish that assignment?" he asks, looking from me to Julia.

I shake my head. "Do I look like I finish assignments?"

"Yes, actually. You're usually quite reliable."

I'm saved from responding by Delaney and Torres, who slide onto the bench across from us. "You talking about the prompts from this morning?" Delaney asks. "I just finished them on the bus."

Ben perks up. "Really? How did you . . ." He flips through his workbook until he finds the right page. ". . . *show the light of God's generosity in the community today?*"

Delaney grins, stabbing her fork into her casserole. "I let some lady go ahead of me in the Walmart checkout line."

"Are you serious?" Torres looks vaguely scandalized. "I spent half an hour chasing carts in the parking lot."

"That's your problem, Torres. I'm not on their payroll."

I bite back a grin as Ben nods. "That's good," he says. "I totally did that checkout thing, too. You all saw me."

"Definitely," Delaney says without missing a beat. "It was really moving."

SAY A LITTLE PRAYER

Ben shoots a finger gun in her direction, grabs a potato chip from Julia's plate, and continues toward the kitchen. I shake my head at his retreating back. There's nothing more frustrating than Ben Young's academic history. As far as I know, he's never once done his homework on time. He's always finishing essays on the bus or memorizing speeches between classes or asking me to quiz him in the fifteen minutes before we leave for school. To this day, I have no idea how he got a 1500 on the SATs without even pretending to study, and I'm not surprised that level of nonchalance extends to camp, too.

After all, there's a reason why no one lectured him for walking back into camp with an armful of shopping bags. Because he's *Ben*, and he has yet to meet a situation he can't charm his way out of.

"Do you think that assignment is mandatory?" I ask, lowering my voice as the chatter swells around us. "Or could I, like, make something up if they ask?"

I glance over my shoulder at Julia, expecting to find her reviewing the prompts we'd missed this morning, but instead, her prayer book sits open in her lap. The page is tilted up, so the only thing I can see is the small butterfly sticker she's placed on the back cover—the freckling of pink wings and gossamer-thin antennae the only thing differentiating her book from the rest of ours. She snaps it closed when she sees me looking.

"I'm sorry, what?"

There's a soft flush sliding over her cheeks, like I've caught her in the middle of something strangely intimate. I shift in my seat,

123

eyes dropping down to my lunch. "Nothing. I was just asking if you did the assignment."

"Oh." Immediately she's back to normal, expression smoothing into casual interest so quickly I can almost believe I'm imagining things. "Right. I should probably get started on that."

Julia drops her prayer book into her bag but makes no move to pull anything else out or start the assignment. She just swirls her straw around her cup of watery soda, takes a long sip, and leans both elbows on the table as Ben slides back onto the bench across from us. That's how we sit for the rest of lunch—Julia laughing with her friends like normal and me trying desperately not to look at the corner of the little blue book that's still peeking over the top of her bag.

Because I know what it looks like to write things you don't want anyone else to see. I recognize the careful way Julia had guarded her page, shielding the paper with her forearm. It's the same way I've been making notes about Pastor Young all week, but I can't, for the life of me, figure out what she could be writing. Or why there's a small obstinate part of my brain that thinks it has something to do with me.

The thing about waking up to a song where a twenty-three-year-old YouTube celebrity rhymes the word "sleek" with "Snapchat streak" is that eventually, the novelty of it wears off. When our alarm sounds the next morning, I'm so used to the screaming guitars and bone-rattling bass that I don't even jump. Maybe it's not so bad, actually. Maybe if I pull my blanket over my head and close my eyes, I can pretend it's one of those cool, edgy EDM songs Ben sometimes adds to our group playlists.

I'm right in the middle of gaslighting myself into believing that "Flexin' on That Gram" might be the greatest song of our generation and possibly of all time when Greer hauls herself out of bed and slams a hand into the power button. The room goes unnaturally silent as she glares down at the alarm, hair sticking up in a frizzy cloud around her head. Then she collapses deliberately back into bed, shoves a pillow over her face, and groans, "Fuck Mike Fratt," loud enough for the entire cabin to hear.

Delaney bursts out laughing, voice gravelly from sleep, and I have to bite my lip to keep from joining in.

Despite our rude awakening, the rest of the morning passes in relative normalcy. I decide very early on that I'm not going to think about Julia or her secret prayer book ever again. I'm not going to consider what had been more important than finishing her assignment, and I'm absolutely not going to wonder if it had something to do with me. That would be ridiculous. I have enough to worry about this week, and whatever Julia's telling God is none of my business.

Dew sparkles under my feet as I make my way toward the showers. The sky is a picture-perfect blue, the cool air a welcome relief after yesterday's heat, and I wonder if Ben has ever thought of painting the camp like this. The open field, the ring of trees, the soft, sloping lines of the cabins. I want to capture it now, to remember this strange, singular moment where I can almost understand what the others see in this place. Where I think I might be able to like it, too, if the circumstances were different.

Julia's still in the cabin when I return. I skip up the steps two at a time, absentmindedly humming our act one finale, and it's not until I drop my shower caddy next to my bunk that I realize she's staring.

"Good morning!" I say.

"Good morning." Her eyebrows lift a fraction of an inch. "You look like you're in a good mood."

I shrug and pull a faded sweatshirt from the bottom of my suitcase. It's not like I'm thrilled to be here, but something about this morning feels different. I've successfully committed two of the supposedly seven deadly sins. I can prove they aren't black and white, that they don't necessarily have to be bad, and Mr. Rider's plan to community-service me into a good, productive member of society is backfiring.

"I don't know," I say, falling into step beside Julia as we head toward the cafeteria. "I just have a good feeling about today."

She blinks. "You do?"

"What, is that not allowed?"

"No, it's totally allowed. I love this for you, but you've never had a good feeling about anything in your life. Last week you thought your math substitute was planning to kill you."

"Well, yeah. He was suspiciously interested in whether I turned in my homework."

"Right," Julia says, flinging an arm over my shoulders. "Because he was your *math substitute*."

It's actually pretty difficult, I realize, to not think about

SAY A LITTLE PRAYER

Julia when we're pressed together like this. We've always been comfortable—fingers interlocking, arms draped casually over each other's waists, hands almost brushing as we walk. It's one of the things I worried about when I came out, that the mere thought of me liking girls would be enough to make her second-guess reaching for me, but nothing's changed. She still puts her head on my shoulder when we watch TikToks during sleepovers, and I still pretend like it doesn't make my heart feel like it's beating somewhere outside my chest.

I used to think it was like this for everyone, that straight girls just got the luxury of *not* overthinking it every time their friend pulled them in for a picture, but I don't think that's true. Hannah and Amanda were close. It's impossible not to be when you spend that much time in the same studio, but even they never reached for each other the same way Julia does for me. They didn't lie together on the same mattress, bodies fused along one side, and stare contentedly up at the ceiling as the other talked about their day.

In a perfect world, I think that would mean something. In a perfect world, I think Julia would feel the same way about me.

I'm sweating by the time we enter the cafeteria, desperate for a tall stack of pancakes and some very strong coffee. I detangle myself from Julia, anticipating the familiar smell of frying bacon and overcooked eggs, but the air is abnormally cold, almost stale. I stumble to a halt, glancing toward the kitchen where a line of campers is usually already snaking through the assembly line. But that's empty, too. No one's grabbing a drink, no one's making coffee, and no one's piling their plate with this morning's breakfast options. Because there are no breakfast options.

There's no food at all.

I whirl toward Julia. "What the hell is this?"

It comes out more accusatory than I mean, but she just shakes her head, lips slightly parted as she stares at the empty kitchen. "I . . . have no idea."

And just like that, my good mood vanishes. Every vaguely positive thought flies right out of my head, and I'm back where I started—infuriated and resentful and all too ready to wrap my hands around Pastor Young's throat. Because this is his doing, obviously. We did something wrong, or he's trying to teach us a lesson and depriving us of breakfast is the only way to get it through our sinful, traitorous skulls.

Unfortunately, it's working. I would do unspeakable things for an omelet right now, including but not limited to accepting Jesus Christ as my personal savior.

Most of the other campers look just as confused as we are, clustered around the tables in nervous packs. When Pastor Young steps into the aisle, the conversation is so woefully subdued that he doesn't even bother with the microphone.

"Good morning, campers! I hope you're all feeling energized and refreshed after yesterday's field trip." I flinch as his too-bright voice echoes off the walls, and I drop onto a bench near the back. "As you can see from the lack of buffet line, we're doing something a little different this morning. Today's lesson is all about temperance. This virtue is often overlooked in our world of

SAY A LITTLE PRAYER

instant gratification, but I personally think it's one of the most important stepping stones on the path to enlightenment. Which, of course, is one of the reasons we'll be fasting today."

Next to me, Julia slides down in her seat, head barely visible over the top of the table. I close my eyes and resist the urge to join her. Why hadn't I bothered to look ahead at today's lesson? I could have bought snacks during our field trip or at least prepared myself for a day of misery. Judging by the number of nervous, wide-eyed looks flying around the cafeteria, I'm not alone.

"Oh, don't look so heartbroken," Pastor Young continues. "I know it feels daunting, but it's for the best. Like the other virtues, temperance has a darker counterpart rooted in sin—gluttony. It loves indulgence, it loves luxury, and in a world where we're often told more is better, it's easy to fall into its trap. Think of today as a chance to pause and reflect, to gain control over your earthly desires and understand what's truly missing from your life."

If this was yesterday, I might have leaned over to Julia and whispered, *Let me guess, the only thing missing is a relationship with Jesus Christ*. We might have laughed and rolled our eyes when Pastor Young confirmed it, but for once, I don't feel like joking. I'm so lost in my own frustration that I don't notice someone approach until they sit down on Julia's other side.

"Hey."

The last time I'd seen Greer, she'd been actively cursing Mike Fratt's name into her pillow. Now she looks wide awake, hair falling in smooth waves over her shoulders as she braces both elbows on the table. I wonder what sort of dark witchcraft she's

129

using to keep that level of shine under the shower's relentless barrage of hard water. My own hair has started smelling vaguely of sulfur.

"What?" I ask.

Greer ignores me and turns toward Julia instead, lifting a hand to her mouth so the counselors can't see her lips move. "Okay, so this is going to suck, but they did this during my first retreat, too. Most of the seniors still bring snacks in case they try again, so come back to the cabin during lunch and we'll figure something out."

"Really?" Relief breaks across Julia's face. She glances toward the front of the cafeteria, where her father is now leading everyone in a very dejected-sounding prayer. "Thanks, Greer. I'm so sorry about this."

"Don't be. It's not your fault. There should be plenty to go around, so feel free to tell the rest of your group. And don't look at me like that," Greer adds, gaze cutting in my direction. "I'm not trying to poison you."

I scowl down at the empty table. I wasn't aware I'd been looking at her in any particular way, but the thought of sitting in the soft, sun-warmed interior of our cabin and splitting snacks with her and Amanda makes my skin crawl. It's too familiar, too close. Too similar to how things used to be.

"I know," I say. "You're not the one I'm worried about."

"Oh, give it a rest, Riley." Greer scoffs, the sound so brutal and direct that several heads turn in our direction. "You think Amanda likes sharing a cabin with the girl who hit her in front

SAY A LITTLE PRAYER

of the entire senior hallway? You're not the victim here."

My hands curl into fists in my lap, knuckles whitening against the dark fabric of my jeans. "Well, I don't love sharing a cabin with the people who've been talking shit about my sister all semester, so I guess we're even."

It's out before I fully register what I'm saying, a toxic, heady cocktail mixed with four months of pent-up frustration. Greer blinks, drawing back in her seat. "What? I'm not—" she starts, but I don't want to hear the excuse.

I stand so abruptly the bench screeches across the linoleum tile. Up front, Pastor Young's prayer falters. He shoots me a withering glare, but I ignore him. There's something hot pushing against my rib cage, clawing for a way out, and Greer's single throwaway question lights the fuse. *What?* Like she's actually asking. Like she's never stopped to consider the consequences of her actions. Julia reaches for my arm, lips parting like she wants to call me back, but I slide out of her grip. I don't know why I'm coming apart now, why I can't hold my own against *Greer* of all people, but I know if I stay, there's a very good chance I'll combust right here at the table. I might take the entire camp with me.

So I don't listen when Julia says my name again. I don't stop when the rest of our table turns in my direction or when Gabe steps forward, hand outstretched to pull me back. I just inhale a tight, painful breath and push my way out of the cafeteria, leaving the door swinging listlessly behind me.

The girls' locker room is closer than my cabin. It's blessedly empty, quiet except for the soft drip of the leaky faucet in the

131

corner. I sag against the sink and squeeze my eyes shut, gripping the cool porcelain with both hands.

Don't cry.

I won't. I know that, at least. I didn't cry when I left Pleasant Hills, or when I failed my driver's test for the second time in a row, or when Leena dropped half a barricade on my foot during *Les Mis* rehearsal. In fact, I haven't cried since Christmas break, when Mom brought Hannah back from Cleveland and found me wavering in the hallway outside her room.

Oh, Riley, she'd whispered, pulling me into a tight embrace. *I'm so glad she has you. You really are her rock, you know.* She pressed a kiss to my forehead, and I'd swallowed over the tears building in the back of my throat. I could be Hannah's rock if she needed me to be. I could hold it together.

I spent the rest of that week in and out of Hannah's room, watching her stare blankly up at the ceiling until I was half convinced she'd never speak again. When she finally got out of bed, I was there to hand her the homework she'd missed, help review choreography, and drag her on long, chilly walks where we talked about nothing but our favorite unhinged Taylor Swift theories for hours at a time. I was the one who narrowed down a list of in-network therapists, who told everyone at school that she had the flu, and through it all, I didn't fall apart. I didn't cry. Because I was her rock. She needed me, and that meant all of my own messy, unresolved feelings had to stay locked away. If I didn't think about the past, I didn't have to think about Pleasant Hills in anything other than broad, pleasantly neutral strokes. If

SAY A LITTLE PRAYER

I didn't think about Pleasant Hills, I'd never have to confront the part of me that sometimes wishes I could close my eyes and go back to the way things were.

And even though I'm *fine*, even though I left a long time ago, *that's* the feeling coiling in my chest now. Not my anger on Hannah's behalf, not my frustration at Pastor Young's cruelty or my disbelief at Greer's lack of compassion, but the singular heart-wrenching ache of loneliness.

Maybe Greer is right. Maybe I don't believe in God anymore. Maybe I've been alone longer than I thought, floating untethered through a disordered universe with no higher power to guide me.

Footsteps crunch on the gravel outside. The sound trips some distant alarm bell in the back of my mind, and I whirl, hurling myself into the nearest stall. I fumble with the lock right as the door bangs open and hold my breath as someone comes to a stop exactly where I'd been standing a second before. Slowly, I sink onto the toilet lid and draw my knees into my chest.

I stay like that for one minute, two, listening to the ragged thump of my pulse in my ears. Then, right as my nerves are threatening to rattle their way out of my skin, the person outside lets out a soft, shaky sniff.

They're crying. The realization roots me to the spot. Someone else had also ditched our imaginary breakfast to come in here and fall apart alone.

Their back is turned, but I can just make out the shadowy outline of hands gripping the edge of the sink. The faucet creaks, quickly followed by the sound of water splashing into the cracked porcelain, and it's not until they step away to grab a paper towel that I finally catch a glimpse of their feet under the door.

Pristine white sneakers. Lacy ankle socks with two tiny pink sugarplums stamped over the ankle.

My next inhale catches in the back of my throat; I have to clamp a hand over my mouth to stifle it. Because I'd recognize those socks anywhere. Hannah has a pair stuffed in her drawer back home, a gift from her director after her last production of *The Nutcracker*. He got them customized for each senior, so Hannah's came embroidered with a tiny silver snowflake, but there's only one other girl from her studio who attends Pleasant Hills. The same girl who, after years of aggressively pursuing the part, finally got to play the Sugar Plum Fairy.

The same girl I've been actively avoiding since the day she landed me here in the first place.

It's another minute before I hear Amanda's breathing steady on the other side of the stall. Then, without warning, she tosses her wad of paper towels into the trash and storms back the way she'd come. The door slams behind her, leaving me alone in the dark once more. Slowly, carefully, I lower my feet to the ground. Only when I'm convinced she's not coming back do I unlock the door and let myself out of the stall, wondering all the while what someone like Amanda Clarke could possibly have to cry about.

X

If You Read the Gallagher Girls in Middle School, You're Gay Now

I don't know how long I sit in the locker room, one foot propped on the bench and the echo of Amanda's shaky exhale looping in my mind. At one point, I hear the faint crunch of gravel as people file out of the cafeteria and into their groups for the day, and still, I don't move. Because this doesn't make sense. Having a mental breakdown in a church camp locker room should be reserved for people like me, people with actual problems, and I happen to know for a fact that Amanda Clarke—heiress to the Miss Teen Ohio 1998 fortune—has nothing to cry about.

She has, like, a month of high school left. She already got into Indiana University's dance program, and she and Greer are planning a post-grad trip to Paris in July. I know this because Hannah was supposed to go, too, at one point, and because Amanda keeps posting scenes from *Emily in Paris* with the caption "so me" on her Instagram Story. She's *fine*. She's thriving actually, but the thought of her sneaking away to cry in the bathroom kind of shatters that pristine, glossy image.

I don't like imagining my enemies complexly. It really ruins the whole "revenge at all costs" thing I'm doing this week. So instead, when the voices outside fade and silence settles across the locker room once more, I start trying to list options that make sense.

Amanda is crying because:
1. She broke a nail.
2. The lack of proper breakfast got to her, too.
3. The hot water ran out this morning, and she couldn't complete her nine-step skin-care routine.

Normal reasons. Rational reasons. Reasons that make sense within the confines of my universe. None of them feel quite right. It's like someone took a knife to my brain, splicing the version of Amanda I knew with the one I'm avoiding now. Greer might have the longer résumé, status secured by her impressive need to control absolutely everything, but Amanda's power has always felt effortless. She floats through life, seemingly oblivious to the people stopping to check out her shoes or the color of her nail polish. Her hair always looks flawless, her silver cross necklace always sits perfectly in the hollow of her throat, and she's always happy to see you.

She's never upset. She certainly never cries, not even when Hannah invited her over after Christmas break and told her all about Cleveland.

SAY A LITTLE PRAYER

Amanda might not know people's locker combinations or coffee orders by heart, but she understood Hannah in the same innate, bone-deep way I know Julia and Ben. I could picture Greer becoming an acquaintance eventually, someone Hannah reached out to on birthdays or when she was back in town, but Amanda wasn't supposed to go anywhere. Now I'm wondering if their relationship had never been that deep. If maybe all Amanda wanted was to Save her, too.

By the time I leave the locker room, my legs ache from pacing and I feel no closer to finding an answer. The cool air from this morning is already starting to thicken, and I know without looking at the sky that a storm is on its way. I quicken my pace and keep walking, not looking up again until I find my group clustered around our regular picnic table. Gabe's head snaps up when I drop into the seat next to Delaney.

"Riley," he says. "How nice of you to join us. Is there something you'd like to say to the group?"

I grit my teeth and yank my workbook from my bag. "Not really."

Gabe's mouth twists in clear frustration, but this time, he doesn't let me slide. "Are you sure? Because everyone else managed to be here on time. How is your group supposed to trust you if you don't respect them in return?"

There's no way those two things are even remotely connected. There's no way anyone besides Gabe cares that I missed the first half of Bible class, but I feel this morning's leftover anger coil in my stomach. My fingers flex under the table, and I'm about to tell

137

him just that when Pastor Young's face flashes across my mind.

I'd hate for you to become a bad influence.

If I snap now, Gabe won't keep that to himself. He'd tell Pastor Young, who would probably tell Mr. Rider, and then this entire week will have been for nothing. I dig my nails into the tops of my thighs as my expression smooths into something I hope resembles genuine regret.

"You're right," I say. "I'm sorry."

Gabe blinks. His head cocks to the side, and for a minute, I think I've genuinely broken his brain. Delaney saves us both by thrusting her hand in the air.

"Can we go back to page thirty-two?" she asks. "I don't get what that passage is trying to say."

"Right." Gabe shakes his head, gaze returning to his workbook. "Sure. Where was I?"

Only when his attention shifts away do I finally slide down in my seat. I spend the rest of the morning glaring at my lap and pretending not to notice Greer trying to catch my eye across the table. I don't want to talk to her. I don't want to talk to anyone, and the longer Gabe speaks, the more my frustration grows, stoked by the hollow void of my empty stomach. When we finally break for lunch, I'm so annoyed that I don't even wait for Delaney to pack up her things. I just turn on my heel and march down the hill.

I hadn't planned to take Greer up on her offer to share snacks, but I'm so hungry that Satan himself could offer me a bag of trail mix and I'd probably kiss him on the mouth. The porch groans underfoot as I take the stairs two at a time, but when I reach for the cabin door, there's already someone opening it from the other side.

Amanda Clarke, with her perfect white sneakers and sugarplum socks, holding a half-eaten sleeve of peanut butter crackers in one hand.

We freeze—me on the porch, her in the doorway—and despite what happened in the locker room this morning, I think she looks perfectly fine. Sunlight glints off her hair, curls as infuriatingly moisturized as Greer's. Her makeup is the perfect combination of subtle and dewy I've been trying to master all year, and the corner of her mouth is still curled in that same little half smile. Then our eyes lock across the porch, and I think I finally see something crack. It's quick, a barely there tremor, but I catch it before her face smooths. I know that, no matter what Amanda says or how unshakable she pretends to be, we were still the ones in the locker room this morning, trying and failing to hold it together.

"Excuse me."

She pushes past me, shoulder knocking into mine on her way out. By the time I turn around, she's halfway down the stairs, disappearing around the side of the cabin just as Greer and Delaney come to a stop behind us.

"I didn't do anything!" I blurt, instinctively raising my hands as Greer's gaze lands on me.

I brace myself for the accusations, for a repeat of our fight at breakfast, but to my surprise, Greer just sighs. "I know," she says.

"She's been like that all week. She won't talk to me."

That can't possibly be true. Amanda and Greer are always together, whispering behind cupped hands, laughing over the same inconsequential jokes. Except now that I think about it, Greer had been alone at lunch yesterday. She'd been alone this morning, too, and Amanda had been in the locker room with me.

I turn away, absentmindedly rubbing my aching shoulder. "Maybe she finally got tired of the sound of your voice."

If Greer registers the insult, she doesn't react. She crosses the porch and pulls the screen door open. "Maybe," she says. "Or maybe I'm not the person she wants to talk to."

Last year during tech, a sandbag had swung loose from the rafters and nailed me in the ribs. The air had whooshed out of me at once, sudden and quick, and I spent the rest of the night wondering if I'd ever breathe properly again. That's how I feel now, watching Greer's shiny ponytail disappear into our cabin. Like she might as well have reached out and slammed her fist through the center of my chest. I grit my teeth around the ache, push the feeling to the back of my mind, and follow her inside.

Julia and Torres are already sitting cross-legged on the floor, snacks piled between them like a poorly designed summoning circle. Delaney leans down to inspect the haul, but Julia shoots to her feet the second she sees me. "Riley!"

She lurches forward, then stops just short of where I stand in the middle of the cabin. Her hands hover in the space between us, face a portrait of wary concern, and I realize that the last time she saw me, I'd been storming out of the cafeteria. I flash her a casual, toothy grin and hope for the life of me that she can't tell how difficult it is to pull off.

"What's up?" I ask.

"What's . . ." Julia blinks. "Are you okay?"

"Sure. Why wouldn't I be?"

Julia's face shutters, a split second of disoriented confusion, before she shakes her head. "Nothing," she says. "It's just good to see you."

She sinks back into the circle as I turn toward my bunk. The others have piled their workbooks against the side of my bed to make room on the floor, but when I start to nudge them aside, she stiffens again.

"Can you hand me my prayer book, actually?" she asks. "I'll just keep it over here. It's—the one with the butterfly sticker, yes."

I fish Julia's book from the pile and slide it across the floor. She tucks it under her thigh, and again, I try not to think about what she could possibly be writing. Instead, I sink into bed and lift a hand to catch the half-empty bag of cheese crackers Torres tosses my way. The crumbs smeared against the side of the plastic don't look particularly appetizing, but my stomach still growls at the sight. Does this count as gluttony? Is this truly one of the sins Pastor Young is so adamant we avoid?

"I thought the packing list said no food," I say, tearing open the top. "Is that just, like, a suggestion?"

Greer shrugs. "The last time we fasted wasn't exactly enjoyable, so I like to be prepared."

141

Prepared feels like an understatement. She's currently sitting with her back braced against her bedframe, distributing the snacks from her suitcase in color-coded order.

"Were you also learning about temperance last time?" Torres asks bitterly.

"I don't remember." Greer glances at Delaney. "Do you?"

Delaney shakes her head. "All I know is that Miles Briggs's mom threatened to sue because he was diabetic, so they ended up caving at dinner. And then we got a very weird sermon about how a relationship with God cures all ailments."

Julia winces. "I'm sorry."

"Not your fault," Greer says. "You weren't even there."

It's the second time today Julia has apologized for her father's actions. I wonder if she always feels this responsible for him, if she's ever tried to stop him before, or if that's nothing but my own wishful thinking.

"Are the counselors fasting, too?" I ask. "They're all remarkably perky."

Julia shakes her head. "They have a key to the kitchen, so they can just stop by whenever they want."

We all let out a collective groan. Of course the counselors can just *stop by*. Of course the rules don't apply to them. I burrow deeper into my blankets, momentarily overwhelmed by the blatant injustice of it all. How does Pastor Young keep getting away with this? Why am I the only one who seems to care? Sure, the others are annoyed, but they're also sitting in a circle on the floor, passing snacks back and forth like this is some sort of game.

Maybe it is to them. Maybe they genuinely can't imagine a world where things like this don't happen.

I shove another handful of crackers into my mouth and tug my prayer book from under my mattress. Between yesterday's field trip and this morning's breakfast fiasco, I haven't made much progress on my essay. The first few pages are still covered in a collection of random notes, observations from my time under the picnic table and shopping with Julia. Bits and pieces that hardly add up to something substantial. If I want Pastor Young gone, if that really is my goal at the end of this, I need to think bigger.

Of all the virtues we've been subjected to this week, temperance feels the hardest to wrap my head around. I can understand diligence or generosity if I try. I can almost see the point of those, but teaching temperance like this feels mean.

That's fine, I think, reaching down to fish a pen from the bottom of my tote bag. *I can be mean, too.*

It's like I've opened a spigot. Every dark pent-up feeling rushes out of me at once, pouring onto the page in hurried, incomplete sentences. I don't stop to see what I've written or go back to correct the obvious spelling mistakes. I don't pause to consider the implications either. I just write.

I don't understand how people are happy here. It's like they're all lying to me, pretending to believe in this thing that doesn't even make sense, and I'm tired of pretending it doesn't matter. It does. It matters that Pastor Young is still here, preaching his lies and playing the role of the perfect pastor like he's not the one who destroyed everything.

I turn the page and keep going, each word coming quicker than the last.

He talks like he's invincible, like he's the ultimate moral authority on good and evil, but everyone else is just as complicit. They still follow him, they still believe his lies, and they still let it happen. Maybe they're too cowardly to confront the truth. Maybe they don't care. Or maybe I'm the only one smart enough to see through this place. It's not about guidance or community or faith. It's about fear, and I won't let him get away with it anymore.

This isn't an essay, it's a reckoning. And it's time for Pastor Young to go.

I sit back, and underline the last sentence with three trembling strokes. There it is. The thesis I've been chasing since that first afternoon in the chapel. It's not perfect. If this was an AP lit essay, Ms. Nguyen would definitely send it back for "further clarification," but it's also the first time I've written it down. The first time I think I might actually be able to pull this off.

144

Mr. Rider was right, I think as I close my prayer book and lean my head against the wall. *I feel better already.*

"Torres, I swear if you don't stop moving, I'm going to climb up there and *eat you.*"

Delaney hurls her pillow against the bottom of Torres's bunk as the springs let out another squeaky groan. It doesn't help. Torres isn't the only one tossing and turning tonight, unable to get comfortable as the clock ticks past midnight.

"I'm sorry," she groans. "I'm just so *hungry.*"

"I know. I can hear your stomach from here."

I stare at the sagging underside of Julia's mattress and try to force myself into a blissful, dreamless sleep. If I close my eyes, I can almost hear tomorrow's breakfast—the sizzle of pancakes on an open stovetop and the soft crackle of frying bacon.

Or maybe that's *my* stomach now, growling at the thought of something substantial.

Delaney rolls over in bed, blankets rustling as she drags them with her. "This is ridiculous," she mutters.

"*Shhh!*" Amanda hisses from across the room. "I'm trying to sleep."

"No you're not! You're as miserable as we are."

It's ironic, I think, that today's fast was supposed to teach us about temperance. In reality, the only thing it's done is put us at each other's throats. I turn my head in time to watch the clock on the bedside table flip from midnight to 12:01 a.m. Seven hours until our morning wake-up call. It's strange how slow time can move when it wants to, when the only thing separating us from a well-earned meal is a few hours of sleep. Personally, I'd like nothing more than to drift into oblivion and pretend today never happened. Despite my best efforts, I don't think inhaling half a box of crackers and two squeezable applesauce pouches counts as gluttony. The devil probably thinks bigger than that. My prayer book is bursting with new pages of notes for my essay, but it won't matter if I can't figure out a way to commit today's sin in earnest. This whole week, and everything I've been working for, will have been for nothing.

Delaney lets out another muffled groan from across the room. "No, really," she says. "Are we just supposed to suffer until morning?"

"Technically, it's already morning," Greer points out.

I can't see Delaney through the dark, but I'm fairly certain she's rolling her eyes. "Thanks, Greer. Let me know when it's time for breakfast."

It's a throwaway comment, nothing more, but a little thrill zips through me all the same. Maybe I haven't lost the chance to commit gluttony after all. Because it *is* technically tomorrow. Our day of fasting is over, and at this point, gluttony feels less like a sin and more like something that would literally prevent Delaney and Greer from murdering each other in their sleep.

"You're right," I say, rolling over to face the center of the room. "This sucks. We deserve something to eat."

Greer barks out a laugh. "Don't look at me. I gave you all my food this afternoon."

SAY A LITTLE PRAYER

"Sure, but the counselors didn't."

Everyone goes still, the cabin so quiet I momentarily wonder if they're all pretending to be asleep. Then, slowly, Torres sits up.

"What are you talking about?"

I feel her watching me even if I can't make out her face, and I have a feeling the others are doing the same. I shrug and swing my legs over the side of my bed.

"I'm just saying you're right. It's technically tomorrow. Our fast is over, and there's a full, working kitchen, like, five minutes down the path." I reach up and tug on the corner of Julia's blanket. "Do the counselors lock everything at night?"

Julia's been quiet since lights-out, even as the others tossed and turned around us. She doesn't move now, but when I rise onto my toes, I find her staring back at me. Slowly, almost imperceptibly, she nods. "They have to lock everything because of the bears."

"Sure, but they—" I stop. "Wait, *bears*? There are bears here?"

"Why do you think they tell us not to take food to the cabins?"

"I don't know! I thought it was, like, a control thing!" I shudder and push the thought away. "Whatever. Not the point. Do you know where they keep the key?"

"Of course. It's right by the—" This time, Julia's the one who breaks off. "You're not actually going to sneak out, are you?"

I can't see her expression in the dark, but I know her well enough to guess the way she's looking at me. Eyebrows lifted, lips parted, head tilted to one side.

"No." Greer's voice cuts through the dark before I can answer.

147

"Of course she's not. That's literally insane, not to mention against every single camp rule."

"Oh, I know." I reach down and tug a long-sleeved black shirt from the bottom of my suitcase. "But I'm pretty sure withholding meals is against the rules, too, so I think we're even. Who's with me?"

I don't think I'm expecting anyone to say yes. Two of these girls actively despise me, and most of the others don't really know me at all. To them, I could still be an outsider, a fake, the girl who turned her back and left. But they don't know about my plan. They don't know about the sins tucked away in my prayer book or the reason I need to commit this one, too. If I was kind, if I truly cared about their collective souls, I wouldn't drag them into it at all. But when Delaney hauls herself out of bed, over-sized T-shirt hanging off one shoulder and her silk bonnet still wrapped around her braids, it's not guilt I feel coursing through my veins. It's relief.

"Sure," she says. "Why the hell not?"

The ladder at the foot of Torres's bed creaks. She lands softly on the floor and reaches for the robe slung over the top of her suitcase. "I mean, if you're both going, I could come, too? Maybe?"

I let out a breathy laugh and pull my black shirt over my head. I feel like I'm in a heist movie at the part where the leader looks around at their ragtag found-family crew on the eve of their most dangerous job yet. Not that I've thought about what that would be like. Not that I asked my parents for walkie-talkies five birthdays in a row or that I still reread my worn collection of Gallagher Girls paperbacks just to feel something.

I glance into Julia's bunk as Delaney and Torres pull on their shoes. I still can't see her face, but I can picture her lying there, chewing her bottom lip as she runs through the list of potential consequences. Because Julia Young doesn't break rules. She doesn't sneak out of her cabin after dark, and she definitely doesn't steal her dad's key to raid the camp kitchen. She's probably still repenting for the dress she bought yesterday, but some deep, selfish part of me doesn't want to do this without her.

"You don't have to come," I say, lowering my voice so the others can't hear. "If you tell me where the key is, I'll do it."

"You honestly think I'm letting you walk out of this cabin alone?" Julia props herself up on her elbows, and I don't have to see her face to know she's smiling, too. "You're becoming a bad influence, Riley Ackerman."

Bad influence. There's that thrill again, whipping up the length of my spine. This time, it feels like a zipper, like it's deliberately designed to peel me open. Because Julia's right. This is exactly what Pastor Young warned me about—dragging his perfect, obedient daughter into my vortex of sin. I brace a shaky hand against the bedframe. Then, right as the first splinter of doubt starts to slip under my skin, Greer practically hurls herself out of bed.

"Are you serious?" she snaps. "A minute ago you were scared of bears, and now you think you can just waltz around at night?"

We all freeze, and it occurs to me then that Pastor Young might not be my biggest problem tonight. It might be Greer Wilson and her devout commitment to following every single rule. I bite my lip. "Yes?"

"Do you know anything about woodland safety?"

Delaney arches a brow. "Do you?"

"Yes!" Greer cries. "Obviously!"

It's not until she storms across the cabin and stuffs her feet into her sneakers that I realize she's actually planning to come. I glance instinctively at Amanda's bunk. If Greer is here, yanking her hair into a ponytail like it's the most annoying thing in the world, Amanda won't be far behind. They're a pair, a package deal, but when I find her in the dark, she's still sitting on the edge of her mattress.

I remember her in the locker room this morning, fingers curled around the edge of the sink. I remember the spider-thin cracks in her facade this afternoon as she stormed off the porch. And even though I don't care, even though most of me wishes she'd cease to exist, the other part is achingly familiar with what it feels like to be alone.

"You coming, Amanda?"

I feel her stiffen at the sound of my voice. Behind me, the others stop moving, like they're afraid this is some kind of trap. Honestly, I wish it was. I wish I had some elaborate plan to destroy her, too, but for once, my offer is genuine. Amanda glances toward the ladder, weight shifting like she's about to climb down. Then she shakes her head.

"I'm not hungry."

Fine. So much for that. I bite back my frustration and turn to face the others. "Ready?"

One by one, they nod. No one wavers in the middle of the floor, no one second-guesses their decision, and no one hangs back to convince Amanda to join us. For once, I'm in control.

"Excellent." I grin, instinctively reaching for Julia's hand in the dark. "Let's go."

XI

Talk About Forbidden Fruit

There are lots of reasons why I prefer the indoors, and most of them, I realize, have to do with the fact that I've never once encountered a bear in my house. Not that I've seen one outside either, but when we all file onto the porch at 12:17 a.m., it feels like it's becoming a distinct possibility.

Torres is the last one out. She quietly eases the screen door shut, but the porch still groans ominously beneath our feet. It's colder than I thought, the night air crisp with the scent of pine, and I shiver as I pick my way down the steps. Inside, my plan had felt solid. Practical even. But now that we're out here alone, miles of dark forest surrounding us on all sides, it's starting to feel like the opening scene of a very low-budget horror movie.

Camp Thriller Three: The Body of Christ. Five girls, one demonic spirit. May or may not take the form of a Kentucky black bear.

Julia slips her arm through mine as we sneak around the edge of the field, away from the semicircle of cabins. It's so dark I can barely make out the shadow of her presence next to me,

SAY A LITTLE PRAYER

but I feel the tremor in her fingers as she pulls me close.

Once during rehearsal for last year's production of *Macbeth,* a tech kid accidentally tripped a breaker and blacked out the entire auditorium. We kept going as we waited for the lights to return, with Ms. Tina encouraging us to recite the script from memory. It was like every one of my senses sharpened to a singular needle-tipped point. I couldn't see Kev behind me, but I heard him each time he swallowed. I felt the way he lifted his chin ever so slightly before he spoke, and when it was my turn, the other witches and I recited our lines in perfect, uncanny unison like it was the most natural thing in the world.

That's how it feels now, creeping through the woods with Julia at my side. Like even though I can barely see the ground under my feet, I'm still completely, devastatingly aware of her.

I don't think any of us breathe until we emerge from the trees and into the camp's central field. It's significantly easier to navigate without the curtain of branches overhead, but Julia keeps our arms intertwined as she motions us toward the cafeteria. Only when we're all clustered nervously at the back door does she finally release me. She crouches to the ground, fingers gingerly lifting the edge of the welcome mat, and there, lying face up in the dirt, is a single golden key.

Julia straightens, unable to mask her growing smile as she mouths, *Told you*, and slides the key into the lock. The click that follows feels too loud against the night. I wince as it echoes against the trees. The door swings open, and we all pile into the cafeteria, only relaxing when Julia flips the lock back into place.

153

"Oh my god." Delaney sags against the wall. "We did it."

Torres's nervous laugh bounces across the empty cafeteria. "I feel like a spy," she whispers. "Like a . . . secret agent or something."

Greer scoffs, but even her voice doesn't have its usual bite. "You're not spying on anyone. I could hear you breathing halfway across camp."

"That's not fair. I have a deviated septum."

"Okay? You know you can fix that, right?"

Torres rolls her eyes before turning her back on Greer and stomping into the kitchen. My pulse thrums in my ears as I follow. Without the regular bustle of mealtime conversation, the cafeteria feels as cold and eerie as the forest outside. Still, no one dares to turn on a light. Instead, we all feel our way through the room one foot at a time until my hand smacks something solid and cold. *The refrigerator.*

I don't know what Heaven is supposed to look like. I don't know what kind of utopia Pastor Young imagines for himself, but as I yank open the refrigerator door, I think mine would look a little like this—shelves upon shelves piled high with food and glowing with a soft blue light.

Next to me, Delaney lets out a low whimper. "Look." She stretches a tentative hand toward the top shelf. "Cinnamon rolls."

Sure enough, four enormous trays of prebaked pastries stare back at us. I choke on a laugh and quickly scan the rest of the shelves. We don't just have cinnamon rolls. We have *everything*—rows of perfectly good, ready-to-eat food that our good Chris-

SAY A LITTLE PRAYER

tian counselors have been keeping from us all day. Bagels and sodas and baskets of fresh fruit. Pudding cups and sandwiches and more cold cuts than any human person could consume in their lifetime.

I don't know where to start. We're all just standing there, frozen by the overwhelming choice of it all, when Julia reaches down and plucks an Uncrustables sandwich from a box near the bottom.

"Here," she says, holding it in my direction. "It's strawberry. Your favorite."

Her voice must crack through whatever threads of self-restraint have been holding us in place because everyone starts moving at once.

There's a strategy at first—rules we attempt to enforce as we all dive for the food. Don't open anything new. Don't make a mess. Don't take too much or someone might notice in the morning. But when Delaney rips the lid off a brand-new container of potato salad and plops it in the middle of the kitchen table, I think all semblance of order goes out the window. Because why does it matter? There's more than enough food here to get everyone through the week. It's not like the other campers would go hungry. I grab another handful of sandwiches, and by the time we're done, there's a small feast spread across the stainless steel table between us.

For the next several minutes, it's quiet except for the crinkling of plastic and the pop of soda can lids. Julia takes the spot next to me, arm brushing mine each time she reaches for more chips, but for once, I'm too preoccupied to notice the way my skin prickles at the touch. Even Greer looks content with a bag of honey-glazed ham, and it's not until Delaney points a pretzel stick in my direction that the spell finally breaks.

"Can I ask you a question?"

I freeze, every cell in my body tensing instinctively. "Sure?"

It's not a convincing answer, but Delaney doesn't seem to mind. She bites down on the end of her pretzel and asks, "Why did you come to camp this year? It doesn't really seem like your thing."

"How would you know?"

"Well, you've never attended before. And you very clearly hate everything Gabe says."

I'm about to tell her that doesn't count—I'd probably hate Gabe regardless of if I'd attended camp before—when the back of Julia's hand grazes mine. I look down and realize I'm slowly shredding the remains of my sandwich, crumbs scattering across the floor at our feet. I exhale and force myself to stop. Of course Delaney is curious. She doesn't know me. I'm an outsider here, and the question is an echo of the same one Amanda asked me on day one.

Are you ever going to tell us why you're here?

I drop my mangled crusts on top of the sandwich wrappers and mutter, "I got into a fight at school last week. My principal told me it was either this or a suspension."

I brace myself for the inevitable judgment, but Delaney just throws her head back and laughs. "Oh my god," she says. "I miss public school!"

SAY A LITTLE PRAYER

Torres leans forward, bony elbows braced against the table. "Who did you fight?"

"Um . . ." Shame prickles down the back of my neck. I grab a fistful of Julia's chips and purposefully don't look at Greer. "Amanda Clarke?"

"Really? Why?"

I'm honestly surprised Torres hadn't heard about it. Sure, it happened the day before spring break and she's only a sophomore, but I'd assumed news like that would travel—Amanda Clarke, Madison High School's reigning queen of all that is perfect and holy, getting smacked by a girl in a *Shrek the Musical* T-shirt. It's a good story. But if Torres doesn't know why I'd want to fight Amanda in the first place, maybe people aren't talking about me or Hannah as much as I think they are. Maybe they don't care as much as Pastor Young wants me to believe.

"Doesn't matter," I say. "The point is I'm here and I have to write Mr. Rider an essay on what I learn this week."

"Oh?" Delaney grins. "And what have you learned so far?"

My next bite tastes like cardboard, peanut butter too sticky in the back of my throat. I struggle to swallow as I think of the notes scrawled in my prayer book and all the things I intend to do with them. I've learned a lot of things I wish I could share now—that I was right to leave Pleasant Hills when I did, that I'll never understand what they all see in it, that I'm still planning to burn this place down when I leave.

I decide on the safer answer. "I learned I'm never fasting again."

Torres laughs, the soft glow of the refrigerator catching in her dark hair. "So true." Then she straightens. "Wait, who took the nacho dip?"

She lunges in Delaney's direction, hands outstretched as the two of them fumble for the near-empty container. Greer shrieks as someone's elbow nearly upends her bag of ham, Julia snorts out a choked giggle, but I just watch. I think about yesterday, about how the only thing I wanted was more time in that thrift store. If greed is wanting too much, then I think gluttony is excess. It's consuming things until they make you sick, and even though I'm uncomfortably full now, I can't imagine a world where I feel sick of this. Sneaking out and eating cold peanut butter sandwiches in the glow of the camp refrigerator. Feeling the solid press of Julia's arm against mine. Watching Torres yank her jar of dip from Delaney's grasp and scramble toward the other side of the kitchen. Feeling, for a moment, like I might belong.

It's strange, I think, that after a day of being nothing but virtuous and temperate, the five of us are finally coming alive in the afterglow of this singular deadly sin.

By the time the clock above the oven blinks 1:30 a.m., I'm physically incapable of eating another bite. The refrigerator door still swings open, contents slowly dripping onto the tiles below, and despite our initial efforts, there's evidence of our midnight picnic all over the kitchen. I groan, pushing myself away from the table.

"We should head back. And we should probably clean, too."

I grab a roll of paper towels and start wiping down the counters as Julia stuffs everything back into the pantry. It's not perfect.

SAY A LITTLE PRAYER

If anyone looks too closely, they'll probably find our wrappers buried in the trash, but I'm hoping the counselors on the breakfast shift will be too tired to care.

"Want a hand?"

I look up to find Greer on the other side of the table, bottle of disinfectant spray in hand. She's watching me warily, like she's fully prepared to use it as a weapon if she has to, and I wonder why the question feels so much like a truce. I give a noncommittal shrug, and for a minute, we both kind of stand there, scrubbing opposite sides of the same table in awkward, stilted silence.

Last summer, our Student Government Association hosted a car wash to raise money for new football uniforms. And by that I mean incoming senior class president Greer Wilson singlehandedly organized the entire event while her VP made out with his girlfriend behind the band hall. The event was a success, obviously. Greer doesn't do anything halfway, and when she signed me and Hannah up for volunteer shifts, it was with the vaguely threatening air of someone who'd won too many high school debate championships to truly understand the meaning of the word *no*.

The three of us spent the afternoon elbows deep in soapy water, scrubbing the hoods of other people's cars and laughing when Mr. Rider ran over three different cones on his way out of the lot. Greer had traded her usual clothes for a frayed pair of shorts and faded tie-dye, and when we finally packed up at the end of the day, I remember thinking that there weren't many people who could pull off an event like that.

Now the memory sits like a shard of glass in my throat. Impossible to swallow around, impossible to ignore. Maybe it's the bonding experience of creeping through the woods tonight or maybe it's the fact that I'm finally content for the first time all day, but as my fingers curl around the wad of paper towels, all I want is to cut it out completely.

"I . . ." I stop, clear my throat, and take a deep breath before trying again. "I'm sorry I called you a bitch the other day."

Greer's eyes narrow on me across the table, and I get the distinct impression she can't tell if I'm being genuine or not. I can't even tell myself. "Okayyyy," she says, suspicion dripping from every drawn-out syllable. "I'm going to forgive you, but only because it's, like, one in the morning and I'm too tired to think of a good reason not to." She hesitates and then, like it physically pains her, adds, "And I'm sorry for what I said about you, too. It's not . . . *completely* true."

"It's fine," I say. "It was, but I'm not the one you need to apologize to."

"That's not fair." Greer steps toward me, cleaning supplies momentarily forgotten. "I've never said a bad word about Hannah, Riley. Seriously. She's my friend."

I choke back a laugh. "That's bullshit. You've been ghosting her all semester. You've stopped coming over. You've listened to everyone say horrible, disgusting things about her for months, so forgive me if I wouldn't exactly consider you a friend."

Greer flinches, and I see the exact moment her defenses slide back into place. "That's not my fault. I can't control what other people say."

"You could if you weren't such a coward." There's the anger from this morning, simmering in the air between us. "Maybe you were Hannah's friend at one point. Maybe it wasn't your idea to shut her out, but you know how people talk about her and you don't care."

"Of course I care! No one *shut her out*, Riley! She's the one who stopped talking to us."

"Because you're all—!" I stop, voice echoing around the kitchen. Delaney gives us a curious look on her way to the sink, and I squeeze my eyes shut before trying again. "Because you're all still friends with Collin," I whisper. "You know he's the one who asked her to get an abortion, right? Before she'd even decided? He didn't seem particularly worried about the 'sanctity of life' when he thought it would affect his Clemson scholarship."

Greer's hands still on the counter. "He did?"

"Of *course* he did."

I'd never been Collin's biggest fan, mostly because I thought my sister could do better than a guy whose single biggest accomplishment was kicking a twenty-nine-yard field goal once during his junior year, but I'd never thought of him as a bad person. Annoying? Yes. A little manipulative? Maybe. But straight-up evil? I didn't think he had the brain cells for it. And maybe he hadn't meant to be malicious when his parents caught him snooping through their wallets last December. Maybe he hadn't meant for it to go as far as it did, but he still had a choice, and he sold Hannah out the second he could.

Greer shakes her head, gaze dropping to the freshly swept tile. "You'd never guess, you know," she says. "The way he talks about it is . . . It's like he was really hurt."

"I know." I start scrubbing the table again, harder this time. "He's an asshole. And you're all still friends with him."

It's not a question. I know how the world works. Pleasant Hills will always protect people like Greer and Collin—beautiful, talented, promising kids to mold in their image. Hannah and I were two of those kids once. I wonder if everyone knows it's only a matter of time before the tide turns on them, too.

"Was that really your problem?" I ask. "Do you think she's, like, going to hell for what she did?"

Greer shakes her head. "No, that's not . . . I don't care that she got an abortion."

"Then what is it?"

I hear the plea in my voice, tremulous and desperate. I might regret this later. I might look back on this entire interaction through a haze of shame, but I need to know. Greer hesitates. She's still staring at the ground, cleaning supplies forgotten on the table between us. Her fingers twist in the hem of her shirt, and when she speaks again, the words are so quiet I almost miss them.

"I didn't know you could get kicked out of church."

My hand falters, paper towels squeaking across the surface of

SAY A LITTLE PRAYER

the table. I throw a quick glance over my shoulder to make sure the others are still preoccupied. "What?"

"I didn't know you could get kicked out of church," Greer repeats. "I didn't know that was something he would do, and I didn't know it could happen so . . . publicly."

"Yes, you did. He's done it before."

"Not to someone like Hannah. Not to someone like—"

She stops, the rest of her sentence hanging unfinished between us. *Not to someone like me.*

And that's the crux of it all, I think. That's why no one questions Pastor Young's authority. I don't remember the names of the other people he'd cast out. I hardly remember their faces, but I do remember the way the rest of the congregation talked about them—with soft, lowered voices and deliberately pitying expressions. A woman who'd filed a complaint about one of the board members. Another who was raising two small kids out of wedlock. People who already lived on the outskirts of the Pleasant Hills community, who didn't have the time or resources to fight back.

Pastor Young had built an entire congregation around the single intoxicating belief that they were better than everyone else. That they were different, chosen, *blessed*. He can shun whomever he wants in the name of protecting his flock, and there's absolutely no reason for the others to pretend to care. It's not an excuse. It doesn't change the fact that Greer and Amanda have spent the last four months making Hannah's life miserable, but I wonder if they would have been so quick to push her away if they didn't think there was a very real chance they'd be next.

I look up, forcing Greer to meet my eye across the table. "It doesn't have to be like this, you know. He's not God. We don't have to watch him hurt people."

In the faint glow of the refrigerator, the words feel dangerous. A betrayal to talk like this with Julia only a few feet away. Greer sucks in a breath. The sound is loud enough to carry, sudden enough for the others to look up from their tasks, but before anyone can speak, a beam of light cuts through the kitchen window.

I freeze. Greer's head snaps up, and there's a single second of silence as we all watch the unmistakable beam of a flashlight sweep lazily across the opposite wall. Delaney leaps forward, slamming the refrigerator shut. Darkness swallows us whole, and for a minute, the only thing I hear is the rapid, uneven rhythm of my own heart.

And the sound of footsteps steadily approaching the cafeteria.

"Oh my god." Torres's voice turns breathy with fear. "Oh my god, oh my god, oh my—"

"Shut up!" Greer hisses. "Follow me."

With one swift motion, she sweeps all our cleaning supplies into the trash and herds us from the kitchen. Delaney shifts from foot to foot as we huddle against the back door. Julia's hand closes like a vise around my arm, but the only thought running through my head is how completely screwed I am. Pastor Young already gave me a warning. If one of the counselors finds me here, hiding with his *daughter* no less, I can forget about my essay. I'll be lucky if he ever lets me speak to Julia again.

164

SAY A LITTLE PRAYER

Greer peers out the window, then ducks as the beam sweeps back through the glass. I press my back against the wall, directly underneath a painting titled *Jesus Feeds the Hungry*, and try not to think about the irony. When Greer glances back over the sill, her jaw is set.

"It's a counselor," she whispers. "I can't tell who, but I think they're alone. Do you still have the key, Julia?"

Julia nods, nails digging into my forearm as gravel crunches directly outside our open window. The figure stops, turns in a circle, and then, after what feels like ten of the world's longest seconds, they head around the corner instead, toward the front door and away from us. The air leaves my lungs in a shaky exhale. I sag against Julia, but Greer doesn't look remotely finished.

"Come on." She pushes her way between us and grabs the doorknob. "Time to go."

We slip outside one by one. Delaney keeps an eye on the forest as Julia relocks the door and tucks the key back under the mat. I peer around the corner, listening to the footsteps pacing the perimeter of the cafeteria. They'll come back eventually. They'll retrace their steps and find us here, huddled outside with no valid excuse.

Julia straightens, key secure once more. "Locked," she whispers. "What now?"

Greer's eyes flash. I know that look. It's identical to the one she wore when she signed me and Hannah up for car wash duty. The determined, unyielding, slightly deranged expression of someone who's about to execute the world's most complicated plan. "Now," she says, reaching down to grab Torres's wrist, "we run."

And, because she's Greer Wilson, because I think everyone is still a little bit afraid of her, we do.

If the camp felt terrifying on our way here, it's nothing compared to how it feels now. I'm adrift without Julia to guide me, unmoored in the dark with twigs raking down the back of my neck. My trusty Birkenstocks slip over a carpet of dead leaves. There's a shout in the distance, a voice that may or may not be aimed at us, but when I finally risk a glance over my shoulder, the trees block the rest of camp from view.

"Go!" Delaney gasps from somewhere ahead of me. "Get back to the cabin!"

There's a stitch in my chest, pounding in time with my burning legs. Torres is several yards ahead of me, already bursting through the tree line, but I keep stumbling, roots catching under my feet. Then Julia's beside me, hand closing over mine. She yanks me forward and, through gritted teeth, pants, "I cannot *believe* you're still wearing those shoes."

We reach the cabin together and nearly rip the screen off its hinges in our haste to get inside. Amanda bolts upright in bed as it slams behind us. "What the hell?" she asks. "What are you—?"

"Shh!"

Delaney motions for her to be quiet as she kicks off her shoes and scrambles into bed. Torres and Julia lunge for their ladders, and Greer makes a running leap into her own bunk. I dive under my duvet, peeking out just in time to watch two separate flash-

SAY A LITTLE PRAYER

light beams sweep through our windows. Torres collapses into bed, top bunk swaying ominously, but Julia ducks as one of the beams flashes overhead. She's barely halfway up the ladder when our porch lets out a warning groan.

". . . thought I saw them run over here. Just go door to door and make sure everyone's inside."

I don't recognize the counselor's voice floating through our open window. I don't know if they saw our faces back at the cafeteria, but I do know exactly what'll happen if they find anyone out of bed now.

"Julia!" I hiss. "Move!"

The doorknob rattles. Julia lets out a terrified squeak and throws herself into my bed instead. I toss the duvet over our heads right as the door swings open and that same infuriating flashlight sweeps across the cabin. I hold my breath and will myself not to move. If they take another step forward or look too closely, they'll see Julia's empty bunk. They'll notice our shoes scattered across the floor or the end of Greer's robe poking out from under her blankets and start to wonder why we're all breathing like we've just run a marathon.

Next to me, Julia's eyes are wide, nose just brushing mine as we wait. I'm close enough to see the cluster of freckles between her eyebrows each time the flashlight slides over our side of the room, to watch her pulse flutter against the column of her throat. Her breath skates down the side of my face, drawing goose bumps in its wake, and still, I don't move. Not when the footsteps finally retreat and the door closes. Not when the counselors move to the neighboring cabin. Not even when Julia's eyes flutter shut and her teeth slide deliberately over her bottom lip.

The last cabin door slams shut across the field. A sigh floats through our open window, and then the same voice as before says, "Must have been a deer, I guess." Their footsteps fade back down the path. I count to ten in my head once, twice, three times. Only when I'm nearing the end of my fourth does Delaney throw back her blankets and release a trembling breath.

"Yeah," she says. "Must have been."

Her voice is rough, teetering right on the edge of hysteria, but that's all it takes for the tension to snap. Torres snorts into her pillow, Greer lets out a high-pitched giggle, and I bite back a grin as Julia disentangles herself from my blanket.

"Holy shit," she breathes. "I feel like I'm going to combust."

She looks like it, too. Her eyes are bright, cheeks glowing, hair spread across my pillow in tangled waves. She looks, I think, like something else I'd like Ben to paint. Oil and moonlight on canvas. Watercolor blues and purples running into the golden red of her hair.

I don't know how long we stay like that, curled toward each other on the lumpy mattress as we fight not to laugh. Three different times I start to tell her it's safe to go back to her own bed. Three different times I snap my mouth shut. At some point, my eyelids start to droop, and when I wake in the morning with Julia's arm around my waist, fingers splayed against the curve of my stomach, I pretend to be asleep a few minutes longer. Just so I can pretend there's a version of her who wants me like this, too.

XII

The Epic Highs and Lows of Church Camp Capture the Flag

*H*ere is a noncomprehensive list of the most embarrassing things that have ever happened to me:

1. Accidentally calling a student teacher "mom" during a tennis match.
2. Kicking the ball into the wrong net during my short-lived soccer career and losing a tournament game in front of every eighth grader in Madison County.
3. Finishing the mile dead last only to turn around and sprain my ankle on the way back to the bleachers.

I don't think it's a coincidence that all these things occurred during gym class.

It doesn't matter how many times Julia tells me I'd like softball or how often Hannah begs me to try ballet. I know my limits, and I have absolutely no interest in learning all the niche ways I can embarrass myself through team activities. But when we gather in the chapel the next morning, it's with the unmistakable buzz that only accompanies major sporting events—the US Open, the Super Bowl, and apparently, the biannual Pleasant Hills game of capture the flag.

"Oh my god," I say, sliding onto the bleachers next to Ben. "You guys weren't kidding. This is intense."

Ben has always been my unathletic partner in crime, but today, he's grinning up at me through a very unsettling mask of blue face paint. "Told you." He glances up at my hat. "You're on the red team?"

He says *red* like it's an insult, like even though we used to hide under the bleachers to avoid middle school track meets together, he's seriously contemplating breaking my legs. I tug on the brim of the Phillies baseball cap Delaney lent me and grin. "Nervous?"

"Please." Ben snorts. "I've seen you run."

I resist the urge to tell him that I'd actually managed to run pretty fast last night. My knees still ache from the effort, which, now that I'm thinking about it, might be a problem today. I have no idea how the counselors divided us into teams, but this morning, my cabin had jolted awake to another ear-shattering verse of "Flexin' on That Gram" to find a sheet of paper already slipped under our door. Amanda, Greer, and Delaney ended up on the blue team while Julia, Torres, and I were assigned red. Everyone had immediately started digging for color-coded outfits as I sat in bed, wondering if calling this morning's game *intense* was a bit of an understatement.

SAY A LITTLE PRAYER

Now, for example, Amanda sits a few rows ahead of us, dabbing lines of blue paint on Greer's cheeks with the kind of precision usually reserved for complex brain surgery. Her blond curls are held back with a blue headband, and they're both wearing matching pairs of knee-high socks, blue laces woven through their sneakers. Even Julia is fully decked out in head-to-toe red. When she slides into the seat next to me, she spares Ben the briefest glance before leaning in and whispering, "If his team wins, he's going to hold it over our heads for the rest of our lives."

Yes, I think as I watch her loop scarlet ribbon around the end of her braid. *Intense* was definitely an understatement.

I don't know if it's the anticipation or the fact that we actually got a real breakfast this morning, but the mood is noticeably lighter as the worship band finishes their set. Even the sight of Pastor Young jogging onstage in a black-and-white-striped jersey with the words TIME-OUT FOR PRAYER printed across the back doesn't fill me with the usual sense of dread. In fact, I think it's one of the better Jesus-themed shirts he's tried this week.

"Good morning!" he says. "How's everyone feeling?"

The cheer that follows is significantly more enthusiastic than yesterday's. It takes a full minute for Pastor Young to regain some semblance of control.

"That's what I like to hear! I'm not going to keep you long, but I do feel called to share a few words before we head out. Capture the flag is simple, right? It's a fun game, but that doesn't mean there's not a lesson here or that it can't also embody today's heavenly virtue of patience. How many of you play sports?" Most

171

people's hands shoot up. "Great. Now, how many of you have ever let your emotions get the better of you during a game? Have you ever gotten caught up in the moment or made an impulsive decision you later regret?"

Fewer hands, more hesitant this time, but Pastor Young just nods. "I thought so. A casual game at camp might not seem like a big deal, but those emotions can still have serious consequences."

He launches into a sermon about the deadly sin of wrath, and it takes everything in my power not to groan. I've seen Pastor Young watch football. Catch him after the Browns lose, and there's not an ounce of heavenly patience to be found. But if wrath is my sin of the day, if all I have to do is be angry, he might as well have handed me a free pass. Even now, I feel the perpetual ache in my chest, the pressure of keeping my own personal collection of wrath locked where no one can see.

"You good?" Ben nudges my arm, voice soft enough for just us to hear. "You look like you're planning a church arson or something."

Now, there's an idea. I shake my head and force the line between my brows to smooth. "Just thinking about the game."

"Right." Ben smirks. "Riley Ackerman is playing a sport. Who'd have thought?"

I drive my elbow into his ribs.

Twenty-four minutes of preaching later, Pastor Young leads us through a quick prayer and dismisses us from the chapel. Everyone automatically filters into teams as we go. A few counselors motion for the blue group to follow them, but Gabe keeps the

SAY A LITTLE PRAYER

rest of us moving straight ahead. I stifle a yawn. Part of me is still on edge, waiting for one of the counselors to give me a double take or start waving a flashlight in my face, but breakfast had passed without a hitch. No one was whispering about half-eaten containers of potato salad or the mystery girls from the woods, and the longer everything stays quiet, the more I think we might have actually gotten away with it.

"How are we feeling, team?"

Torres throws one arm around my neck, then reaches for Julia with the other. Despite our identical sleep schedules, she looks remarkably well rested. I bite back another yawn.

"Great," I say. "Ready to kick some blue ass, for sure."

Gabe whips around, eyes narrowing on me through the crowd. "Language, Riley. This isn't a competition."

I wrinkle my nose. "I'm pretty sure it is, though."

"What was that?"

"Nothing!" I call, ignoring the way Julia turns her head into my neck to hide her grin. "I meant I'm ready to engage in some completely chill, low-stakes athletic activity. In the name of the Lord."

I flash Gabe my sweetest smile. Torres snorts out a laugh, and soon the three of us are struggling to hold it together, arms inter-locked as we continue across a narrow stream and deeper into the woods. Eventually, we stop in front of a single wooden tower.

"Here you go," Gabe says. "You know the rules. Just wait for the whistle."

Bold of him to assume I know anything about what's

173

happening here. He leaves us clustered in a circle, and I lift a hand to squint toward the top of the base. The tower looks like it's been ripped from a children's playground. There's still an opening at the top where a slide should go and a rickety-looking staircase winding its way up the side. Someone's hung an array of little glass ornaments from the balcony—angels and crosses and birds caught midflight—and dangling from the roof is a single red scarf.

Torres takes one look at it and nods. "Okay, team, here's the plan."

To my surprise, no one argues. I know Torres plays volleyball back home. I know she'd been good enough to make the varsity team as a first-year, and looking at her now, I can tell why. Her arms are corded with lean muscle, and even though she's the shortest one here, I have a feeling she could take me to the ground no problem. Even Patrick, who'd spray-painted his hair a concerning shade of red, steps back and lets her lead.

"Patrick, Jace, and Lydia—when Pastor Young blows the whistle, you'll take our flag and hide it somewhere on our side of the river," Torres says, pointing at people as she goes. "It has to be visible, but that doesn't mean it should be easy to get. You'll be the first line of defense, too, so make sure you're ready. Liam, Eli, Rosanna, and I will start on border patrol and try to tag anyone who crosses into our territory. April, Sav, and Matty will stay here to guard the base, and the rest of you will fan out to find the other team's flag. Any questions?"

I raise a tentative hand. "So what are the rules, exactly?"

SAY A LITTLE PRAYER

Torres's head cocks to one side, like she can't tell if I'm kidding, but Julia waves her off. "Don't worry," she says. "It's not hard. We want to get the blue flag and bring it back before the other team finds ours. That river we crossed was the dividing line—if you're on this side, you're safe. If you're on the other, the blue team can tag you out."

I nod in a vain attempt to look interested and not like that summary feels pulled from my darkest gym class nightmares. *Wrath*, I think. *The point of today is wrath, not abject terror.* Julia puts a reassuring hand on my arm, but before she can elaborate, three short whistles sound from somewhere in the distance. The clearing falls silent as Torres holds up a hand. Then there's another whistle, longer this time, and everyone scatters.

Patrick scales the side of the tower, legs pumping beneath his bright red shorts, and tosses our flag down to Jace. His group takes off into the woods, Torres makes a beeline for the river, but I waver in front of the tower, suddenly unsure of what to do. Then Julia's hand closes around my wrist, as steadying as it had been last night, and she yanks me toward the trees.

"Go!" she cries. "Over here!"

And just like last night, just like always, I take her hand in return.

This morning, the worship band had strummed their way through three different songs about weathering the storm. Most Christian rock songs are like that—a combination of metaphors and annoyingly catchy melodies that usually circle back to God being a lighthouse or something. But as I run after Julia, dodging

175

weeds and fallen branches, I think that's what she feels like, too. A beacon. A light. Something I'll always be able to find.

This far into the woods, the ground is damp under our feet, but I can already feel the afternoon heat pressing through the branches. Yesterday's cool spell was short-lived, and even though the sky is clear, I still feel a storm hovering on the horizon. I hop over another patch of mud and ask, "Is this usually an all-day thing?"

Julia arches a brow. "Why? Have somewhere to be?"

"Somewhere with air-conditioning, preferably."

"Oh, come on, Riley." She turns and plants both hands on my shoulders, face tipping up to the sky. "Don't you feel it?"

"I . . ." Honestly, the only thing I feel right now is the press of her thumbs against my collarbones. I swallow and try again. "Feel what?"

"*That.*" Julia waves a hand in the general direction of the forest. "The sun. The air. The trees. It's beautiful, isn't it?"

The thing about having a Big Gay Crush is that it makes you do very silly things. One year, I'd braided Rebecca Delgado's hair every night for our production of *Mamma Mia!* just so I could know what it felt like between my fingers. Last summer, I spent my entire allowance on iced caramel lattes so I'd have an excuse to talk to the new barista, and now, when Julia closes her eyes and tips her face toward the sky, there's a part of me that genuinely thinks, *Yes, there* is *something beautiful about being in the middle of the woods with no amenities. Why didn't I think of that?*

"Sure," I say, stepping deliberately out of her grasp. "It's nice."

SAY A LITTLE PRAYER

By the time we reach the stream that divides our territories, my pulse has almost returned to normal. Julia looks up and down the muddy embankment before hopping across, and after a brief second where I picture myself landing in the murky water below, I follow. When I straighten, Julia has a finger pressed to her lips.

"Quiet," she whispers. "Keep a lookout for the blue flag."

I nod, mime zipping my lips, then promptly trip over a gnarled root. Julia bites back an exasperated sigh, but as she turns to go, I swear I see the corner of her mouth lift in another faint, stomach-flipping smile. I tug the brim of my hat down over my eyes and hurry after her.

"Do you know where to look?" I ask after several minutes of picking our way through the trampled underbrush. "Where do people usually hide flags?"

Julia shrugs. "It's different every year. No one uses the same spot twice, but there are a few trees up here I want to scope out. Maybe we could—"

A twig snaps somewhere to our left. I whirl toward the sound, but before I can get a good look, Julia yanks me behind the nearest tree. My back slams into the trunk, and I manage to suck in a single surprised breath before my brain short-circuits at the feeling of her hip pressed against mine. Slowly, we both peer around the trunk.

A length of blue silk is tucked in the hollow of a nearby tree, the end barely visible through the leaves. It's a good spot—the flag just high enough that someone would have to climb or jump to reach it. I picture the end of it wrapped around my fist, trailing

177

behind me on my way back to base. Then I glance to the left, and my victorious daydream evaporates.

Amanda stands in front of the tree, jaw set in steely determination. She's traded her cap sleeves and tennis skirts for a pair of navy leggings and a cropped *Swan Lake* T-shirt. The blue lines drawn across her face bring out the sharp green of her eyes, and I cannot *believe* that out of everyone currently attending this camp, she's the one standing between me and victory.

I glance at Julia, eyebrows lifted in silent question. The flag is right there. It's two versus one. Julia chews on her bottom lip. She sneaks a glance around the trunk, but before she can respond, the bushes to our left start to rustle. We turn around right as Greer appears on the path behind us, followed by another boy from her team.

For a second, we all freeze, eyes locked on each other across the clearing. Then Greer jabs a finger in our direction. "Get them!"

"Run!"

Julia pushes me in front of her, and we tear through the forest with Greer hot on our heels. I'm going as fast as I can, feet slipping through the mud, and I have a sudden flashback to last night. Our mad dash through the trees with flashlights bobbing behind us. I'd barely made it then, and I'm definitely not quick enough now.

"Faster, Riley!" Julia cries.

I grit my teeth, but it's like my muscles are physically revolting. Twigs rip through my hair as we round a corner and find the stream directly in front of us. Safety. Our footprints are still visible in the mud on the other side, and at the last second, Julia pushes me forward. I make a wild leap right as Greer's hand closes on the back of Julia's shirt.

"Got you!"

"No!" I whirl. "Julia!"

But it's too late. She's stuck, standing on the opposite side of the stream with Greer on one side and the boy on the other. "Go!" She waves a hand in my direction. "Save yourself!"

Greer rolls her eyes. "She's literally already safe, but okay."

She still has one hand fisted in the back of Julia's shirt, but when she turns to go, I think she's smiling, too.

The three of them head back into the forest, Julia glancing over her shoulder every few steps, and after a minute of trying and failing to catch my breath, I start walking back toward our base. I have no idea where Patrick hid our flag. I don't know who's winning, and at this point, I'm not even sure I remember the rules. There's a stich in my side, throbbing in time with my ragged pulse, but when Torres jogs into the clearing a second later, she's barely winded. Maybe I'm not giving the Madison High School volleyball team enough credit.

"Hey." She scans the tree line over my shoulder. "Where's Julia?"

I shake my head. "Blue team got her after we saw their flag."

"You saw it? Where?"

I point and describe the area as best I can. Torres considers me for a minute, then looks back at our sparsely guarded base. "Okay," she says. "Let's be aggressive while we still can. Liam,

Will, Mason, you come with me. Riley, stay here and guard the prisoners. Chase down anyone who tries to free them."

The fact she thinks I'm capable of chasing anyone down is kind of sweet. I give her a mock salute, then stroll toward the base, taking inventory of our prisoners as I go. There aren't many, but I do a double take when I spot Ben sitting near the middle. "Wow," I say. "What happened to holding your victory over our heads forever?"

"Don't mock me," he groans. "I forgot Torres is superhuman." Then his gaze slides to the edge of the clearing. "They've been gone a while, haven't they?"

"They've been gone, like, thirty seconds."

"You sure? You don't want to go after them and check?"

I shake my head. "I'm good, thanks."

"What if they need your help?"

"I promise you they don't."

Ben leans back on his elbows, the picture-perfect image of casual nonchalance. "Suit yourself," he says. "I just know I'd feel *terrible* if something happened to my teammates while I was standing around, doing nothing. We don't need supervision, you know. You could always—"

I pick up a nearby stick and smack it against the side of the tower. "Silence, wench."

To my surprise, Ben actually jumps. "Jesus Christ," he mutters. "Fine. You would have been a menace in the Stanford prison experiment, you know that?"

"Thank you."

SAY A LITTLE PRAYER

"That's not a compliment!"

I flash him my most innocent grin, and even though this game is supposed to mean nothing, even though I'm not supposed to care, I still feel the tension of it spiraling through every limb. Because this is almost fun and I'm definitely not losing to *Ben* of all people.

Footsteps pound between the trees, and I look up in time to watch Torres burst into the clearing. "Whoa!" I steady her as she sags against me. "What happened?"

"Ambush," she pants. "Blue team got the others."

"Oh no." Ben crosses one ankle over the other. "Sounds like you're in a real pickle."

I shoot him a pointed glare before turning back to Torres. "Everyone else is out?"

She nods. "You were right, though. Amanda's still the only one guarding the flag."

Of course she is. I grit my teeth at the thought of Amanda holding our flag above her head, beaming down at her crowd of adoring followers. She shouldn't get to win this, too. I won't let her. I grab Torres's arm and wheel her away from the base.

"Let me come back with you," I whisper. "I think I have a plan."

I wait for her to protest, to remind me that I barely understand the rules, much less game strategy, but to my surprise, she nods. Maybe fleeing through the forest at night bonds people more than I thought. We set off down the path, arms still locked together as I explain what I'm thinking. Torres

181

nods in all the right places, and when I finish, her jaw is set.

"Got it," she says. "I'm in."

My calves ache in protest as we leap back across the stream, but I force myself to keep up, pulling Torres behind the same tree Julia and I had used before. Sure enough, there's the blue flag hanging from the hollow several feet above the ground and there's Amanda, still standing beneath it. If Torres and I had more people, we could take her no problem. But right now, it's just the two of us. And if I'm being honest, it's mostly Torres.

I glance over my shoulder, eyebrows raised, and Torres nods. *Ready*. I brace a hand against the trunk as we watch Amanda pace the clearing. One lap. Two. Then, when she finally turns her back on us, I move.

I burst from our hiding spot and make a wild dash for the flag. There's no way I'll get it. There's no way I actually make it out of this unscathed, but I jump anyway, barely managing to catch the end of the silk between my fingers. It flutters to the ground, and I have just enough time to feel a hot rush of victory before Amanda's hands slam into my back.

"You're out!"

The force of her hit sends me stumbling into the tree. I catch myself on the trunk, rough bark scraping down both palms. "Okay, okay," I say. "Chill. God forbid anyone have fun around here."

Amanda's eyes flash, and for a minute, I think I see that same crack spreading beneath her demure expression. "So this is *fun* for you now?"

SAY A LITTLE PRAYER

"Maybe." I wipe my palms against my thighs. "Miracles happen every day, right?" Then, before Amanda can react, I change the subject. "What were you doing in the locker room yesterday? Must have been something pretty upsetting to make you cry like that."

I might as well have slapped her again. Amanda goes still, face turning as white as her sneakers, and I wish more than anything I could enjoy this. That there's not a part of me that still feels the tiniest bit guilty. She opens her mouth, but before she can speak, there's a blur of color to our right.

Torres tears from her hiding spot, snatches the flag off the ground, and makes a U-turn around the base of the tree with a speed I didn't think human beings possessed. I swear she ruffles the hair on my arms as she goes.

A frustrated sound breaks in the back of Amanda's throat. "Greer!" she calls. "Tori! Help! She's getting away!"

But it's too late. Somewhere in the distance, a whistle sounds. Cheers rise up from our side of the stream, and I picture Torres sprinting up the tower steps, flag clutched victoriously in her fist. *We did it*, I think as Amanda whirls to face me. *We won.*

I wonder why it doesn't feel like a victory.

"Sorry," I say, giving my hands one last brush against my thighs. "Better luck next time."

I don't stay to hear if she has a response. I don't want one. Instead, I turn and jog back the way I'd come, leaving Amanda Clarke rooted to the forest floor behind me.

183

XIII

Some Light Property Destruction, as a Treat

When I'd boarded the camp bus last week, it had been with a looming sense of dread. It didn't matter how many times Julia told me it would be okay or how excited the others were—I was never supposed to come back to Pleasant Hills. I never wanted to stay. But when our team huddles together beneath our base and Julia cries, "You did it! You played a sport!" before tossing my baseball cap into the air, I think this feeling is something I wouldn't mind getting back.

It's not until we start heading toward the cafeteria that I realize I've completely forgotten about channeling wrath. In fact, I feel lighter than I have in weeks.

Before I can dwell too much on the implications, Ben slides up behind me and throws an arm over my shoulders. "Riley! You played a sport!"

I shove him away. "Why does everyone keep saying that?"

"Because you famously faked bronchitis to get out of running the mile last year?"

SAY A LITTLE PRAYER

That's fair. At the time, I thought the excuse was brilliant, but now, there's something like pride lurking beneath my aching muscles. It's similar to how I feel after a long day of rehearsal or finally nailing a solo, like I've really accomplished something great. I grin and reach up to tug on the brim of my hat, stopping only when my fingers close around empty air.

"Oh shoot." I stumble to a halt. "I think I left Delaney's hat at the tower."

Julia glances over her shoulder. "Want us to come with you?"

"No, I'll be quick. Just save me a seat at your table."

I break away from the group, making sure to remain just off the path so the counselors don't notice me turning around. It only takes a few seconds for everyone's footsteps to fade and the trees to swallow the sound of their retreating voices. Then I'm alone, walking uninhibited beneath a canopy of gently swaying leaves. A warm breeze wafts through the branches, drying the sweat on my forehead. It's quiet here, almost peaceful, and for a second, it makes me think of dusty church pews and well-worn hymnals. I don't miss what Pleasant Hills became, but sometimes, in these strange, in-between moments, I miss what it had the potential to be.

The thought shivers down my spine as I duck back into the clearing. Sure enough, there's my borrowed baseball cap, lying a few feet away. I scoop it up and am just about to leave when a different sound floats toward me from the other side of the tower.

A rough, shaky inhale followed by the distinct sniff of someone crying.

185

I freeze, a dozen half-remembered folktales flashing across my mind. There are creatures lurking in the Kentucky wilderness. That's just common sense, and I'm sure there's at least one who lures unsuspecting girls to their deaths with the sound of tears. Mothman, probably. He's always seemed a little shifty.

Slowly, hat still clutched in one hand, I peer around the side of the tower. When I finally catch sight of who's keeping me company, I almost wish it *was* Mothman. That, at least, would be easier to deal with.

Instead, I find Amanda perched halfway up the wooden steps, legs tucked against her chest as her shoulders shake with silent sobs.

I pull back, heart slamming against my rib cage. Either the universe has a twisted sense of humor or I'm cursed with the absolute worst luck known to man. There's no other explanation for why this keeps happening to me. I'm just debating whether I should hide under the tower until she leaves or retreat into the woods when a twig catches under my heel. It snaps, the sound echoing comically loud around the clearing, and I stumble away from the tower as Amanda's head whips in my direction.

"Sorry! I'm not . . . I was just grabbing my hat."

The excuse sounds unconvincing, even to me. It's not like I'm spying on her. It's not like I care, but this is the second time in two days I've seen her like this. I'd be lying if I said some deep, twisted part of me wasn't morbidly curious as to why.

Amanda's cheeks flood with color. She stands and swipes the back of her hand over her face, but when she straightens, her expression is still frustratingly neutral. "Can I help you with something? Or are you physically incapable of minding your own business?"

So that's what we're doing, then? I shrug. "I'm just enjoying the view."

"Of course." Amanda flicks a dismissive hand at the trees behind us. "Just go, Riley. I think we're done here."

"You don't own the forest."

"Neither do you."

"Then I guess we're both out of luck."

I know I'm antagonizing her, pushing as many buttons as I can in the hopes that something will give, but I don't care. This is what I've been craving for months—a moment where it's just the two of us, where there aren't any school administrators or counselors to run to. Just her and me and whatever truth I can drag to the surface.

"What is it, then?" I ask, leaning one shoulder against the base of the tower. "What's wrong?"

Amanda shakes her head. "Nothing."

"Doesn't seem like nothing. Did Jeremy dump you? I always thought he could do better."

A flash of movement on the stairs—Amanda's hands curling into fists. "No. He's not . . . We're fine."

"Are you failing a class, then?" My eyes widen in mock concern. "It's physics, isn't it? You know you need four science credits to graduate."

"I'm not failing—"

"Then what is it? Did your nail tech cancel an appointment? Did you accidentally commit a deadly sin? Did someone—?"

"Enough!"

Amanda rounds on me, white-knuckled fingers gripping the wooden railing, and there it is. Something other than pleasant indifference curling the corner of her mouth. For a second, I think it looks suspiciously like fear. I reach for it, digging my claws in one final time.

"You don't need to get defensive. I'm just trying to help."

"I don't need your help."

"You sure?"

Amanda exhales through her teeth. *"Positive."*

"Okay." I make a show of looking around the empty clearing. "It's just that none of your other friends seem to be here at the moment, so if there's anything you want to share—"

"Oh my god!" Amanda drags a frustrated hand through her hair. "Fine! I didn't get into Indiana's dance program. Are you happy?"

I don't know what I'd been expecting her to say. I don't know what, exactly, I thought I'd find when I finally cracked her open. Dark, terrible secrets, maybe, or an itemized list of every sin she's ever committed. Something that proves what I've known for months—that Amanda Clarke is not the good Christian girl everyone believes her to be. But as she glares down at me from the steps of the tower, it's not satisfaction I feel curled in the pit of my stomach. In fact, the only thought running through my head is *That's it?*

SAY A LITTLE PRAYER

"You . . . You didn't get into IU?"

"That's not what I said," Amanda snaps. "I got into the school, of course, but apparently I'm 'not a good fit' for their dance program. So forgive me if I'm a little upset for wasting fifteen years of my life on a hobby that went exactly nowhere."

"But Greer thinks you got in. She told me this week."

"Well, I lied. To her and everyone else."

"Why?"

"It's not . . . You wouldn't understand."

I roll my eyes. "Because you're *sooo* much more interesting than the rest of us? Try me."

Amanda folds her arms over her chest. The movement is too tense to be casual, nails digging into her forearms, but when she speaks again, her voice is barely audible. "I'm not good at anything else. I'm not like Greer or Hannah or you. Dance is the only thing that's ever been easy for me."

It's such an obvious, self-pitying lie that I bark out a laugh. Because Amanda is good at *everything*—school, ballet, leading the youth congregation in minutes-long versions of the same inauthentic prayer. It's her whole thing, the reason people stop when she passes in the hallway, and watching her try to twist herself into some poor, pitiful victim is infuriating.

"Really?" I choke back another laugh. "You don't want to workshop that a bit?"

Amanda's face flushes a delicate shade of pink. "Fuck you, Riley."

There it is. I grip both sides of the railing and casually pull

189

myself up the first step. "I'm just saying that even in the weird alternate universe where that's remotely believable, it's still not true. You applied to other dance programs. I know you got in. Why does this one matter so much?"

I don't tell her how I know which programs she'd applied to, how I remember hearing her and Hannah on the phone last fall, brainstorming which variations to pull from Amanda's repertoire. *What about* Coppélia? *Do you remember Esmeralda from that one summer intensive? I might still have the tambourine. If you send in an audition that doesn't include the fouettés from the Black Swan Coda, I will literally strangle you.*

Amanda shakes her head. "I can't . . . I'm supposed to go to IU. I *want* to go to IU."

"Doesn't sound like it," I say.

"I do." There's a note of desperation in her voice, a switchblade edge that sharpens as I haul myself up another step. "It's a great school. I like it, and it's the one my parents said they'd pay for. They wouldn't even have to know I was dancing. All I had to do was get in, but if I can't do that at a school where my dad has a literal *building* named after him, how the hell am I supposed to make it anywhere else?"

She drags a hand down her face, smearing the blue paint still caked beneath her eyes. An uncomfortable pressure settles between my ribs, an ache that feels suspiciously close to guilt. I grit my teeth and push it away.

"Why are you telling me this?" I ask. "I mean, I know I kind of forced you to, but I didn't think you'd actually say anything."

SAY A LITTLE PRAYER

Amanda lets out a watery laugh. "I don't know. Because you already hate me, I guess? I don't really have anyone else to tell. My mom doesn't care. Jeremy has exactly two brain cells, both of which are devoted to memorizing hockey stats and looking down Greer's shirt when he thinks I'm not around. Greer's never lost anything in her life, and I just want . . ." Her voice catches in the back of her throat. She squeezes her eyes shut. "I *miss* her."

There it is again—the fist to the gut. The sudden, airless sensation of drowning. Because I know she's not talking about Greer or Jorgia Rose or any of their other friends.

"Good," I snap. "You should miss her. She's amazing. She was your friend and you just left."

"I know."

"No, you *don't!*" I grip the railing, ignoring the splinters sinking into my palms. "You don't know. She trusted you, Amanda. She needed you. I can't do everything. I'm trying and I . . ."

My throat closes, and I cannot believe that after months of holding it together, Amanda Clarke might be the one who sees me cry. I swipe an angry hand across my face and force myself to meet her gaze. "Why?" I ask. "How could you just stop caring?"

Will it happen to me, too? Is it only a matter of time before Julia's the one shutting me out?

I don't recognize the way Amanda's looking at me. It's distant, almost unsettling, and it's not until her eyes flutter closed that I realize it's because I've never seen her truly unguarded.

"I wish I stopped," she whispers. "That would be easier, I

think. It's all just so *much*. It's so much all the time, and I can't fix it because every time I think about what happened I feel so . . ."

"Angry?" I supply.

Amanda flinches, then shakes her head emphatically. "No, of course not."

It's funny, I think, that out of all the things I've accused her of so far, that's the one that crawls under her skin. "Why not?" I ask. "You're angry at me. Or you were a few minutes ago."

"That doesn't count. You're a very specific brand of irritating."

"I like to think of myself as an acquired taste." I hesitate, then add, "You seemed pretty mad at your parents, too."

Amanda's cheeks flush. "No, I'm not. Pastor Young said it this morning—it's wrong to be angry. It's a sin."

I think of Greer standing next to me in the kitchen last night, the way her eyes had widened when she whispered, *I didn't know he could kick people out of church.* Maybe we all feel like this, deep down. Maybe everyone at Pleasant Hills is just as angry as me, and maybe we're all just waiting for someone to break that place wide open.

I hadn't felt particularly wrathful during our game of capture the flag, but I certainly feel it now, standing face-to-face with Amanda Clarke in the middle of the woods. The last four months rewind through my brain in sickening flashes. Hannah coming home from church in tears. Amanda ignoring her calls that night. The first day back at school when Jorgia Rose had conveniently taken the last open seat at their lunch table and left Hannah standing alone. Every snide comment, every whispered

SAY A LITTLE PRAYER

rumor, every time Amanda had averted her eyes in the hallway instead of facing what she'd done.

If this is the kind of rage Pastor Young is talking about, I can almost understand why he's so afraid. Right now I feel like I could tear the world apart.

I release a ragged sigh and start climbing the stairs, shouldering Amanda out of the way as I go. "Follow me."

She doesn't answer, but after a second of wary hesitation, I hear her footsteps behind me. We come to a stop on the tower balcony, and I reach up to trail a finger over the decorative glass ornaments dangling from the ceiling.

"Here's a secret," I say. "I'm angry, too."

Amanda's still hovering by the stairs, like she thinks I'll toss her over the railing if she gets too close. She lets out a dismissive snort. "That's not a secret."

I ignore her, grabbing one of the ornaments and yanking it toward me until the string snaps.

"Lately, it feels like I'm one wrong move from exploding," I say. "Like there's too much inside me with nowhere to go. And it doesn't feel fair to talk about it because I'm fine, all things considered, but I'm still so angry all the time." I raise my voice so it rings across the clearing and hurl the ornament over the side of the balcony. "I'm angry at Principal Rider for making me come here!"

Glass shatters against a nearby tree with a satisfying crunch. Amanda sucks in a surprised breath, but I don't look at her. I just reach up for another. "I'm mad at Pastor Young for making

193

Hannah a target when she did nothing wrong. I'm mad that everyone else just let it happen, and I'm *livid* at you and Greer for doing his dirty work for him."

Something in my chest unlatches as I hurl the glass into the trees. A release that feels as natural as breathing. I whip around to glare at Amanda. "Your turn."

"Oh!" She takes a shaky step back. "No, I . . . I can't."

"Really? You don't want to break something? You're not still annoyed with me?"

"I mean, a little, but—"

"But nothing." I pull a little glass angel from its string. "Here."

I don't know why I'm so insistent. It's not like I need Amanda to commit this sin with me for it to work, but some dark, vengeful part of me wants her to. I want her to be angry. I want to know she's capable of feeling *something* other than bland indifference for the things she's done.

Amanda hesitates, weighing the angel in her hand, then gently lobs it over the balcony. It arcs through the air and bounces harmlessly off another tree before landing in the grass in one piece. She blinks down at it, and despite myself, despite everything, I almost smile.

"Nice try."

Her face reddens. "This was a bad idea. I can't—"

"No!" I grab the back of her shirt as she starts toward the stairs. "It's fine! I'll go again. I'm still mad they didn't feed us yesterday."

I hurl another ornament across the clearing and bite back a

SAY A LITTLE PRAYER

satisfied grin when it disintegrates against the ground. Amanda squares her shoulders. "Fine," she says. "I'm mad about that, too, I guess."

She tears another bird from its string, and this time, her aim is true. Glass falls to the ground in a glittering shower, and the locked doors in my chest swing wider. "There you go!" I cry. "I'm mad no one understands autonomy in this town!"

Amanda's gaze narrows across the clearing. "I'm mad at my parents for assuming they know what I want."

"I hate that I'm missing rehearsal this week!"

"I can't believe I lost capture the flag!"

"I'm mad no one else seems to hate Pastor Young as much as I do!"

The instant my ornament shatters on the grass, I wish I could take it back. It's one thing to be angry about the tangible way Pastor Young treated Hannah, but that last confession feels too personal. I shake my head as Amanda turns to look at me. "I'm kidding. That's not . . . I don't hate him."

"Yes, you do," she says. "Everyone does, a little bit."

I snap a faceless angel off its string and take aim. "You don't."

"And how could you possibly know that?"

"Because I don't think you'd spend the last four months actively terrorizing your best friend based on the whim of someone you hate."

I hurl the angel as hard as I can into the woods. Its broken pieces catch in the sun like fallen stars, but when I look back over my shoulder, Amanda's still watching me.

"You weren't there that day," she says, voice lowered like she's afraid someone might be listening. "The way he talked to Hannah . . . It was like a warning. Like he could do that to anyone at any time. No one wanted to be next."

"That's not an excuse."

"I know. That's not what I'm trying to say."

"What are you saying, then?" I snap. "Please, enlighten me, Amanda, because I've been trying to figure it out for months, and I can't think of a single acceptable reason why you'd treat her like that."

"There's not!" Amanda turns in a frustrated circle. "Of course there's not! You think I don't know that? You think I don't wish I could go back and do something different? I'm *sorry*!"

She lets out a choked, guttural scream and smashes her last ornament on the ground at our feet. I jump as glass sprays over the balcony. The woods fall silent, and when I look up again, Amanda's eyes are a shade too bright, shoulders heaving like she's still playing capture the flag.

I'm sorry.

A week ago, I would have tossed the apology back in her face. I would have shredded the words before they left her mouth, but Amanda is the second person to look me in the eye this week and talk about Pastor Young in a way that's not wholly devout. She and Greer both said they didn't feel like they had a choice, and even though my first instinct is to scoff and ask how neither of them saw this coming, there's another part of me that remem-

SAY A LITTLE PRAYER

bers what it feels like to believe in something so desperately. I'd listened to Pastor Young preach about sinners and consequences for years without putting a face to the victims he condemned. Maybe I'm just as terrible and selfish for not noticing the flaws in his sermons until they started ripping me apart, too.

I swallow over the sudden lump in my throat. "Thanks. But that's not my apology to accept."

Amanda nods, gaze dropping to the floor. "Yeah. I know."

For a minute, the only sound is the breeze wafting through the remaining ornaments overhead. I take a deep breath, and to my surprise, the pressure in my chest is gone. It's like the anger unlocked something inside me, like putting a voice to the things that haunt me has somehow robbed them of their power. I wonder if Amanda feels the same way, if maybe she'd just needed someone to give her permission.

I turn to face her and, before I can second-guess myself, blurt, "I'm sorry I hit you."

"Oh." Amanda blinks, like she'd somehow forgotten the whole reason I'm here. "Thanks. I'm sorry you had to."

In that moment, I think she actually might be. There's a wary truce forming between us, made of broken glass and shouted secrets. Not enough to bridge the gap these last few months have carved, but enough to make me wonder what could be waiting on the other side.

This is what wrath can do, I think. *This is what everyone is so afraid of.*

"Come on," I say, waving her toward the stairs. "Let's go to lunch."

And as we walk back through the woods together, I desperately wish Mr. Rider could see me now. I think he'd probably give me an A.

XIV

Anyway, Here's "Wonderwall" (the Lord's Version)

"I hate to be the one to tell you this, but Patrick Davies has a guitar."

I peer over Delaney's shoulder and squint toward the bonfire on the other side of the field. Sure enough, Patrick is perched on the edge of a folding chair with a midnight-blue guitar braced on one knee. His hair is still spray-painted red from this afternoon, and there's a group of girls sitting at his feet, watching him with barely concealed adoration.

"Oh no," I say. "Should we help them?"

Delaney shakes her head. "Listening to some guy play guitar at the campfire is a canon event, Riley. We can't interfere. Just ask Torres how obsessed she was with Ethan Brady last year."

"I was not!" Torres protests, but the flush staining her cheeks says otherwise.

Ethan had been our drama department's resident tenor for the past four years. After last spring's production of *Les Mis*, he'd treated the entire cast to Steak 'n Shake on his dad's credit card, tearfully told us that playing Jean Valjean had been "the honor of his life," and said he'd think about us every day at college. He'd quit the University of Michigan theater department within a week and now spends his time uploading embarrassingly earnest guitar covers to TikTok and tagging John Mayer in the comments.

"Ethan Brady?" I bite back a grin. "Come on, Torres. You can do better than that."

She groans. "That's not . . . We were *friends*."

"Please." Delaney scoffs. "He played 'Wonderwall,' like, six times a night, and you willingly sat through them all."

I laugh, partially because Torres is turning a concerning shade of pink and partially because I know exactly what Ethan Brady's version of "Wonderwall" sounds like.

The three of us come to a stop at the edge of the bonfire, just outside the ring of flickering light. Usually, we'd all be in separate cabins by now, finishing up any lingering assignments and getting ready for bed. Tonight, however, is a party. The counselors have hauled in giant bags of marshmallows and graham crackers— treats that were conveniently absent from our midnight kitchen run—and set up a semicircle of collapsible camping chairs around the firepit. Most of them are already occupied and the campers who hadn't managed to grab a seat are lounging across various picnic blankets. Maybe it's leftover camaraderie from this morning's game or maybe it's the fact that our afternoon lessons had been cut short to accommodate tonight's festivities, but the mood is noticeably lighter than it has been all week.

Torres shuffles through the pile of abandoned skewers until

she finds one clean enough for her liking. She jams a handful of marshmallows on top and slides up to the firepit, right next to where Greer is meticulously turning her own skewer every few seconds. She looks up when we approach and asks, with absolutely no preamble, "Do you think we should tell them he has a girlfriend?"

At first, it's unclear if she's talking to us at all. Greer's gaze is laser focused on the golden-brown crust slowly forming around the outside of her marshmallow. Even Amanda, who's hovering on her other side, is looking anywhere but at me, like she's afraid I'm going to jab her with my skewer and announce to the entire camp that she'd dared to experience a single human emotion. I raise a brow. "Who has a girlfriend?"

Greer jerks her chin over the open flame to where Patrick is still strumming his guitar. In the few minutes it had taken us to cross the field, the cluster of girls at his feet has nearly doubled. Some of them are singing along. I think Alexis Waddy is trying to harmonize.

"Does he?" I ask.

Greer nods. "He literally asked Aisha McKenzie to prom last week."

Delaney heaves a sigh. "It won't matter. They all think they can *fix him*."

"Well, does he take requests, at least? If I hear 'Closing Time' again, I'm going to scream."

Torres folds her arms defensively. "Some people like 'Closing Time.'"

"No one likes 'Closing Time,' Torres," Greer says. Then she raises her voice and calls, "Hey, Patrick!" loud enough to get his attention through the chaos.

Patrick looks up, music unfaltering as he jerks his chin in her direction. "What's up?"

"Do you take requests?"

"Not usually, but I'll take one for you, baby."

I grimace and shove the end of my skewer into the open flame. There's no way that line has ever worked on anyone, let alone someone who'd been ready to make a camp-wide announcement about his relationship status, but when I look back at Greer, her mouth is hanging half open. She blinks, eyes glazed, and I'm just coming to the startling realization that one of the smartest, most competent people I know can still be overcome by some guy with a guitar and semidecent biceps when Amanda pushes her way between us.

"Do you know 'Flexin' on That Gram'?" she asks.

Patrick's grin falters. "Uh . . . don't think so?"

"What about 'Wonderwall'?"

Torres grimaces, physically cringing away from the suggestion, but Patrick's face lights up. There's a split second of silence as he adjusts his fingers, then the familiar chords start drifting across the circle. Delaney and I let out a collective groan as Greer gives her head a little shake.

"Why would you say that?" she asks, rounding on Amanda. "That's just as bad as 'Closing Time.'"

SAY A LITTLE PRAYER

"I had to do something, Greer. You looked like you were about to throw yourself across an open flame."

"I was *fine*."

"Your marshmallow is on fire."

Greer looks down in time to watch her perfect golden marshmallow burst into flames on the end of her skewer. She shrieks, frantically trying to blow it out, but by the time it subsides, the only thing left is a charred husk.

Amanda gives her a sympathetic pat on the back. "And that," she says, "is why we don't listen to boys with guitars."

The others fall into easy conversation around me, laughing as the remnants of Greer's marshmallow drip into the pit with a soft hiss. I remain at the edge of the circle. I haven't talked to Julia since lunch. I assumed she'd gone ahead to help set up the bonfire, but I don't see her on any of the blankets. I spot Ben a few yards away, momentarily drawn by the copper glint of his hair, but he's surrounded by a group of boys from his cabin, his sister nowhere to be found. She isn't digging through the pile of skewers either. She's not constructing s'mores or playing cornhole on the other side of the firepit or sitting with the cluster of girls at Patrick's feet.

It's not until I glance over my shoulder that I finally spot her sitting alone on an overturned log at the edge of the clearing. She's wearing one of my old drama club T-shirts, the stretched-out collar hanging loose from one shoulder as she bends over the prayer book in her lap. The fire casts a warm orange glow across

203

the side of her face, etching her unbound hair in layers of gold, and the sight of it makes my heart go miserably, traitorously soft.

"I'll be right back," I say to no one in particular.

I duck away from the fire without waiting for a response. Julia looks up as I approach, and just like last time, she closes her prayer book a little too quickly at the sight of me. Just like last time, I pretend not to notice.

"Here." I hold my skewer in her direction. "For you."

Julia eyes the burned hunk of marshmallow clinging to the end. "Thanks," she says dryly. Then she glances over my shoulder. "Were you just talking to Amanda? Like, on purpose?"

I snort. "Something like that."

Julia's log isn't really meant for two people, but she scoots over the best she can to make room. I drape one leg over each side, straddling it so I can face her directly, then follow her gaze across the clearing. The others are still deep in conversation, laughing at some joke we can't hear. Greer has her head thrown back, physically holding Amanda's shoulder to remain upright, and my chest squeezes at the sight. How many times had I watched them laugh with Hannah like that, arm in arm on the couch or piled together in the back of a car?

"I don't know what we're doing," I say, gaze dropping back to the log beneath me. "We ran into each other this afternoon when I went back for my hat."

Julia's eyebrows fly up. "Really?"

"Yeah. She . . . apologized."

"For what she said about Hannah?"

SAY A LITTLE PRAYER

"For everything, I think."

"Oh." Julia leans back, weight braced on one hand. "And you believe her?"

"I want to. I think Hannah deserves to hear it." I trail a finger over the rough bark between us, tracing invisible lines as I try to untangle the knot inside me. "It's weird, though. For so long, I couldn't do anything about Pleasant Hills or . . . how it works, but I could blame her. I'm not sure what to do with that now."

Too much, I think as the words hang suspended between us. *Too real.* I bite the inside of my cheek as Julia stiffens beside me. This might be the closest I've ever come to talking about Pastor Young's role in all this, and still, I feel like I'm tiptoeing around the truth. Like the topic is breakable and I'm one wrong word away from shattering with it.

Years ago, I accepted that I would never completely understand how Julia's brain works. She's always been several steps ahead of me, but that doesn't mean I can't still read her like a book. Now, for instance, I watch her brow crease with something between frustration and torment. When she speaks again, every word is deliberate.

"I love bonfire night. I always have. It feels like the first time all week everyone's happy."

I laugh. "Yeah, because no one's making us do weird survivalist activities."

"Sure," Julia says. "There's that, but it's also the first time I feel like these trips have a purpose."

"And what's that?"

205

A wry smile lifts the corner of her mouth. "Being together. Finding each other. I know camp isn't perfect, but I've always loved having a place to come back to, and I love when it feels like this. This should be the point of everything, you know? I don't think people like Amanda know that yet."

My nails dig into a patch of crumbling moss. "That's not an excuse."

"I know." Julia's expression turns distant. "But I don't think it's like this everywhere. I think there must be places where people genuinely care about each other. Delaney's family belongs to this church over in Franklin where people actually laugh during the sermon. Did you know that? They're supposed to. I went with them once a few years ago, and their pastor talked for twenty minutes about how Jesus would have been a socialist if he was alive today. Which is, like, objectively true, but the only thing I could think about was how much trouble I'd be in if anyone ever found out I was there, and sometimes I wonder what would happen if we had someone other than—"

She stops, but I feel the confession hanging on the tip of her tongue. It lingers between us, deliberately unsaid, and I resist the urge to lean forward and take it. To make her state, out loud, what we're both thinking. I know Julia and Ben don't agree with most of the things their father does, but I didn't realize how much I've needed to hear her say it until now. I wait, but after a second of strained silence, Julia just ducks her head.

"Sorry," she mutters. "The point is, I don't like Amanda. But maybe she's never had anyone tell her things could be different."

SAY A LITTLE PRAYER

It's the same thing I've been telling myself all week—the idea that if I can just get people to listen, if I can pull together real, tangible proof of Pastor Young's lies, then everything will be fine. It has to be. I've come too far to second-guess my plan now, but as I watch Julia tilt her head toward the bonfire, I wonder if basing my entire strategy on the idea that our congregation is inherently good might come back to bite me.

Maybe it's not that simple. Maybe everyone is more complicit than I want to believe.

"Could it really be different, though?" I ask. "Could things actually change? I left a year ago, Julia. Isn't it all still the same?"

When Julia looks at me again, her expression is painfully gentle. "No," she says. "They're not the same. You're here. You came back."

I shake my head. "I'm not back."

"You could be, though."

"Is that what you want?"

The question slips out before I can stop it. *He still thinks we can Save you.* That's what Ben told me on the bus. That's what I'm afraid Julia is thinking now.

She blinks, lashes fanning across her cheeks as her head cocks to the side. "What do you mean?"

"I mean . . ." I swallow over my rapidly tightening throat. "What if this week is it? What if I never come back to church and nothing you say will ever convince me? Would you still want . . . that?"

I can't bring myself to voice the real question—*would you still*

207

want me? But when Julia reaches for me in the dark, hand settling purposefully on my knee, I wonder if she hears it, too.

"Always."

My next inhale catches in the back of my throat. Somewhere behind us, Patrick launches into the slow, twangy chorus of a song I almost recognize. It's slower than 'Wonderwall,' more intimate than anything he's played all night, and there's a split second between heartbeats where it feels like Julia and I have slipped out of time.

Because we're not alone here. The bonfire is still flickering several yards away. There are plenty of reasons for me to keep my distance, but as I watch the flames drag gold-tipped fingers down the side of Julia's face, I can't remember a single one. In fact, every scrap of my remaining attention is focused on the way her hand still lingers on my knee, like she can't imagine a world where she ever lets go. Then her gaze drops to my lips, and for a single aching second, I think she wants to kiss me.

No. I push the thought away. *You're being delusional.*

But how am I supposed to think anything else when she's looking at me like this?

Her grip tightens around my knee, and I have to dig my fingers into the bark to avoid reaching for her, too. I want to touch her. I want to tuck her hair behind her ears and memorize the soft curve of her waist, and I want, more than anything, to know if what she said earlier is true.

If she really thinks I can change things.

The fire pops, sending a shower of sparks arcing into the

SAY A LITTLE PRAYER

night. Julia blinks at the sound. She shoots a quick glance over her shoulder, then stiffens. I hear her suck in a sharp breath, and then she's on her feet.

"It's late," she says, barely looking at me as she scoops up her things. "I think I should call it a night."

I teeter on the log, caught off guard by her sudden absence. "I . . . What?"

Julia's face is inscrutable as she grabs her prayer book from the ground. "It's late," she repeats. "Sorry. I'll see you back at the cabin."

And then, before I can form a coherent sentence, she's gone.

Rationally, I know no one else is watching us. There are too many people milling around the clearing to tell who's coming and going, but it feels like every eye is suddenly trained on me. Like the entire camp knows exactly how much I wanted to kiss her and how, for a second, I thought she wanted to kiss me, too.

I squeeze my eyes shut as Patrick starts strumming his way through another song. It's not like I haven't considered the possibility of kissing Julia. It's not like I haven't overanalyzed the feeling of her hand in mine or the way she'd curled against me last night and thought, *Could we?* So far, the answer has always been a firm and deliberate *no*. No, Julia isn't queer. No, she would have told me if she was. No, I'm not willing to risk our friendship on feelings she probably doesn't reciprocate.

But as I watch her disappear into the night, the answer shifts in the back of my mind. Instead of *no*, it sounds a little more like *what if?*

I groan and bury my face in my hands. This, I think, is why I'd been so hesitant to come out—because no matter how supportive my friends and family have been so far, it still feels like something that will fundamentally change the way people see me. There are a decent number of queer students at Madison. There's an LGBTQ+ club, too, but that didn't stop Kyle Anderson from getting quietly scrapped from the homecoming court ballot when the rest of the baseball team found out he was dating a boy from his temple. It doesn't stop the handful of volleyball girls who still make jokes about changing in front of Emma Perez or the teachers from misgendering Angie Harrison for the third year in a row.

Maybe Julia has sat through too many of her father's "this is why God hates gay people" sermons to ever truly consider an alternative. Or maybe the desire had been too clear on my face tonight, too vulnerable, and she decided I wasn't worth it either.

I slide off the log and reach for my bag, suddenly desperate to be anywhere but here. I've just started back toward the others when a chill prickles down my spine. I risk a glance over my shoulder, and there, standing on the other side of the firepit with his hands casually tucked in his pockets, is Pastor Young. He's back in his counselor T-shirt and baggy jeans, identical to the cluster of people around him. In fact, I might not have noticed him at all if he wasn't watching me through the flames, eyes narrowed on the empty space Julia just left.

I drop my gaze, heart slamming against my rib cage. *How long has he been standing there, watching us?* It shouldn't matter. There

SAY A LITTLE PRAYER

wasn't anything to see, but shame still hooks itself under my skin. I hate how familiar it feels. I hate the part of me that still wants to apologize, to throw myself at Pastor Young's feet and beg for his forgiveness, even though I've done nothing wrong.

That's something they train into you early at Pleasant Hills. It's something, I've found, that's even harder to clear out.

Delaney looks up when I approach, then tugs me back into the circle like I never left. Torres offers me a perfectly toasted s'more, Greer grimaces each time a new girl joins the circle at Patrick's feet, and through it all, I smile, trying very hard not to notice Pastor Young still watching me across the open flame.

XV

Lust and Found

I sleep fitfully that night, wading half asleep through dream after dream where Pastor Young watches me, unblinking, from every corner of the room. When I run into him in the cafeteria the next morning, it takes me a solid thirty seconds to realize it's not an additional part of the nightmare. It is, unfortunately, real life.

"Morning, Riley," he says, stepping back so I can stack my empty tray on the counter behind him. "Nice win yesterday."

It's another minute before I remember our game of capture the flag. I feel like I've lived a thousand lifetimes since then, each more draining than the last. "Thanks," I say. "It was a team effort."

"That's not what I heard." Pastor Young nods toward the door, motioning for me to walk with him. "Do you have a minute? I feel like I haven't seen you all week."

Yes, I think. *There's a reason for that.*

Out loud, I say, "I don't have long. We're meeting in the chapel today, and Gabe will probably kill me if I'm late for today's lesson on"—I flip open my workbook, hastily fanning through the pages until I find where we left off—"lust and the way it consumes us."

I snap the book closed. On second thought, maybe I should take my time.

Pastor Young comes to a stop just outside the cafeteria doors, but I waver on the threshold. Every Sunday for as long as I can remember, he stood in front of the Pleasant Hills chapel and greeted every member of the congregation by name. He always remembered the details, too, like when the McHughs' next baby was due or where the seniors were going to college. He does the same thing here, offering every passing camper a wave and a smile. After a year away, I'd forgotten how intoxicating it is to watch, how chosen and favored and special his attention makes you feel.

"So," he says, turning the full force of that warmth on me. "How have you been?"

I shrug. "Can't complain."

"I'm sure you could."

I bite the inside of my cheek to stop my lips from quirking into a traitorous smile. "Okay, fine. I didn't *love* the day we fasted."

Pastor Young laughs. "Fair. But that was the point, right? To reflect on your earthly desires?"

"Sure."

He turns to greet a new wave of campers, and I lean one shoulder against the doorframe, trying to remember that this whole kind, caring, man-of-God routine is a lie. He wants something, and the second I refuse, he'll go back to looking at me the way he did that first day on the path. Like I'm something to be fixed.

"Well, I'm glad to hear you're having a good time," he says. "I've been praying for you this week, you know. Have you given any more thought to rejoining our Sunday congregation?"

There it is. I give another noncommittal shrug. "Maybe."

It's a lie, of course, but Pastor Young's expression instantly brightens. "That's great to hear. Truly, I can't express how much everyone misses having you around." Then, before I can think of an appropriately neutral response, he lowers his voice and adds, "Your family's sins aren't yours to bear."

Usually, my anger comes out hot, molten fury bubbling in the pit of my stomach. Now, however, all I feel is cold. It crawls up my spine like ice, freezing my smile into place. "I think we might have a different definition of sin, Pastor Young," I say.

"Let's hope not." His hand lands on my shoulder in a way I think is supposed to be reassuring. "Your sister made her choice. That's not your burden to carry, and I would hate for her bad decisions to impact your relationship with the Lord."

I step deliberately out of his grip. "And what if I don't want a relationship with the Lord?"

That gets his attention. Pastor Young steps back, brow pinched, and when he looks down at me again, I see the exact moment his perfect, white-toothed veneer cracks. "If that's the case," he says gravely, "then we'd be having a very different conversation. I would hate to think I've failed you somehow, that I missed your cries for help. I don't want that, Riley, and I definitely don't want

SAY A LITTLE PRAYER

to have to tell your principal that this week didn't work out the way we hoped."

My head snaps up. "What?"

"That's why you're here, isn't it? To repent for the way you acted? To move forward with the grace of salvation? I want that for you, believe me. I was ready to give you a glowing report when we got home, but now—"

"Now *what*?" I ask. It comes out bitter and harsh, but I don't care. If he's done pretending, I am, too. "I've done everything you asked."

"Careful." Pastor Young holds up a placating hand. "There's no need to get angry. I'm not upset with you, Riley. I'm just being honest. All I've ever wanted is to set you on the right path and help your family out of the dark."

The worst part is, I think he really means it. He truly believes he's doing this for my own good, to help me, and something about that feels worse than if he was being actively malicious.

"No offense," I say, offense implied in every syllable, "but my family is fine. I came here because Mr. Rider gave me a choice, not because I want a place in your congregation. I'm writing the essay he assigned. *That's* the deal. You don't get to change the rules because you don't like me."

It's not until the words leave my mouth that I think I might have gone too far. Pastor Young is used to me pretending, to my forced smiles and agreeable nods. It's how we've communicated all year. It's how I'd planned to survive this week, too, but when

215

Pastor Young sighs and shakes his head, the disappointment couldn't be clearer.

"No," he says. "I can't. At this point, it looks like all I can do is keep you in my prayers and hope that, one day, you'll see that everything I'm doing is for your own good. All of it. I care about you, Riley. I still think you can be Saved."

I let out a dismissive snort and tug the strap of my bag over my shoulder. "And I still think you're full of it."

He doesn't try to stop me when I leave. Instead, he remains in the doorway, head bowed like he's already starting to pray for my soul.

Clouds gather overhead as I stalk toward the chapel. The sky is thick with them, storm finally brewing on the horizon, and I think that's how I feel, too. Dark and tempestuous and ready to burst. It's not until I reach the door that the first drops of regret start to prick against my skin. *What did I do?*

I'm already on thin ice. I'd spent all week looking over my shoulder, hiding my thrift store finds and outrunning the counselor night patrol so Pastor Young wouldn't have an excuse to shut me out. *But he doesn't need one now*, I think bitterly. I've just confirmed every suspicion he's had and handed him a perfect, infallible reason to keep his children far, far away from me.

I bite back a strangled curse and push my way into the chapel. When I look up to find a PowerPoint titled CHASTITY: SAVE YOUR SOUL BY SAVING "IT" already loaded onto the mainstage projector, I momentarily consider flinging myself off the bleachers.

I drop into the first empty seat I find as Cindy jogs onto the

SAY A LITTLE PRAYER

stage. "Hey, ladies!" she calls directly into the mic. "How's everyone feeling this morning?"

She doesn't sell it the way Pastor Young does. The enthusiasm in her voice doesn't quite reach her eyes. I glance over my shoulder and realize, with a jolt, that the chapel is only half full. There's no sign of Gabe or Ben or the other boys from my group, and after a hurried scan of the bleachers, I realize it's because none of the boys are here at all. No, today it's just us, Cindy, and Cindy's informational sex PowerPoint.

She clicks over to a new slide titled LUST AND FOUND. I wonder if it's possible to physically sink through the core of the earth.

"As you can see, it's just us girls today," Cindy says, flashing us a conspiratorial grin. "And even though we're talking about something that might feel a little embarrassing, I want you to know that this is a safe space. Sound good?"

A few heads bob unenthusiastically as I slide down in my seat and fish my prayer book from my bag. Cindy's still talking her way through the slides, but I've stopped listening. I know how this goes. She'll preach about abstinence and "just saying no" like we'll always have a choice. She'll talk about how Jesus will keep us safe without giving any real advice or mentioning that condoms can expire, so maybe you shouldn't use the one your boyfriend has been carrying in his wallet for six months because it might break, you might get pregnant, and then if you decide not to be, multiple grown adults will still try to burn you for it.

It's so much. That's what Amanda had said yesterday, head in her hands, blue paint streaked down both cheeks. *It's so much*

217

all the time. The last thing I want is for her to be right, but that's exactly what it feels like now, watching Cindy talk. Like it's *too much*. Like the things I've brushed aside all year are finally coming to a head.

The pointed looks and whispers from people who didn't know why I left Pleasant Hills in the first place. Being back here after all this time. Listening to Cindy run through a list of abstinence talking points and pretending not to notice every time her gaze slides surreptitiously toward me. Watching Julia leave last night, wondering if I'd somehow broken the last thing holding us together.

How is anyone supposed to endure it? Why was I so convinced I could escape this place unscathed?

My fingers wrap instinctively around the corner of my prayer book. I start to tuck it away, then freeze, realization zipping up my spine. *This is how.* My original plan might be built on the impossible notion that people might actually listen to me, but it's still something I can control. A way to keep Julia, to shatter the shiny, impenetrable facade of this place wide open, and finally prove I was *right*.

I just have to see it through.

I open the book, reading page after page until the words stick behind my closed eyelids. There's more here than I thought, a collection of scribbled notes and observations from the week. Sitting under the picnic table with Greer and Delaney. Smashing decorative glass into the forest floor. Watching Julia try on vintage gowns in the back of a rural thrift store, wanting more,

SAY A LITTLE PRAYER

wanting *her*. Small things. Deceptively simple things. Things Pastor Young had told us, in no uncertain terms, were the worst of the worst sins.

"You with us, Riley?"

I look up to find Cindy standing at the end of my row. Her PowerPoint is still running behind her, now paused on a slide that reads LUST: NOT SO LIT. I hastily close my prayer book and set it aside. "Sorry."

"That's better." She hands me a stack of sticky notes and a box of dull golf pencils. "Take one of each and pass it down."

I swallow my unease and take one of each. When I pass the supplies down, I finally spot Julia a few rows above me. She'd taken an early breakfast, so I haven't really seen her since last night's bonfire, but the minute our eyes lock above the crowd, I feel the pit in my stomach start to close. She unfolds her sticky note to reveal a giant frowny face already sketched in the middle, and I choke back a laugh.

"Okay," Cindy says when she returns to the mic. "Time for a little activity. Everyone write your name in the middle of the sticky note."

She looks pointedly around the room, waiting for everyone to complete the task. I bite back a sigh and scratch out my name in the tiniest, most illegible letters I can manage, just in case it's a trick.

"Good," she says. "When you're done, I want you to crumple the note in your fist."

I half-heartedly scrunch the paper and when I look up, Cindy's beaming triumphantly, like we've all fallen right into her trap.

"Now try to smooth it out. Put it back to the way it was before." There's a faint rustle as everyone smooths their hands over their sticky notes before giving up. Cindy gives us a knowing grin. "It doesn't work, does it? See how a part of it will always be crumpled? That's what lust does, ladies. It tarnishes. It changes you; it wears you down. It means you won't be able to give your future husband the best version of yourself, and that's not something you can take back."

The bleachers let out a soft groan as people shift uncomfortably in their seats, but for once, I don't move. When I uncurl my fist, the pink sticky note sits right in the center of my palm. Bold of Cindy to assume there's a best version of myself to give.

I turn my hand over and let the crumpled paper fall to the floor.

It's still cloudy by the time we break for lunch, humidity hanging thick between the trees. Cindy had called Julia to the front on the way out, so I hang back as the rest of the girls stream past me, waiting for her to catch up. I want to see her. I want her to look me in the eye, to tell me that last night was nothing more than a silly, inconsequential fluke, and I want, more than anything, to believe her when she does.

I lean against the side of the chapel, tossing my crumpled sticky note from hand to hand. I'd grabbed it on my way out the door as a physical reminder of what I'm fighting against, but the longer I stand here, waiting for Julia to emerge, the more it starts

SAY A LITTLE PRAYER

to feel like an omen. I'm about to give up and toss it in the trash on the way to lunch when I spot Ben walking toward me down the path. His face lights up when he sees me.

"Congrats on surviving lust day," he says, breaking away from his group of friends. "How do you feel?"

I roll my eyes and toss the wadded-up paper in his direction. "Here. Take my virginity."

"No thank you!"

Ben swats it away with surprising accuracy, and despite everything, I feel myself lighten. I turn to face him, one shoulder propped against the wall. "What was your lesson? I'm assuming you didn't write your name on a sticky note to learn about purity?"

"Oh." Ben immediately looks guilty. "No, that's definitely what we did."

I lift a brow, and it takes exactly half a second for him to break.

"Okay, fine. It was, like, twenty minutes of Gabe monologuing about a time his girlfriend's bikini almost caused him to stumble, and then we got to wander the woods to journal about our urges."

"What kind of urges?"

"Sexual, I'm assuming."

"Gross." I wrinkle my nose. "All we got was a weird Power-Point about how Jesus hates the female orgasm."

Ben straightens. "Really?"

"No, but it was totally implied."

He laughs, and as he relaxes against the wall, I catch a glimpse of something solid and rectangular stuffed in his pocket. My eyes immediately narrow. "Is that your phone?"

"What?" Ben stiffens. "No."

It definitely is. I make a grab for his pocket, but Ben gets there first. He's taller than me, so when he thrusts his hand in the air, the phone hangs just out of reach. I jump for it anyway, grabbing his wrist and accidentally smashing his glasses into his face in the process.

"Ow!" he cries. "Okay, okay! It's my phone. Cindy gave it back this morning."

I shove him away. "Are you serious? I had to sit through her sex PowerPoint, but she let you have your phone? Why?"

"I wanted to check the weather."

"You . . . What?"

"The *weather*," Ben repeats. "There's a storm coming. I heard Dad and the counselors talk about driving home early if it doesn't go around us."

I glance up at the sky. Of course it's going to rain. Even I could tell him that, but there's no way he sweet-talked Cindy into breaking camp rules to look at the weather. "So what does it say?"

Ben's throat bobs. "What?"

"What does it say?" I wave a hand in the direction of his phone. "If you spent all morning looking at the weather, you should have a pretty good idea of what we're dealing with."

"I . . ." Ben's face is slowly turning the same color as his hair. "See, this is why it's so important to keep up, Riley. If you bothered to read the forecast—"

"Liar." Suspicion tips down my spine. "Who are you talking to?"

"No one!"

The answer is too quick. I plant both hands on my hips. "Ben."

To his credit, he really tries to keep it in. I can tell. His gaze shifts from side to side, like he's searching for an escape route, and after a few seconds, I see him actually start to sweat.

"Okay, fine," he gasps. "I'm texting Hannah."

I throw up my hands. "Yes, Ben! I know! *Everyone* knows. You literally could not be more obvious about it!" Then I hesitate as the full implication of what he's saying sinks in. "Is she . . . texting you back?"

He nods, gaze locked determinedly on the ground. "We've been talking all morning."

I don't know why that surprises me. Hannah and Ben are friends. We're all friends, but it's not like the two of them have a "text all morning while one of them is at church camp" kind of relationship. I wait for the familiar protective rush, for something jealous and dark to worm its way into my chest, but nothing comes. This, I think, feels like something that was bound to happen sooner or later.

"Good," I say. "I'm glad."

Ben ducks his head, cheeks still glowing a concerning shade of pink. "I like her," he says, like it's a secret confession and not the most obvious thing in the world.

I put a reassuring hand on his shoulder. "I know." Then I tighten my grip, drop my mouth close to his ear, and whisper,

"But if you even *think* about hurting her, I swear to God and Jesus and all the holy spirits—"

"There's only one Holy Spirit," Ben interrupts weakly.

"—I swear to the singular Holy Spirit that I will hunt you down and bury you in the Pleasant Hills cemetery. You won't even have a headstone. No one will ever see you again."

Ben has gone remarkably still under my fingers. "I know," he says. "I actually think about that all the time."

"Good." I give his shoulder another reassuring pat before pushing him away.

Ben still looks wary as he brushes the wrinkles from his shirt, but when he looks up again, something about his expression is significantly lighter. "Are you heading to lunch?" he asks. "I need to stop by the cabin first, but I'll walk with you."

I shake my head. "I'm waiting for Julia. But can you take this back to my cabin on your way?" I slide my bag down my arm. "I hate carrying it around."

Ben takes it with a barely concealed grunt. "I have no idea how they make those books so heavy."

"I think it's the weight of our sins."

"Hmm." He slings the bag over his shoulder. "That explains a lot."

He sets off toward the cabins, sparing me one last nervous glance over his shoulder. I bite back a grin. I don't have to wonder what Hannah sees in him. They've always been two sides of the same coin, a pair that make sense. It's the same way I feel about Julia.

SAY A LITTLE PRAYER

At the thought, I sneak another glance toward the chapel, but the door remains tightly closed. Unease curls unbidden in my chest. Maybe Julia already left. Maybe she slipped past me in the crowd or snuck out the back to avoid me entirely. I kick my heel against the wall and tell myself it's fine. I'll give her another minute. The seconds tick down in my mind, and when she doesn't appear, I give her two more, just to be sure.

Only when I reach zero a third time do I let out a rough groan and stalk back into the chapel, ignoring the way Crucified Jesus #4 rattles in time to the slamming door.

XVI

What If We Kissed in the Church Camp Chapel? Haha, Just Kidding. Unless . . . ?

I find Julia sitting on the corner of the stage, back propped against the gilded pulpit. It's dark without the spotlights, but I'd recognize the shadowy outline of her profile anywhere. She has one leg folded beneath her, the other swinging off the stage as she flips another page in her prayer book. It's not until I clear my throat that she notices me standing between the bleachers.

"Oh!" She closes the book and sets it aside. "Sorry, I didn't realize you were waiting."

"It's okay," I say. "I didn't know you were busy."

"I'm not, really. I just needed a minute to think. Lessons like that are always . . . frustrating."

I nod, some of the tension rolling off my shoulders as I approach. It's like last night, like I didn't realize how much I needed to hear her say that until she does. "Do they talk like that every year?" I ask, lowering myself to the stage beside her. "I know we used to get a version of it in Sunday school, but I don't remember it being that . . . harsh."

Julia runs a finger down the spine of her prayer book, tracing the outline of the butterfly sticker across the back. "Sometimes. You get used to it after a while, though. One year, we all got flowers and Cindy made us pick the petals off one by one."

"Why?"

"To show how undesirable our future husbands would find us if we sullied ourselves before marriage or something."

She waves a hand, clearly trying to make a joke, but I don't find the image particularly funny. I try to picture Julia sitting through these presentations year after year, rolling her eyes at terrible PowerPoint puns, but never voicing her opinion out loud. I rub a hand over my forehead.

"How do you do it? How are you okay with something like that?"

I really don't mean for this to be, like, a *moment*, but the question slips out before I realize what I'm asking. Behind us, the screen goes dark, shadows pushing further across the stage. Julia tips her chin toward the vaulted ceiling. She's quiet for so long that I'm not entirely sure she's going to answer until she shakes her head.

"I don't always think he's right, you know."

My hands go still in my lap. I wait, suddenly afraid to breathe as she continues.

"I think when you get down to it, this whole . . . *thing* is just about being kind and having faith in something bigger than yourself. That's it. That's what I want to believe, anyway. So when they give us lessons like this or when Dad gets a little too preachy,

I have to remind myself that it's not important and it's not why we're here."

Her voice is steady, like she's been forming this particular thought for years and finally found the right words. Like we're having a regular conversation and not potentially dismantling the structure of our entire lives.

"I'm glad you can do that," I say. "Really, but what about everyone else? What about the girls who just sat through that presentation for the first time? How are they supposed to know it's not important when everyone's telling them differently?"

Julia's hands tighten on the edge of the stage. "I don't know. I try to guide them when I can."

"And when you can't?"

"Then I have to hope they find their own way."

"Those can't be the only options," I say. "What if you said something? What if you or Ben actually talked to your father? You're the only people he might actually listen to."

"He doesn't listen to me." There's an edge to Julia's voice now, something that feels suspiciously like panic. "You get to go home this weekend, Riley. You don't have to think about this place again, but I live with it."

"I live with it, too!" I cry. "We all do!"

I've been out of this world for a year, and still, Pleasant Hills has its claws in me. I don't think I'll ever get them out. I'm going to feel the effects of this week long after I get home, and I'm willing to bet the others will, too. Maybe the fear of Pastor Young's wrath will linger in the back of their minds and make them

228

SAY A LITTLE PRAYER

second-guess every choice. Maybe it'll rot them from the inside out, turn them against anyone who feels a little bit different.

I lean forward, forcing Julia to meet my gaze. "What is it?" I ask. "What's stopping you?"

There's a sad little smile playing across her face now, half reluctant, half resigned. When she speaks again, her voice sounds far away. "When you were little, did your parents tell you that they'd always love you no matter what? That you might fight or make mistakes, but at the end of the day, you were family?"

I let out a soft, unexpected laugh. Of course my parents said that. They're sentimental and overbearing and *involved*, and the thing is, they really, truly mean it. They hugged me when I came out, like it was the most natural thing in the world. They drove Hannah across the state for better medical care without question, and I know, without a doubt, that if I said I needed them now, they'd get in the car and drive straight to Kentucky.

"Yeah," I say, voice sticking in my throat. "They said that."

Julia gives a sad little smile. "Mine did, too. Except the thing is, I know it's not true. There *are* things I can't do, things that would absolutely make them stop loving me."

I feel the conversation shift then, a tiny jolt under my feet. The chapel stage is big enough for us to sit comfortably, but here we are, Julia's knee pressed against my thigh, my hand a breath away from hers. Drawn together by the same unknowable gravity that pushed us last night.

"Like what?" I ask.

Julia shrugs. "Like steal the communion wine."

229

"You wouldn't do that anyway. You think wine is gross."

"Okay, true. But I also can't miss curfew or sneak out to parties."

"Boring. They'd totally forgive you for that. What else?"

I don't mean for it to sound like a challenge, but there it is. Julia's fingers slide over mine, the slightest, featherlight brush, and every cell in my body pulls taut.

"I can't forget an assignment," she says. "I can't fail a class."

There's another confession here, I think, something delicate. I lean in, ignoring the flush creeping over my chest. "That's all?"

"I can't . . ." Julia's gone still next to me, face indistinguishable from the carved busts staring down at us. A marble statue. A frozen saint. She clears her throat and tries again. "I can't skip church. I can't talk back, I can't wear certain clothes, I can't—"

She breaks off, biting her lip like she's physically preventing the words from tumbling out. I tilt my head. "Can't what?"

She's touching me on purpose now, she must be. I know what her hands feel like. I've held them a hundred times, so when one of them slides up my thigh now, when I feel the heat of it all the way through my denim shorts, I don't quite know what to make of it. In fact, I'm still looking down, distracted by the sight of her pale pink nails against my bare skin when Julia leans in, slips her other hand around the back of my neck, and kisses me.

It's clumsy and fast, like she's afraid I'm going to vanish beneath her. And even though part of me wondered, even though I hoped this might be where we were heading, I'm so surprised that I fully forget to kiss her back until she pulls away.

SAY A LITTLE PRAYER

"Oh," I say, brain gloriously, completely blank. "I see."

Then I grab the front of her shirt and pull her toward me.

This kiss is softer, more hesitant. I slide my hand along the curve of Julia's waist, pulse leaping when she leans into the touch. I wonder how long we've both wanted to do this, how long Julia's been telling herself not to. Her thumb skims down the line of my throat, and I have the brief, terrible thought that she can probably feel the blood pumping embarrassingly fast under my skin before she pulls me against her.

There's a certain irony, I think, to doing this in a chapel. There are a dozen different Jesus statues looking down on us. There's a pulpit at Julia's back with an open Bible on top. There are dozens of people who have told me, in explicit detail, how wrong this kind of desire is, and I do not care. I brace a hand against the carved wood as Julia's mouth opens under mine. Her fingers skim up the back of my shirt, tracing the groove of my spine, and I think, briefly, that if this is lust, if this is some deadly, unforgivable sin, I'll gladly burn for it.

Julia pulls back, breath shaky in my ear. I want to keep her like this. I want to memorize the wild look in her eyes and the feeling of her hair tangled between my fingers, but when she straightens, something cold slips into the space between us.

"Oh," she whispers. Then, softer, "Oh no."

She shoots to her feet, and I throw out a hand just in time to avoid toppling after her. "What's wrong?"

"Nothing!" Julia presses a trembling hand to her mouth. "It's nothing, I just can't. I'm sorry. This is a mistake."

I flinch, surprised at how much the word stings. *Mistake.* I wait for her to stop, to realize how that sounds and correct herself, but Julia keeps pacing, each step more agitated than the last.

"This can't happen," she whispers. "If anyone knew . . . If my father . . ."

She trails off, and my chest squeezes into a fist. Because I remember how it felt last year to hear Pastor Young tell the entire congregation that it was impossible for gay people to enter the kingdom of Heaven. God simply wouldn't allow it. It didn't matter how many years I'd spent memorizing prayers or singing in the worship band. It didn't matter that I'd done everything right. This was something I couldn't control, something that would forever change the way certain people thought about me.

"It's okay," I say, sliding off the stage to join her. "I get it. He doesn't have to know. I won't tell anyone, if that's what you're worried about."

Julia ignores me, fingers twisting in her hair as she turns to pace another lap. "It doesn't matter. It still happened."

"And you think that's a bad thing?"

"Yes! I'm not you, Riley! I can't walk around kissing whoever I want."

I suck in a sharp, surprised breath. Julia's eyes widen. She stumbles to a halt, hands flying to her mouth.

"I'm sorry," she says. "That's not what I meant."

But I think I know exactly what she means. That this is wrong, even if no one can see us. That it's still a sin because her father said so. The revelation is strangely numb in the hollow cavern of

SAY A LITTLE PRAYER

my chest, like I'm watching it happen to someone else. I swallow over the painful lump in my throat. "'I don't always think he's right, you know.'"

Julia blinks. "What?"

"That's what you said." I wave a hand at the stage. "'I don't always think he's right.' Doesn't that extend to this, too?"

"That's not . . ." Julia's mouth presses into a thin, pale line. "This is different."

"No, it's not." I step forward, reaching for her even now. "Do you remember what he said that first day? That the seven deadly sins are like a one-way ticket to hell? He said they were absolute, that there's no room for nuance, but he was wrong. He's been wrong about so many things, Julia. Yesterday, Amanda and I broke all those little ornaments hanging from our base in the woods. It was wrath, sure, but it felt *good*. And the night before when we all snuck into the kitchen? That was gluttony, but the alternative was literally starving until morning. That's not a bad thing!"

It feels good to talk about this after a week of silence. My words tumble over each other like they're afraid of getting left behind, and when I reach for Julia's hand, she lets me take it.

"I'm supposed to write that essay, remember? Mr. Rider wants to know what I learn here, and this is it. That it's not all black and white. I've been committing the seven deadly sins—sloth, greed, gluttony, wrath, lust." I tick them off on my fingers. "They're not necessarily bad, and it's way more complicated than he wants us to believe."

Julia's gaze flicks over my face. "You're doing what?"

"It's fine," I say. "They're just empty threats, Julia. Something your dad uses to control the people around him, and I can finally prove it."

"Oh." Julia's face is unreadable, but her hands have gone cold. Slowly, she extricates herself from my grip. "So that's why you kissed me? To check another sin off your list?"

She might as well have slapped me. "What? I'm not—"

"No, go ahead." Julia waves a hand at the empty chapel. "Make your sermon, Riley. Tell us what you learned this week. Was it all at my expense?"

She starts pacing again, and it occurs to me that even though I've seen Julia angry before, she's never really been angry with me. It makes me feel wrong, off-balance, like the entire chapel is slowly listing to the side.

"It's not like that," I say. "I just want to show people he's wrong. He's ruined so many lives, and we don't have to listen to him if we don't want to. He doesn't have to be in charge. That's it."

"That's it?" Julia whirls to face me. "So it's not at my expense, you're just trying to ruin my family? That's your defense?"

"You just said you don't agree with him! You can't even kiss someone without thinking about what he'd do. Wouldn't it be easier for everyone if he wasn't here?"

Julia's jaw tenses. "Show me."

I blink. "What?"

"Show me," she repeats. "All the proof you've been gathering this week. I want to see it."

SAY A LITTLE PRAYER

I open my mouth, then close it. There are a lot of things scrawled in the pages of my prayer book that I don't want her to read. "I can't. Ben took my bag back to the cabin."

Julia turns without looking at me and marches across the chapel. "Then, let's go get it."

"Wait, I don't—"

But she's already gone, pushing through the doors and onto the path. I bite back a curse and scramble to follow. Sure, I can understand how it looks from the outside, but this is *Julia*. She knows me, and I can't, for the life of me, figure out why she's this mad.

The others are already back from lunch by the time we reach the cabin. They look up when the screen door flies open, eyes widening as it smacks the opposite wall with a sharp bang.

"Show me," Julia says before anyone else can speak. "I want to see it."

Vaguely, I'm aware of Delaney rising to her feet, but the others seem rooted in place. I swallow over my rapidly closing throat. "Can we just—?"

"*Show me*," she repeats. "It's the only reason you're here, right? Let me see what you wrote."

I shoot a glance toward my bunk. My bag sits on the floor next to my suitcase, both workbooks still tucked inside. Slowly, like I'm caught in a dream, I reach down and tug the prayer book free. Julia snatches it from my grip and flips it open, eyes skimming from page to page.

"'Sloth was easier than I thought,'" she reads aloud. "'I told

235

Delaney and Greer to sit under the table this morning instead of building Gabe's stupid shelter, and it worked. Maybe this won't be as hard as I thought. Maybe everyone else will be just as easy to trick.'"

I wince. Hearing it out loud makes it sound ten times worse. Julia flips a page and continues.

"'I don't understand how people are happy here. It's like they're all lying to me, pretending to believe in this thing that doesn't even make sense. I knew I was right to leave, but I didn't think I'd be the only one smart enough to see through all this.'"

Torres takes a hesitant step forward. "Did . . . you write that?" she asks.

"No." I shake my head. "I mean, *yes*—I wrote it, but it's just a first draft."

Julia closes the book and tosses it onto my bed. In the time it takes to land on my pillow, I feel my chance to defuse the situation vanish. "But you still wrote it," she says. "You said it yourself—you've been tricking all of us into carrying out your personal vendetta while pretending to be our friend."

"I'm not pretending!"

"What would you call it, then? Because I don't think my friend would write those things."

My hands curl into fists. "Why? Because I said your dad is a piece of shit? That's not really a surprise, Julia."

Julia stiffens. Behind me, Greer mumbles something that sounds suspiciously like "Yikes," but Torres is the one who steps between us.

SAY A LITTLE PRAYER

"Enough," she snaps. "What's going on?"

For a second, something like fear flashes across Julia's face. *She thinks I'm going to tell them*, I realize. She thinks I'm going to tell everyone we kissed like it's some terrible secret. For some reason, the fact she thinks so little of me hurts more than her dismissal.

"It's nothing," I say. "That was harsh. I'm sorry, but it's not about you."

Julia folds her arms. "No, it's just about how much you hate my dad, apparently."

I can't help it. I let out a rough, high-pitched laugh. "Of course I hate him! He's the reason I left, Julia. He's the reason Hannah can't come back. Did you honestly think I was okay with that?"

"I don't know what to think! You never talk about it! It's like this secret, taboo subject you never bring up."

"But you know," I say. We're straying dangerously far from our original argument, every emotion I've ignored for months suddenly rising to the surface. "Do you just not care?"

Julia's shoulders slump, expression softening ever so slightly. "Of course I care," she whispers. "It's . . . complicated."

"Why? Because you're scared he'll turn on you next? Because you're afraid of what'll happen if he finds out you're not as perfect as you pretend to—"

"*Don't.*"

The edge in her voice is back, grating against my rapidly fraying self-control. It's definitely fear driving her now. I recognize the way it pinches the corner of her mouth, but I don't care. "You can't have it both ways," I say. "You can't tell me how much you want things to change when it's convenient and then do nothing about it."

Julia shakes her head. "That's not my responsibility."

"It's not mine either! I don't want to be here, but I also don't want to live in a world that lets people like him do whatever they want. He's going to hurt you, too."

It's the one thing I'm sure of. Maybe our kiss meant nothing. Maybe Julia was just curious. Maybe she'll shove herself so far back in the closet that none of this will matter, but I don't think she can deny it forever. Eventually, something will slip, and the very people she's defending will turn on her, too. I wait, breath tight in my chest, but when Julia's gaze drops to the ground, I realize this conversation is over.

This time, no one's coming to save me.

"Fine," I say, reaching for the door. "Ignore it. Maybe you're safe here, but this place is hurting me, too. I don't think my friends would be okay with that."

"Then, maybe we aren't friends."

Julia still isn't looking at me. She's standing with her head down, hands balled at her sides, but she might as well have shouted in my face. There might be a world where I salvage this somehow, where I let Julia rage and acknowledge this as the defense mechanism it so clearly is. But I'm tired of giving everyone the benefit of the doubt. I'm tired of no one standing up for me, so when I open my mouth again, it's to say the one thing I know will end this once and for all.

"I know you think you're different," I whisper, watching her shoulders tense with each word. "I know you think you're this great person and amazing ally, but that's not true. You've always been just like him."

The color drains from Julia's face in a single vivid rush, but I don't stay to see the aftermath. I came here to destroy this place, didn't I? Maybe I can't do that without taking Julia down with me. So when her hand twitches at her side like she wants to reach for me, I pretend not to notice. Instead, I walk straight out of the cabin and back into the sticky afternoon as thunder rumbles ominously overhead.

XVII

POV: You're Watching Me Have a Proper, Full-On Gay Crisis

*T*he first thing I notice the next morning is the silence. There's no alarm, no thumping bass, no jumbled mess of lyrics. Then there's a hand on my shoulder, someone leaning over me in the dark, and I jolt upright. Because Amanda Clarke is standing next to my bed with her too-sharp nails casually resting on my collarbone.

"What—?"

Our cabin door flings open to reveal Cindy on the porch, pen tapping rhythmically against her clipboard. "Let's go, girls," she calls. "Time to get moving."

I groan and drag a hand down my face. "What's going on?"

Amanda releases me. "We're leaving," she whispers. "They want us to pack."

Maybe I'm still dreaming. The sky outside the windows is a heavy shade of gray, like the clouds are physically pressing against the trees. But maybe that's a dream, too. Maybe everything that happened yesterday was a product of my guilty, over-

SAY A LITTLE PRAYER

worked imagination. Maybe Julia and I are still speaking.

Then Cindy flips a switch and floods our cabin with cold, unforgiving light. "I'm not kidding," she says. "There's a huge storm system heading our way, and Pastor Young wants to make sure we all get home safe. I know it's a bummer, but there's a light breakfast in the cafeteria. You can grab your phones on the way out, but we really need to be on the road in an hour, okay?"

She doesn't wait for confirmation before hopping off the porch and making a beeline for the next cabin. The screen door slams behind her, and it's like the sound finally breaks through our collective fog. Everyone moves at once, scrambling out of bed to gather toiletries and fish lone socks from the corners of the room. I do a quick sweep of my surroundings, tugging my sheets off the bed as I go, but it's not until I stuff them in my suitcase that the reality of the situation hits me.

We're leaving.

We're leaving with my essay incomplete, any chance I might have had to fix things slipping through my fingers.

I'd eaten dinner alone last night, tucked in the back corner of the chapel where no one could see. I had looked down at the spot where Julia kissed me just a few hours earlier, and for the first time in over a year, I tried to pray. *Where did it go wrong?* I was supposed to fix things. I was supposed to help, but all I'd done was hurt the people I care about. I'd sat with my hands clasped and my eyes squeezed shut, waiting for some omnipotent, disembodied voice to break through the walls, but nothing came. There was only quiet.

241

Julia doesn't look at me as she finishes packing her suitcase. Torres trails her onto the porch, backpack hanging off one shoulder, but Delaney pauses in the doorway. For a second, I almost think she's waiting for me. Then she sighs and leans over to rest her chin against Greer's shoulder.

"I hate that I'm going to miss this place," she murmurs.

Greer rolls her eyes. "I know. It's embarrassing."

She slings an arm around Amanda's shoulders as the three of them take in the cabin one final time. My gaze drops to the floor. It's like I'm interrupting, like I'm once again lingering at the edge of a group no one asked me to join. By the time I wrestle my suitcase closed, they're gone. I sigh and push myself to my feet. I've just turned toward the door when our alarm blares to life. I jump, heart pounding as the familiar chorus bounces off the walls, and for a second, I genuinely consider smashing the entire thing against the floor. A destructively fitting end to the week.

Instead, I grit my teeth and seize the handle of my suitcase. The last thing I hear before the door slams shut behind me is the second earsplitting verse of "Flexin' on That Gram."

I think the lowest point of my life was the time I got food poisoning at Scheana Mayville's tenth birthday and threw up on top of her cake. But when I board the bus home and find that the only open seat is next to Patrick "Guitar Guy" Davies, I think this might just be up there. Especially when he nudges my shoulder and says, "Bummer about the storm, right, Renée?" as if he hasn't sat in front of me in homeroom every day for the last three years.

SAY A LITTLE PRAYER

"Yeah, Patrick," I say, sliding down in my seat. "It's a real bummer."

I text Mom the update as soon as we pull onto the road. Her response comes less than a minute later. Got it—can the Youngs give you a ride home? I'm finishing up some reports for work.

My chest aches at the casual question. They probably could, but there's no way I'm asking. I bite my lip and type, no, they're all staying to help unpack.

It's probably not a lie. I'm sure there are church things to do when we get back, and I'm sure they don't want to do them with me. In fact, I think Pastor Young would be perfectly happy to never see me around his children ever again.

By the time we pull into the parking lot, Patrick is on his second consecutive listen of a playlist titled "Songs I've Crashed My Car To," and I'm two seconds away from tossing his enormous pair of definitely not soundproof headphones out the window. Mom is already waiting for me, standing outside the car despite the drizzling rain. I drag my suitcase across the parking lot, and she immediately scoops me into her arms.

"Rough luck with the storm," she murmurs into my hair. "Did you have a good week?"

In that moment, it takes everything in my power not to laugh. "It was fine."

She helps me tug my suitcase into the back, grimacing as cold rain drips down the sleeves of her jacket. When I slam the trunk, I find Pastor Young watching me from across the parking lot. He lifts a hand in our direction, mouth set in a pleasantly friendly

243

smile, and Mom offers him an acknowledging wave in return.

"What an asshole," she mutters.

Any other time, I might have cracked a smile.

Hannah's in the kitchen when we arrive, physics textbook open on the counter before her. She jumps up when we enter.

"You're home!" she cries, wrapping me in a crushing hug. Then she pulls back, eyes narrowing like she's somehow absorbed my bad mood through osmosis. "What's wrong?"

I shake my head. "Nothing. Just tired. We were up pretty early this morning."

Again, it's not technically a lie.

"Why don't you go unpack?" Mom says. She runs a hand through my hair, then grimaces when her fingers catch in the tangles. "And take a shower while you're at it. We have leftovers for lunch when you're done."

She doesn't have to tell me twice. I drag my suitcase upstairs, then turn and flop face-first onto my unmade bed. Clothes are still scattered across the floor from my disastrous attempt at packing. There's a pair of socks on the pillow next to my face, but I don't care. I close my eyes and get exactly three seconds of peace before my door flies open.

"Hey!" I snap. "That was closed!"

Hannah ignores me. She just shuts the door and turns to face me with both hands planted on her hips. "What's wrong?"

"Nothing!"

"Bullshit. You might be able to fool Mom, but you can't fool me. What happened? Are you and Julia in a fight?"

SAY A LITTLE PRAYER

I push myself into a seated position and clutch the nearest pillow to my chest for support. "Why would you say that?"

"Ben texted me before you got back."

I roll my eyes. "Of course he did."

"Riley—"

"It's fine, Hannah. I just called her dad a piece of shit, she said she doesn't want to be my friend anymore, and that's it. There's nothing to say."

To my horror, my throat burns with something that feels suspiciously close to tears.

"Oh." Hannah's gaze softens. She takes a tentative step forward. "I thought you two didn't talk about him?"

"Yeah, well." I rub a hand over my face. "Maybe we should have, because she seems to think that just because I'm not marching through the streets demanding her father's head on a spike that I'm just, like, fine and cool and completely over everything he did to us."

My voice breaks on the last word. I sink my teeth into my bottom lip, but it's too late. There's a tremor, then a crack, and everything just sort of collapses. I'm crying. Like, *actually* crying for the first time in months, and I realize, with a sickening jolt, that I don't know how to stop.

"Oh no." Hannah flies across the room. She wraps me in her arms, and even though I spent the last week longing for the comfort of her beside me, I can't seem to catch my breath now.

I can't stop crying either, and it's so embarrassing that all I can do is bury my face in her shoulder and wait for it to stop. When I

245

finally pull it together long enough to drag a hand over my face, Hannah's sitting on the bed next to me. I have the strangest feeling that her arms are the only thing holding me together right now, so when she looks me in the eye and demands I tell her everything, I do.

I tell her about this year's camp theme and our opening sermon and how I'd seized the opportunity to prove Pastor Young wrong by committing all seven deadly sins. I tell her about the big things—like my essay and all the ways I planned to blast it out—but I also tell her about the small in-between moments, too. Sneaking into the kitchen at night, watching Torres win capture the flag, laughing with Delaney and Greer at the bonfire. I tell her about Julia kissing me in the chapel and all the secret, dangerous things it ignited in my chest.

When I finally stop for breath, Hannah's eyes are wide. "Wow," she says. "That's a lot." Then, after a second, she adds, "Is Julia okay?"

"Oh my god, Hannah." I shove her away. "This is supposed to be about me."

"It is! Sorry, I'm just saying that you've had time to come to terms with who you are. You could go to anyone in this house right now and say, 'Hey, I kissed Julia,' and we'd help you through it. She doesn't have that. This might be completely new for her."

"I don't care. I *literally* came out to her a year ago. She could have talked to me."

Hannah lifts a brow. "Like how you talked to her about Pastor Young?"

246

SAY A LITTLE PRAYER

Fair point. I scowl and shove the pillow over my face, momentarily blocking out the light. There's something else clawing its way through me, a confession I've never been able to put into words. I don't even know if I want to say it now, but Hannah places a hand on the pillow and gently lowers it back into my lap.

"What is it?" she asks.

I grit my teeth and wish, for the hundredth time, that she wasn't so goddamn perceptive. "I think . . ." My voice catches. "I think I'm still mad at her for things that might not even be her fault. And then I get mad at myself for being mad at her because that's not fair, but I still feel it right here." I press a hand to my chest. "I was so mad at Amanda and Greer for how they treated you, but Julia is your friend, too. She didn't stand up for you that day, and she's never stood up for me either. And I get that it's different for her, but it's been a year and I'm still so *angry* about it."

Hannah runs a soothing hand down my arm. "Are you more upset for you or me?" she asks. "Because I don't blame her for what happened. No one stood up for me that day."

"I would have," I say. "I should have been there. I should have stopped it."

"Don't. That wasn't your fault, Riley. None of this is your fault."

But some dark, twisted part of me still thinks it is. I bite my lip as a fresh wave of tears threatens to choke me. "I was supposed to be there for you," I whisper. "I'm supposed to be your rock."

"Says who?"

"Mom," I say. "Everyone."

"Well, that's not fair." Hannah pulls away from me, just

247

enough to spread her arms. "Do I look breakable to you? Seriously, Riley. Is there something I'm missing?"

I shake my head. "I don't think that's what she meant."

"I know what she meant. I know what she's trying to do, but I'm fine. I don't regret any of the choices I made, and the fact that you and Mom keep blaming yourselves for not being able to protect me is, frankly, insulting."

She glares at me over the pillow, and for the first time in months, I think she might be right. I've been treating her like something delicate, trying to piece her life back together as best I can, but Hannah has never been weak. I nod, swallowing back tears as the knot in my chest finally starts to loosen.

"I know. I'm sorry. I just really wanted you to be okay."

Hannah's gaze softens. "Has it ever occurred to you that I think the same thing about you?"

"I don't know what you're talking about. I'm obviously, like, extremely fine and stable."

"Right," Hannah says. "Totally. So, what are you crying about, again?"

I don't even know, at this point. I let out a choked laugh and for a minute, we just sit there, pressed together in the corner of my bed. Eventually, I sigh and swipe the back of my hand across my face. "I hate that I still miss it, you know," I whisper. "Pleasant Hills, I mean. Isn't that weird?"

Hannah shakes her head. "No. I miss it, too. Mostly the little things, like hearing Patty Perkins sing 'O Holy Night' on Christ-

248

SAY A LITTLE PRAYER

mas Eve or the really good soap in the women's bathroom."

"Or that room behind the treasurer's office where we found that *Playboy* collection," I add. "Or the powdered donuts they serve before Bible study."

"Oh my god." Hannah laughs. "What did they put in those?"

"Salvation, probably." I take a deep, steadying breath and look up at the ceiling. "Do you still believe in God?"

Her answer is immediate. "Of course."

"How?"

"Well, realizing that Pleasant Hills Baptist Church doesn't have a monopoly on the Christian faith was a big part of it." Hannah leans back on her elbows. "I like the idea that we're not alone. I think it's better to assume the best and treat people well than worry about Pastor Young's arbitrary rules for skipping hell."

I glance at her out of the corner of my eye. "It's that easy?"

"No, of course not. I really hate what that place has become, but I like to think it's not everything."

It's so similar to what Julia said yesterday that I wonder if the two of them have discussed this before, if they've been finding ways to help each other through, a little at a time. I don't know if I'll ever be able to unwind the concept of faith from the way Pastor Young preaches it. The two are so intertwined that I wouldn't know where to start, but Hannah, like usual, is already several steps ahead.

There's a knock on my door, and I look up to find Mom hovering in the doorway. I straighten, hurriedly wiping the tears from my face, but she makes no move to cross the threshold.

"Sorry to interrupt," she says. "But you have a visitor downstairs."

Her voice is carefully neutral, but her jaw is tense, like she's pushing the words through gritted teeth. My brow furrows. "Who?"

"Amanda Clarke."

Hannah stiffens beside me. I groan and slide off the bed. "It's fine. I'll take care of it."

Mom shakes her head. "She says she's here for Hannah, actually."

"She's—" I blink, instantly suspicious. "Why?"

"Excellent question." Mom looks like she's about three seconds away from busting through the floor and taking Amanda out herself. "You don't have to," she says as Hannah sits up on my bed. "Trust me, I'm more than willing to say you're not here and send her home."

Hannah shakes her head. "No, it's okay. I'll see her." She stands and offers me a small smile. "Assume the best, right?"

I swallow over a sound of protest and strongly suspect Mom is doing the same. She watches Hannah walk downstairs before shaking her head and muttering something that sounds suspiciously like "too nice."

Maybe she's right. Maybe Hannah is about to get her heart broken by the same girl who'd ripped it out in the first place. Maybe everything Amanda told me this week had been a lie.

I think it's better to assume the best and treat people well than

SAY A LITTLE PRAYER

worry about Pastor Young's arbitrary rules for skipping hell.

I haul my suitcase onto my bed and start unpacking. It would have been nice if just one member of the Pleasant Hills congregation had thought that way about me. If they'd smiled and assumed the best and held out a hand when the loneliness turned insurmountable. Things might have been different.

It's not until hours later, when I come downstairs to find Hannah and Amanda still sitting together on the porch with soft, hesitant smiles tugging at the corners of their mouths, that I think they still could be.

XVIII

Breadstick Slut

The summer before eighth grade, Julia and Ben went to Greece with their grandmother. It was before any of us had phones, and I'd spent the three weeks we were apart writing increasingly detailed letters about everything they'd missed. When they finally got home, I found that Julia had done the same. That's how much we missed each other. Now, though, I don't think this weird silent purgatory has an easy way out.

On Monday, I watch from the safety of my bedroom window as Ben and Julia leave for school twenty minutes earlier than usual. It's hard not to think of the choice as personal, another ploy to avoid me, too. That morning, I leave my newly completed essay on Mr. Rider's desk on the way to first period. It's not my best work, but I'd shredded the notes in my prayer book the day I got home, just tore the pages from the binding and let them pile in the corner of my room. They didn't matter. Those notes caused more trouble than they were worth, and I hadn't even finished what I set out to do—two sins short of seven. Instead, I'd typed three double-spaced pages full of things I thought Mr. Rider

SAY A LITTLE PRAYER

wanted to hear, things that would make him sit back and con-gratulate himself for saving another Godless, delinquent student from the dark path of cynicism. It's nothing like the passionate, vitriolic speech I'd imagined, but I can't bring myself to care.

Bold of anyone to assume I'd be the one to change things, any-way.

When I take my seat in homeroom, I find that even though I feel irreversibly different from the girl I'd been last week, every-thing else remains the same. Patrick Davies still looks like he can't quite remember where he's supposed to know me from, Leena and I still pass notes in the back of our calculus class as Mrs. Rockwell explains derivatives, and Kev still spends our lunch period frantically finishing his homework.

"It's the first day back," Leena says, watching him scribble a list of French verbs on the back of his hand. "How are you already behind?"

Kev shrugs and flips to the back of his textbook. "The better question is, how do I already have three French assignments?"

But it's nice, I think, to know that some things don't change. It makes the rest of the week easier to bear. When I show up for tech rehearsal Monday night, I know that Rex Blythe will miss his opening cue no less than three times, someone's going to forget the choreography we cleaned up before spring break, and Ms. Tina is going to end the night on the verge of a mental breakdown. It's comforting. Honestly, the only difference in my day-to-day schedule is that Torres sometimes offers me a tenta-tive wave when we pass each other in the hall.

253

And Julia isn't speaking to me. There's also that.

"Please, Ben," I say when I finally catch him pulling into the driveway on Wednesday night. "I just want to talk to her."

He's still in his school uniform, dark green slacks speckled with paint, and I wonder if he's working on a new piece for his summer program. I wonder if he'd tell me if he was or if we're also not speaking by default. He sighs and drags a hand through his hair. "What happened?" he asks. "She changes the subject whenever it comes up."

So he doesn't know. Julia usually tells Ben everything, and I don't know if it makes me feel better or worse to learn she's not talking now. I could tell him about the kiss. I could tell him about what Julia said or about how I still remember the way her jaw tensed right before she said, *Then, maybe we aren't friends.* I could tell him there's a part of me that wants to write her off completely for that, just relegate her to the back of my mind and never think about her again.

Instead, I kick the toe of my shoe into the grass. "It's . . . complicated."

"Clearly," Ben mutters. "Fine. I'll see what I can do, but you know how she is. She'll talk when she's ready."

But as the week drags on and my phone remains stubbornly quiet, I wonder if either of us will ever feel ready for this. By the time Sunday rolls around, the despair I've languished in all week has slowly but surely hardened into anger.

"It's not fair," I say, flopping back against Hannah's pillows. "Why do I have to be the bigger person?"

SAY A LITTLE PRAYER

It's just past nine, way too early to be awake on a weekend, but I can't sleep. Opening night is four days away, I've barely studied for my upcoming econ test, and I can't concentrate even if I wanted to because every spare moment is currently dedicated to being very annoyed at Julia Young. Hannah watches me in her vanity mirror as she pins her hair into a tight bun. She also has a show next week, and judging by the open dance bag on her bed, she's planning to spend this afternoon in the studio. I wonder if Amanda will be there, too.

"It sounds like you both said things you regret," Hannah says. "Maybe she feels guilty."

I roll my eyes. "She should. But she could at least say it to my face."

"Well, you're not exactly the poster child for forgiveness, Riley. You're still mad at Liam Robertson for stealing your lunch money in third grade."

"Because he deserves to suffer for that!"

Hannah lifts a brow, and I hear how it sounds a second later. "Okay, fine. I get it. But are we just supposed to do this forever? Am I supposed to avoid her until I go off to college or die?"

My phone vibrates against the pillow, cutting off Hannah's measured response. Ben's name flashes across the screen, and I scramble to answer it.

"Hello?"

"Hi," he says. "Are you going to church this morning?"

"Um, I think you have the wrong number."

"No, we have that camp thing, remember? They're throwing

some sort of party since the seniors didn't get their last day." He heaves a sigh when I don't respond. "Do you ever check your email?"

I don't have the heart to tell him I unsubscribed from the Pleasant Hills email list ages ago. "I'm not going to a church party, Ben."

"It's not about the party." He lowers his voice and adds pointedly, "*Everyone* will be there."

Only then do I realize what he's saying. That Julia will be there. That we could finally talk. She might be able to avoid me out here, but the last thing she's going to do is cause a scene in the Pleasant Hills chapel.

"Fine," I say. "Be right there."

Hannah looks up as I push myself off the bed. "What was that about?" she asks.

I grimace. "How would you like to drive me to church?"

Mom and Dad are already sitting around the kitchen table when the two of us walk downstairs. There's a pot of freshly brewed coffee steaming between them, and when I take a deep breath and announce, "I'm going to church," Mom nearly knocks it over in surprise.

Her eyebrows lift over the top of her newspaper, gaze darting between me and Hannah like she can't quite tell if I'm being serious. "Oh," she says eventually. "Okay."

And it's funny because I know if I actually did want to go back, if I told her I found a new appreciation for Jesus Christ in the Kentucky wilderness, she'd still support me. She'd drive me to

SAY A LITTLE PRAYER

service herself if I wanted. Last week, Julia asked how I knew my parents loved me. I didn't have a solid answer then, but I think if someone asked me now, I'd say it's because of moments like this.

"I'm not actually going to church," I add when Mom opens her mouth. "They're just having this camp party, and I want to talk to Julia. I'm not, like, converting or anything."

"You were already baptized," Dad says without looking up from his breakfast. "You don't have to convert."

"Gross."

Hannah wrinkles her nose. "Humbling."

Mom rubs a hand over her forehead. "Julia will be home in an hour, you know. You could talk to her then."

I hesitate. "It's . . . not that simple."

"So you'd rather corner her at church?"

"Okay, when you say it like that, it sounds dramatic, but I promise it's not! I won't even stay for the service; I just need to see her."

Mom looks from me to Hannah, like her desire to let us make our own choices is warring with her bone-deep instinct to keep us safe. Eventually, she sighs and sets her newspaper on the table. "Okay. Whatever you need to do. But behave," she adds, jabbing a finger in my direction. "And text me if you need a ride home."

I reach over and squeeze her hand on my way out the door. "I will."

It's not until Hannah drops me off in the Pleasant Hills parking lot that I realize I'm still wearing last night's pajama shirt. The jeans I pulled off my floor are technically clean, but the faded

257

BREADSTICK SLUT graphic tee is starting to feel like a poor choice.

"You look fine," Hannah says, waving me out of the car. "Jesus loves bread. That's his whole thing."

I glance over my shoulder as she shifts the car back into drive. "I think his whole thing was *being* bread, actually."

"Even better."

She blows me a kiss through the window and pulls out of the parking lot with ease. I suck in a breath as I watch her go, and then before I can second-guess my own rash decision, I turn and march purposefully toward the front doors.

Someone's updated the sign so it now reads GOD WANTS YOU ON YOUR KNEES. I don't think anyone thought about the implications of that particular statement, but when I open the door and step into the lobby, I immediately stop thinking about it, too. It's been over a year since I've been inside Pleasant Hills Baptist Church, but it still smells the same. Flowers and incense and the dull tang of lemon furniture polish. The air outside is cool and fresh, but it's warm in here, almost stuffy, as everyone files into the lobby. Heads turn as I slink along the back wall, and even though I'd love to think it's because of my incredible shirt, I know it's probably because I'm me. Because there's nothing the Pleasant Hills congregation loves more than a good story.

Did you see Riley Ackerman this morning? Do you think she's back for good?

I'll be the topic of every upcoming prayer request just so people can fish for information while simultaneously feeling good about themselves. I try to breathe, but just get more of that

SAY A LITTLE PRAYER

cloying, too familiar musk straight up my nose. I'm suffocating between the curious stares, and for the first time since getting in Hannah's car, I start to wonder if this is a very bad idea.

"Riley?"

I whirl to find Delaney making her way through the crowd. She's wearing a bright yellow slip dress, her braids pulled back in a high bun. It's a bright contrast to the rest of the congregation, and it takes me a minute to realize why it feels so strange. Because Delaney doesn't attend Pleasant Hills. She's probably here for the party, like me, and even though there are countless things I could say to her now, my first instinct, laughably, is to warn her about her bare shoulders. Someone's going to have a problem with it. They're going to offer her some passive-aggressive lost and found sweater or tell her to leave.

She comes to a stop in front of me, eyebrows lifted in hesitant curiosity. "I didn't think you were coming today."

"I'm not back," I blurt.

"Okay?"

"No, I mean . . ." I squeeze my eyes shut. *Excellent start.* "I just meant that I'm here to see Julia. I don't want you to get the wrong idea."

"Oh, right," Delaney says. "I forgot you think I'm easy to trick."

I wince at the memory of my prayer book notes, all the hurt pieces I'd tucked away. It's not just Julia I need to talk to. "I'm sorry about that."

"I know." Delaney looks me up and down. "I'd probably be more annoyed if you weren't so obvious about it."

259

"Obvious?"

"Please, Riley." She takes my arm and steers me toward the chapel. "All the writing in your prayer book when you thought no one was looking? All the times you casually-not-casually managed to do the exact opposite of what Gabe was trying to preach? You're not as sneaky as you think you are, and neither is Julia."

I look up, chest tightening at the sound of her name. "What do you mean?"

Delaney squeezes my shoulder, then pushes me down the main aisle. "Go. I just saw her walk in with Ben."

It's not an answer. It honestly just raises more questions I don't have time to ask, but I keep moving as Delaney drops into a pew near the back. More people are staring now, eyes tracking me as I weave my way past them. It's not until I reach the front that I finally spot Julia a few rows away, shuffling into a pew with her mother and Ben.

"Julia!" I practically throw myself across the aisle to reach her. "Wait!"

She whips around. Ben follows her gaze, and I watch their eyes widen in unison before Julia's expression smooths.

"What are you doing?"

Her voice is a careful, respectable whisper, but it's still enough to make Mrs. Young glance over her shoulder. She motions Julia forward, then does a double take when she sees me. "Riley!" she cries. "What a lovely surprise. How have you been? I feel like I haven't seen you in weeks."

SAY A LITTLE PRAYER

I plaster on my best church-friendly smile and lie through my teeth. "Great! So good to see you, Mrs. Young."

If it was anyone else, the conversation would have ended there, but Mrs. Young, unfortunately, is a goddamn delight. I've always thought so, and as her face splits into a grin, I think I might be stuck.

"I heard you all had a great week at camp," she says. "I'm sorry it was cut short, but I hope you still managed to enjoy yourself."

I wave a hand. "Oh, it was perfect. We had the best time, right, Julia?"

I risk a glance in her direction, but her face is carefully blank. "Sure did."

"Do you think we should talk about the after-party, maybe? Before service starts?"

If she has any idea what I'm trying to say, she doesn't show it. She just tucks her hair behind one ear and gives me a weak little half shrug. "I don't think that's necessary."

My heart sinks at the vague disinterest in her voice. "It won't take long."

"Sorry." She steps around Ben and follows her mother into an empty pew. "I think we're about to start."

"Julia, I'm—"

The rest of my sentence falters as an organ blasts through the chapel. All around me, people rise to their feet, and I realize, with a sickening jolt, that I'm trapped in the pew behind her, three rows from the front with no way out.

"Didn't expect to see you here."

The voice in my ear is soft, familiar, and I turn to find Amanda Clarke standing at my other side, gaze fixed deliberately on the front. "What are you doing?" she asks.

I grit my teeth. "Nothing."

"You look like you got dressed in the dark."

"You look like a cupcake."

It's true. Amanda's crochet top is roughly the same color and volume of a generously frosted strawberry cupcake. She lets out a soft, unexpected laugh, and when I steal a glance in her direction, I see her parents, standing stiff-backed and silent beside her. Mrs. Clarke shoots me a pointed glare, and I pull back, refocusing on the front as Amanda clears her throat.

Despite my time away, I know exactly how this service will go. I can practically predict the acolytes' steps as they make their way down the aisle toward the array of candles. Pastor Young walks in last, striding toward the pulpit in his billowing white robe. He nods at a few people as he goes, but when he lays a hand on his wife's shoulder, Julia's gaze drops to her lap, like she doesn't want to look at him either.

We stay standing as he leads us through the call to worship, and I hate that I still know every word to every prayer. I hate that I can recite them now, lips barely moving along with the people around me. There's something hot working its way up the back of my throat, and when I try to swallow it down, I think it feels suspiciously like envy. I don't want to come back to Pleasant Hills, but I hate how easy it is for everyone else to believe in something I don't think exists anymore. I didn't real-

SAY A LITTLE PRAYER

ize how much I missed that comfort until now.

Ironic, I think, that I'm still checking deadly sins off my list even now. If I was still at camp, I'm sure I could figure out how to spin this one, too.

Amanda leans back against the pew, arms folded, but I stay perched on the edge of my seat as we creep toward the sermon. Pastor Young can't seem to relax either. He hasn't opened with his usual bad joke or corny pun, and when he looks up from the pulpit, I swear there's a second where his gaze slides deliberately over me. Like he's seeking me out. Like he wants to make sure I'm here for what happens next.

He opens his mouth, and something twists in the pit of my stomach, the anticipation of a coming storm.

"Beloved congregation," he says. "Today, my heart is heavy. It's weary with disappointment, but I want you to know that I stand before you not as an accuser but as a shepherd who deeply loves his flock."

The chapel goes unnervingly silent as people stiffen in their seats, brows furrowed in silent question. I risk a glance at Amanda and find her looking just as confused as me. *What the hell is happening?*

"As most of you know, we had our spring youth retreat down in Rhyville, Kentucky, last week," Pastor Young says, bracing both hands on the podium. "Our time was unfortunately cut short, but it was still immensely rewarding. It's one of my favorite parts of this calling—guiding young minds as they learn to walk with the Lord. Watching them spread God's word within their own communities. This year, however, it appears some of our youth have chosen to walk a different path, one that leads away from his grace."

My pulse quickens. It's too loud in my ears, but I think he's talking about me. He has to be. I'd given Mr. Rider a perfectly innocent, well-written essay on Monday, but maybe that wasn't enough. Maybe Pastor Young had somehow learned about my original plan or read the things scribbled in my prayer book.

Julia could have told him.

The thought is chilling, slicing right down to my bones, but the more I think about it, the more it makes sense. Julia was the only one who'd known the specifics of my plan. She knew I wanted her father gone, and she must have sold me out to protect her own secrets.

"My disappointment doesn't come from a place of self-righteousness," Pastor Young continues. "Truly. Instead, it comes from a deep concern for this congregation. It hurts me when people purposefully squander God's love, and I hope it hurts you, too. We're all sinners, of course, but those ways don't have to define us. In fact, the Lord calls upon us every day to repent, and that's what I encourage you all to do now."

He turns away from the podium, digging for something within the folds of his robes. I tense, muscles quivering as I wait on the edge of my seat. What could he possibly have on me? The contents of my prayer book are scattered across the floor of my room back home, hidden from his prying eyes, so I should be safe.

I should be safe, right?

SAY A LITTLE PRAYER

I'm still running through the events of last week, trying to pin-point where I could have gone wrong, when Pastor Young finally straightens and holds the mysterious item up to the light. In that instant, it's like my brain disconnects from my body, unable to process what I'm seeing.

Because he's holding a prayer book all right, but it's not mine. The familiar blue cover reflects the flickering candlelight as he waves it around, and if I didn't know better, I'd think it could belong to anyone. It looks exactly the same as the one in my trash can back home except for one thing. The single butterfly sticker pressed onto the back.

Julia's sticker. Julia's book, now clutched firmly in her father's hands.

XIX

I Accidentally Unionize a Midwest Baptist Church

I'm not lost for words often. In fact, every teacher I've ever had has described me as "precocious," which everyone knows is code for "can't shut up to save her life." But when Pastor Young holds Julia's prayer book up for everyone to see, it's like my brain is physically unable to process words.

"A counselor found this in one of the girls' cabins after everyone left," Pastor Young says. "Every camper was given a prayer book like this at the start of the week. It was supposed to be a place for reflection, somewhere to communicate with God, but I'd like to share what this one says instead."

I don't think Julia is breathing. What little I can see of her face has gone bone white, hands gripping the edge of her pew. I remember how secretive she'd been with her writing, how she always made sure to shield it from prying eyes. She hadn't even shown me, and I doubt she wants it read aloud now, in front of the entire congregation.

I swallow and try to force my scrambled brain to think, to *do*

SAY A LITTLE PRAYER

something. But Pastor Young flips open the book before I can. He stops at a page near the middle and leans toward the mic.

"'I feel like I'm standing at a crossroad of who I am and who I've been taught to be,'" he recites. "'There's this thing that happens when she takes my hand. I don't even know if she realizes she's doing it, but every so often, she'll run her thumb down the underside of my wrist, like she's just reminding herself I'm there. I know it's supposed to feel wrong. I've heard that my entire life, but there are days where I think I'd give this up completely if it means she'll keep touching me like that.'"

My next inhale slices me open, a knife lodged somewhere around my sternum. I feel Amanda shift forward in her seat, and I know she recognizes the book, too. We both saw Julia writing in it. Everyone in our cabin did. If Pastor Young wants to know who wrote it, it won't be hard to get someone to spill. I clutch for Amanda's hand, desperate for something to hold on to, and before I fully realize what I've done, she squeezes mine in return.

Pastor Young continues, derision dripping from every stolen word. "'How could something be wrong when it feels like that? How am I supposed to believe it's a sin? I don't know if I believe in a God who enforces that, but I do know I want to kiss her. It might be the only thing I've ever wanted, really.'"

When he looks up again, something like triumph blazing behind his eyes, I don't think I've ever hated him more. I want to storm the stage. I want to tear that book from his hands and tuck it away where no one can see because I know what those realizations feel like. I remember how alone I'd felt when I came out last

267

year, how absolutely petrified I'd been to say the words out loud, and here's Pastor Young, reading someone's private journal like they're on trial. Like he's already decided the writer is guilty.

My muscles tense, and Amanda's hand locks around mine. She can probably feel how much I want to launch myself over the pews, but I think I could make it. I'm only three rows from the front.

Slowly, Pastor Young closes the book and sets it back on the podium. "I'm sure I don't have to lay out the problem here," he says. "We just spent a week learning about the dangers of sin, and I still failed to keep one of our youths from falling off the path. I accept responsibility for that. I seek forgiveness, too, but we need to move forward together." His gaze sweeps over the congregation and again, I have the strangest feeling he's looking directly at me. "Girls—if this book is yours, or if you have any idea who wrote it, please come forward. Lay your sins before our Creator. Acknowledge your faults and ask for forgiveness."

No. Terror fists itself over my heart. He can't do this. He can't out Julia in front of everyone. She'd full-on panicked after we kissed. She hadn't been able to explain why she'd done it or say the word "gay" out loud, and she shouldn't have to if she's not ready. She's still sitting right in front of me, so close I could reach out and touch her if I wanted to. Her shoulders are too stiff, gaze fixed purposefully ahead like every cell in her body has gone rigid, and she's squeezing Ben's hand like it's her last remaining lifeline.

He shoots a glance toward her white-knuckled grip, and when

SAY A LITTLE PRAYER

he looks up again, something like realization dawns across his face.

If Mrs. Young is at all aware of the emotional crisis happening next to her, she doesn't show it. Her posture is still casually relaxed, hands folded in her lap, but she's staring firmly at the hymnal in front of her. Like if she doesn't acknowledge her husband's request, it won't affect her. All around us, people are shifting uncomfortably in their seats, shooting quick, nervous glances at the pews around them before averting their gazes, too.

I wonder, briefly, if this is what happened the day Pastor Young kicked Hannah out, too. If everyone just looked away and pretended like she didn't exist.

Pastor Young sighs, drumming his fingers on the podium as the silence stretches before him. "This isn't a punishment," he says. "Remember the words of Psalm 51:10. 'Create in me a clean heart, O God, and renew a right spirit within me.' That should be a reassurance, not a warning. Seek forgiveness. Humble yourself in the name of the Lord."

I have the strangest feeling that Amanda's grip on my hand is the only thing keeping me seated. *Strange*, I think. *Who would have thought?*

When Pastor Young speaks again, his frustration is clear in every word. "There is no sin that can't be forgiven. We know this to be true, but lying? Covering up the sins of others? That's wrong, my friends. Let's support the sinners in our midst today. Let's walk with them together into the light." He picks up the book again, shaking it toward the crowd. "Who wrote this?"

269

For all Pastor Young's talk about learning and growing in the spirit of the Lord, there never seems to be any grace to do so. It's perfection or nothing, faith based on fear, and I don't think he has any intention of stopping now.

I watch Julia's shoulders sag, like she's exhaling a breath, and in that instant I know she's going to confess. She'll admit the book is hers and face whatever consequence comes her way because she's physically incapable of letting someone else take the blame. It's her fatal flaw, one of the things I love about her, and it's going to ruin her life.

But I don't think it would ruin mine.

I suck in a breath and before I can think better of it, I drop Amanda's hand and shoot to my feet. "It's mine," I say. "I wrote it."

If I thought the chapel was quiet before, it's nothing compared to what happens now. It's like my words hang in the air, suspended between the panes of stained glass. *It's mine. I wrote it.* Amanda slides down in her seat, gaze averted like she's trying to put as much space between us as possible. At the altar, Pastor Young's face softens into a slow satisfied smile.

"Riley Ackerman," he says. Straight into the microphone so everyone can hear my name. "I should have known. We gave you a second chance, and you returned to poison the flock."

His voice is too prepared, too collected, and I wonder, briefly, if this was his plan all along. Maybe he always thought the book was mine. Maybe he was only hosting a camp party to ensure my return, and maybe this is a punishment for all the things I'd said

SAY A LITTLE PRAYER

last week. For every part of me he couldn't control.

That's fine, I think, hands curling into fists at my sides. I'll gladly be his scapegoat if it means Julia walks out of this unscathed.

I can feel her watching me, open-mouthed from the next pew. Slowly, she shakes her head in the smallest back-and-forth motion, but I don't back down. I don't want to. In this moment, I think I finally understand the strange, elusive truth I've been chasing since the day I left Pleasant Hills.

Pastor Young only has the power people decide to give him, and right now, I'm not afraid.

"Well?" Pastor Young holds up the book, and I realize he's expecting me to speak. "Is there something you'd like to say to your congregation?"

There absolutely isn't. I'm not repenting for a single thing, but before I can tell him, *No, actually, I'd rather drown myself in your vat of holy water*, there's a shuffle of movement behind me.

"She didn't do it. That's my prayer book, actually."

I whip around so fast I nearly lose my balance, and when I see Greer Wilson standing a few rows behind me, there's a moment where I seriously wonder if I'm hallucinating. Maybe I fainted a while ago, and this is just a product of my panicked imagination. Because there's Greer with her shiny brown hair and silk ribbons, polished cross necklace gleaming against the front of her designer dress. There's Greer with her chin lifted and the beginnings of an "I've Won Two High School Debate State Championships, You *Will* Lose This Fight" smile etched across her face. Her

271

father gapes up at her from the pew, but Greer keeps both hands planted on her hips. She shoots me a fleeting glare, and I hear her voice as clearly as if she'd shouted.

See? I'm not a coward.

Pastor Young looks back and forth between us. His brow furrows, mouth falling open, but Julia flies out of her seat before he can speak.

"Don't," she says. "They had nothing to do with it. It's mine."

I clamp a hand over her shoulder, trying in vain to push her back down. "It's not. It's mine, she's—"

"Enough!" Pastor Young slams the prayer book against the podium. "Sit down, Julia."

She shakes her head. She's trembling under my grip, but her jaw locks in steely determination. "No."

For a second, I think something like fear flashes across Pastor Young's face, right behind his careful mask of calm. "Sit down," he repeats, and as the words leave his mouth, I wonder if anyone has ever had the audacity to tell him *no.*

"This is so weird." Somewhere in the back, another pew creaks. Delaney rises to her feet, arms casually stretched over her head. "I specifically remember having a bunch of gay thoughts last week and writing them down in my prayer book. I kind of thought it was between me and God, though, as in *private*," she adds pointedly. "But anyway, that book is mine."

She flashes me a wink, and I hate that she's too far away to push down. This isn't supposed to be a statement. I'm supposed to take the blame, move on, and keep everyone safe. But when I

SAY A LITTLE PRAYER

watch Pastor Young's fingers curl around the edge of his podium, I think it might be too late.

"I admire your loyalty, girls," he says, voice silky with exaggerated patience. "But this is clearly Riley's book. It was found in her cabin, under her bed."

"It was our cabin, too," Greer points out. "That evidence would never hold up in court."

"But this isn't a courtroom, Miss Wilson. This is a community. All I want is for Riley to humble herself in the eyes of the Lord. She can be punished accordingly, and we can all move on. Her sins don't have to affect you."

Delaney folds her arms. "Wait, I'm confused. Do you want to punish whoever wrote that book, or do you want them to lay their sins before our Creator? I feel like you can't have it both ways."

I glance over my shoulder, silently willing Delaney to sit down and leave it alone. The people around her keep shifting in their seats. They're exchanging strained, uncomfortable glances, but the longer I try to catch her eye, the more I don't think they're aimed at us. In fact, as I listen to whispers swell around me, jumping from one side of the chapel to the other, I think their judgment might actually be aimed at Pastor Young.

"Hold on!"

I hadn't seen Torres before, but there's no mistaking her voice now. She jumps to her feet, then clambers on top of the pew so she can glare at Pastor Young over the crowd. "That's mine. I remember writing it."

273

Next to me, Amanda lets out a muffled groan. She drags a hand down her face and whispers something that sounds strangely like *What the hell?* before pushing herself to her feet.

"It's not hers," she says. "I wrote it."

Mrs. Clarke looks like her daughter just admitted to kicking orphaned puppies for fun. She flashes a brilliant Miss Teen Ohio 1998 smile at the congregation before wrapping a hand around Amanda's wrist and hissing, "*Sit down*," through clenched teeth.

Amanda shakes her off. "What? If he wants me to repent, I'll do it. They shouldn't get in trouble for something I did."

"Yeah!" Ben leaps to his feet. "Same. I wrote it, too."

"Sit *down*, Benjamin."

Pastor Young's voice cuts through the growing whispers and just like that, the crowd goes still. Ben drops back in his seat, but Pastor Young is still glaring at me. "I'm going to ask you again," he says, voice trembling with silent fury. "Did you write this?"

"Yes," I say, but the word seems to echo around the chapel. I realize too late it's because the others answered, too, still speaking in unison.

In front of me, Mrs. Young finally meets her husband's gaze. I watch her throat bob as she gives her head a single shake, like she's silently urging him to let it go. I know he won't. We're alike in that way, I think. We'll hang on until resentment rots us from the inside out, until we don't recognize the person we used to be. Pastor Young takes a deep breath, and when he speaks again, his words are finally directed at someone else.

"Amanda," he says, and I feel her flinch beside me. "You've always been a faithful servant of the Lord. You come from a good family with good values. I know this wasn't you. Why don't you tell me what you know?"

For a second, I think she might. Her shoulders tense, folding in on themselves as I watch, and I take her hand again. I hold her in place like she'd done for me, and slowly, I feel her fingers close around mine.

"I told you," she says, lifting her chin ever so slightly. "It's mine."

Last week, there was a chapter in our camp workbook about the virtue of humility in opposition with the deadly sin of pride. It made it seem like pride was a bad thing, something to fear, but as I stand here now, I think Pastor Young was just afraid of what we could do with it. Of what would happen to the church if everyone looked up and thought, *No, I like who I am*.

I don't think I ever needed an essay to take him down. I don't think it would have worked. It's one thing to write about what needs to change, but it's another to stand up for it here, in front of everyone, and show them there might be another way. Maybe Pastor Young will do this again next week. Maybe by then, everyone will have forgotten about us, but I know one thing for sure. He won't get away with it today.

I take a deep breath and meet his eye over the podium. "Exactly," I say. "It's mine."

Then I reach over the pew and grab Julia's hand, tugging her and Amanda into the aisle. Vaguely, I'm aware of the new rush of whispers, of the others following us out of their seats, but I don't look back. I don't give Pastor Young the chance to send us away. Instead, I lift my chin, flash him one final grin, and walk out.

XX

Our Lord and Savior Tom Hanks

There's this painting in the Pleasant Hills women's bathroom everyone hates. It shows a sobbing acrylic Eve clutching a half-eaten apple to her chest as the depiction of God, who looks strangely like Tom Hanks for some reason, throws her from the Garden of Eden. It's not the subject of the painting that freaks people out; that's standard practice around here. It's just that the entire thing, from the way God Tom Hanks's nails dig into Eve's bloody arm to the expression of pure, unadulterated terror on her face, is so eerily lifelike that I always wonder how the artist put it together in the first place.

But that's why it's here, I guess. Another chilling reminder of what happens to women who disobey.

It's the first thing I see when I yank Julia into the bathroom, and even though a year away has dulled the memory, the sight of it reflected in the mirror still makes me jump.

"Jesus Christ," I gasp, clutching a hand to my chest. "That thing gets me every time."

Julia doesn't answer. She doesn't even look up as I sag against the wall, directly under the painting in question. She just braces her hands on the edge of the sink and bows her head. Her ponytail falls over one shoulder, temporarily hiding her face, and for a second, I think she looks like the girl in the painting—broken and miserable and utterly alone.

Then the door flies open. I whip around, ready to fight, but it's just the others piling into the bathroom behind me. Amanda with her cheeks still tinged the same shade of pink as her ridiculous cupcake shirt. Greer in her perfectly pressed church clothes. Delaney, who looks seconds away from putting her fist through a wall, and Torres, who has both hands resting on her knees like she needs to catch her breath.

The bathroom is too small for all of us, but as I look from face to incredulous face, I realize I'd been wrong before. Julia's not alone. None of us are.

"Holy shit," Torres whispers to no one in particular. "That was *so* fucked."

I choke back a laugh, and I don't know if I'm more surprised at the sound or the fact that Torres, of all people, is the one swearing. Julia sucks in a shaky breath, and then she's laughing, too, head thrown back as she clutches the sink with her free hand. It's a wild sound, almost hysterical, like she doesn't know how to stop.

I step toward her. "Julia . . ."

"No, it's fine," she says, laugher still trembling through the end of every word. "I'm good. Everything's good; I'm *fine*."

She's not. That couldn't be more obvious. Her fingers tighten

SAY A LITTLE PRAYER

around the edge of the sink, but when she straightens and runs a hand down the front of her dress, she's almost pulled herself together enough to sell it. If I didn't know her so well, if I hadn't also spent the last year suppressing my own pain, I might believe her.

"Thanks for checking on me," she says, voice unnaturally steady. "But you should go back inside. The sermon isn't over yet, and it'll be a lot worse if you stay here."

Amanda rolls her eyes. "Honestly, Julia, I'd rather spend all day in this bathroom than listen to anything my mother has to say right now."

I glance over my shoulder. "You don't think Miss Teen Ohio 1998 would be impressed with your behavior?"

"Miss Teen Ohio 1998 hasn't had a complex thought in decades."

"Well, I'm definitely not going back," Delaney says. "I don't even go here."

Torres nods. "Exactly. I mean, I *do* go here," she adds. "Obviously. But I'm not walking back into that."

Julia looks like she wants to protest, but before she can start, there's a loud knock on the bathroom door. Greer immediately slams herself against it and yells, "*We're busy!*" in a way that makes me think she might have been a club bouncer in another life.

"Chill! It's just me!"

Ben, his voice barely audible through the wall. I motion for Greer to let him in, and when she opens the bathroom door, he

279

looks just as flustered as the rest of us. He's panting, a thin layer of sweat already forming on his upper lip.

"What's going on?" Greer demands. "What are they saying?"

It's comforting to know that Greer Wilson's intrinsic urge to gather every piece of gossip known to man still works in situations like this. I haven't thought about the congregation since I walked out the door, but now that she brings it up, I am curious what we left behind.

Ben shakes his head. "It's nothing, really. He's still preaching and pretending your walkout was all part of his bigger lesson, but people are wondering where you went."

I glance down at my phone. It's almost ten thirty. The service will be ending soon, and I don't want to be here when the congregation gets out. Maybe the others can go home with their parents, but I'm not sending Julia back to her father now.

Ben looks like he's reading my mind. "We should probably head out before this is over," he says, nodding in Julia's direction. "How did you get here?"

"Hannah," I say. "We can call her or my mom. Someone will come get us, and then you can hide in my room as long as you need."

"Thanks." Ben looks up, past me to where Julia still stands next to the sink. "You good, Jules?"

Julia doesn't move. She just stands with her feet planted on the cold tile, arms wrapped around herself. Ben takes a careful step forward. "Julia," he murmurs. "Look at me."

She does. Her next inhale catches on the tail end of a sob, and

SAY A LITTLE PRAYER

I see the exact moment her resolve crumbles. She sags into her brother's arms, fingers curling in the fabric of his shirt as he carefully turns her away from us.

I've seen Julia cry, of course, but it's always been from something visible. When a rogue softball broke her nose during practice. When we saw *Little Women* in theaters. When her childhood dog died. I knew how to comfort her then, what to say and how to say it, but this is uncharted territory. Ben whispers something into her hair, and even though I can't make out the words, I see Julia nod ever so slightly. It's another second before he finally lets her go.

"Okay," he says, turning to face us. "Why don't we figure out how to get home? Riley and Julia will meet us outside in a minute."

I look up. "We will?"

"Yup. See you in a bit."

He ruffles my hair as he passes, holding open the bathroom door so the others can file outside. Then it falls shut, and it's just me and Julia, alone in the church bathroom with a very graphic depiction of female sin.

The irony, of course, is not lost on me.

I brace a shoulder against the wall as Julia turns back to the mirror, wiping her face with the back of her hand. Despite everything, her mascara is still perfectly in place, her slightly puffy eyes the only sign she's been crying at all. There are only a few feet of cold bathroom tile between us, but for some reason, she feels miles away. She feels like a stranger. We've never gone this

281

long without speaking, and our last conversation had been more than a little contentious. I'm not sure how to unwind the hurt still tangled between us, so maybe we don't. Maybe whatever comes next is the beginning of the end.

I tense as Julia turns to face me, mentally preparing for a dismissal. Then she takes a deep breath, looks me dead in the eye, and says, in a practiced, matter-of-fact tone, "So. I'm gay."

A surprised laugh bursts out of me. I can't help it; she says it so casually, like we've had this conversation a hundred times before. Like hearing her say it doesn't light my skin on fire.

"I'm actually a lesbian, if we're being specific," she adds quickly. "I'm pretty sure. Because I don't think I've ever liked anyone who wasn't a girl, but I also never thought I'd ever say it out loud, so, guess my dad's good for something, you know?"

She flashes me a wobbly smile, but the fact that she's trying to make a joke now, when everything so far has been at her expense, makes me furious. "He's not," I say, more forcefully than I mean to. "It's none of his business."

"He seems to think it is."

"Yes, well, he also thinks that economic recessions are caused by having gay people in government. You don't ever have to talk about it if you don't want to, Julia. You don't owe it to anyone."

It's what Mom told me the day after I came out, when she found me in the driveway, trying to figure out how I was going to handle everyone at school. She'd sat down next to me, looked up at the darkening sky, and said, *You don't owe anyone a piece of*

SAY A LITTLE PRAYER

yourself, you know. It's okay to have it be just yours for now, and that doesn't make it any less valid.

Julia looks down, bottom lip caught between her teeth. "I think I owe it to you, though," she whispers. "I kissed you and then . . . Oh my god, Riley. I was so horrible to you."

She buries her face in her hands and something in my chest crumples. I push myself off the wall, stopping just short of where she stands on the other side of the sink. Close enough for either of us to touch if we wanted to. "Yeah," I say. "You were, but I think you're allowed to be a little horrible when you're having a gay crisis at church camp. It's not like I was a shining example of good friendship either."

"No." Julia wipes the back of her hand across her face. "But I know what you were trying to do. I know it wasn't personal."

"Then why did you act like it was?"

She hesitates, gaze fixed somewhere between the toes of her shoes. When she speaks again, every word feels deliberate. "I know you hate the way my dad talks about being gay. I know you're angry at him, and that makes sense. You're allowed to be because he hurt you directly, and if I admitted that he hurt me, too, that I was also angry with him, it felt like I might as well write *lesbian* across my forehead. Because everyone would know."

She leans back against the sink, shoulders angling toward me ever so slightly. It feels like an invitation, like a crack in the door, but I don't know how to open it the rest of the way.

"I know you probably hate me, too," she continues. "You prob-

283

ably think I'm a coward or that I don't care about what happened to you or Hannah, but that is so far from the truth. I hate that you've been hurting all year. I hate that you didn't feel like you could tell me, and I hate that I can't do anything to fix it now."

My hands ache, and when I look down, I realize I'm gripping the edge of the sink, too. I let go and rub my palms against my jeans. "I wanted to tell you everything," I admit. "I thought about it so many times, but it didn't seem fair. What were you supposed to do? Listen to all the reasons I hated your dad and then tell me he's a piece of shit?"

"No, that's your job, apparently."

"Right." I almost smile. "I'm sorry about that. And I'm sorry for comparing you to him. It's not true."

Julia's shoulders sag with obvious relief, like that particular condemnation was still plaguing her. "Thank you. I want us to talk, you know. I want us to help each other."

"Me, too," I say. "I miss you."

"I miss you, too." For the first time all day, a genuine smile tugs at the corner of Julia's mouth. "You know how many things happened this week? You know how many times I started to text you before I remembered we weren't speaking?"

I look up. "What sort of things?"

"Like, did you hear Mike Fratt got arrested?"

"What?" I surge forward. "No! *Why?*"

"Tax evasion, I think. He never reported any of that money he won last summer."

"Oh my god." I laugh. "You know how many bad albums

SAY A LITTLE PRAYER

he's going to drop now? He's in debt, Julia. That's how everyone makes money these days."

She laughs, too, hand flying up to cover her mouth, and I feel the pressure between us snap. I wonder then if we're ever going to talk about the rest of it. All the deep, secret feelings Pastor Young had pulled from her journal and poured into the chapel. I meant what I said earlier—we don't have to—but that doesn't stop me from wondering if the things Julia wrote are true.

I think she senses the shift in the air because she bows her head, hair temporarily shielding her face from view. "Those things I wrote . . ."

"You don't—" I start, but Julia holds up a hand.

"I was writing about you. I think you probably know, but I'm sorry you had to hear it like that and not from me, because you . . ." Her voice breaks. "You are, without a doubt, one of the best things in my life. I can't lose you, so if that means we forget I ever wrote that and just keep being friends, I don't care. But I can't take another week of you silently hating me."

My throat aches. "You thought I hated you?"

"You hate a lot of people, Riley. It's not an unreasonable conclusion."

"But this is *you*," I say. "I don't hate you. I've never hated you. I was angry, sure, but mostly at myself because I don't want to lose you either." I hesitate and add, "Did he really think that book was mine?"

Julia winces. "Probably. He didn't think it was mine, that's for sure. If he did, we would have handled it privately."

285

"Do you think he knows it's yours now?"

"I don't know."

I nod, and even though every aspect of the movement hurts, I take a careful step back. "Then maybe you should give yourself some time. Just to process everything and figure out a way forward that's not, you know, totally detrimental to your entire life. And if you need me to *not* be around while that happens, I get it. I won't be mad."

Julia chokes out a laugh. "Don't tell me what I want."

"I'm not! I'm just trying to—"

"Riley."

There's her hand, next to mine on the sink. Last time we touched had felt accidental, like something that was bound to happen sooner or later, but when Julia slides her fingers through mine, firmly lacing them together, I think it's purposeful. Like this time, she means it.

"Don't," she whispers. "I can do it."

And when she reaches up to cup the side of my face, I know the instant her lips brush mine that she means this, too.

The kiss is soft, a gentle exploration. It feels like a prologue, like there's a world where I kiss her a million more times just like this and each time means a little bit more. Julia's fingers slide into my hair. Something about having that first kiss in a chapel and this one in a church bathroom makes me feel powerful. Like if I can do this here, in front of Biblical Tom Hanks, and not burst into flames, how many other rules could I break?

SAY A LITTLE PRAYER

How many other choices could I make for myself, away from the chains of this place?

When we break apart, her cheeks are flushed, eyes wide.

"What?" I ask. "Was that too much?"

Julia shakes her head, fingers brushing lightly over her lips. "No. I just didn't know it could feel like that."

And god, if that doesn't make me feel *alive*.

She's right, of course. She always is. There's a voice echoing in the back of my mind now, a relentless beat of *This is how it's supposed to feel*. Like I've only just now figured out how to take a real breath. I squeeze her hand and finally, gently, pull her away from the sink.

"Ready to go?"

Julia glances over her shoulder, gaze skimming from the painting to the line of stalls to her own reflection etched in the bathroom mirror. Her expression solidifies. "I think I've been ready for a while now."

And in that moment, I think she's talking about more than leaving the bathroom. Again, she laces her fingers through mine. Again, I squeeze her hand. Then we finally open the door and walk out of Pleasant Hills Baptist Church together.

XXI

Amen.

The summer before sixth grade, Ben cleared a patch of grass in the corner of his family's backyard, tilled the soil until it came up clean and fresh, and planted an obscene number of sunflowers. The first batch died in an early frost. The second perished to a family of rabbits, but eventually he got it right. They grew little by little until they towered above the fence, a few square feet of sunshine in a dreary Ohio suburb. They come back every year, right as summer drapes itself over the city, and that's where the three of us have taken every group photo of the last four years.

Birthdays, holidays, middle school dances. There's a picture of Hannah holding her first college acceptance letter, one of Ben posing with a blue-ribbon portrait, and another of freshman year Julia lifting her shirt to show off her appendectomy scar. There's one of me before a middle school dance, wearing a truly hideous teal chiffon dress with one finger held in the air in an effort to replicate the *Hamilton* poster, and countless pictures of the four of us tangled together on the lawn.

It was always a group effort, our parents standing together

on the Youngs' back patio snapping photo after photo as Mom called, "Riley, honey, focus! Look at the camera!" every five seconds. It didn't work. I'm not looking at the camera in most of the pictures, but she still stuck them to the fridge anyway—a scrapbook of sun-soaked memories set against the backdrop of those same familiar flowers.

So it's strange, I think, for the four of us to be dressed up for one of the most important events of our high school careers and *not* be picking our way through the Youngs' backyard toward Ben's sunflowers. Instead, we're all standing at the top of Torres's circular driveway, feet aching in too-tight prom shoes, waiting for the limo her mom ordered to whisk us away.

Torres's mom is, apparently, always doing things like this. Hosting sleepovers and movie nights in the backyard when the weather turns warm, letting her children deck out the pool house to celebrate their friends' birthdays, and ordering her daughter a custom prom dress from Milan, just because she can. They live in the same gated community as Greer's family, but while the Wilsons walk around expecting everyone to know exactly who they are and what they do, Mrs. Torres had welcomed us into her home from the minute she buzzed us through the gate.

I have no idea how people end up with this kind of money, but since neither of them have told us what they do for a living, part of me likes to think it has to do with organized crime. That's certainly more interesting than Mr. Wilson giving people new noses.

"You having fun?"

I look down as Torres sidles up next to me. Even in her heels, she's several inches shorter than the rest of us, the hem of her pink gown barely skimming the top of the cement. She cut her hair sometime last week, and now it stops just below her chin. I think the effect is striking, a girl who knows exactly what she wants, and that's probably how she ended up here in the first place—a sophomore who'd effortlessly convinced some junior basketball player she'd never spoken with to ask her on a date.

"Yeah," I say. "I can't believe your mom got a limo."

Torres waves a hand. "Please. That woman doesn't need an excuse to get a limo. She said, and I quote, 'You only go to senior prom once.'"

"You're not a senior," I point out.

"Sure, but Hannah is."

We both glance over to where Hannah stands a few feet away, brushing grass off the hem of her dress. Ben crouches next to her, and when he straightens, there's a moment where I genuinely think the rest of us could cease to exist and he wouldn't care because he'd still be looking at her.

They're not dating. Hannah has made it perfectly clear that she's going to California alone, but I also don't think she'd be here tonight if Ben hadn't shown up on our porch last week with half a dozen roses and a charmingly earnest handwritten poster. I think she likes him more than she wants to admit. I think the thought of trusting someone like that again will always be hard for her, but when she'd pinned a boutonniere of pink carnations to his chest, I had to physically restrain myself from pumping both fists in the air.

SAY A LITTLE PRAYER

After an entire semester of agonizing over her well-being, jumping to protect her at every possible opportunity, it's nice to know she'll be okay without me. That she can be her own rock if she has to.

Julia's watching them, too, standing far enough away from me to feel casual but just close enough that I can brush my hand against hers between the folds of our gowns. Her hair is braided across the crown of her head, pulled back in a low twist. The dark maroon of her dress makes the auburn color pop, complementing the subtle makeup shimmering across both eyelids. Ben said the look was very "Mickenlee Hooper at the Grammys," and I nodded like I totally understood what that meant.

Now there's a knowing little smile spreading across her face. When she turns to look at me, I know exactly what she's going to say before the words leave her mouth. "They look good together."

I nod, and then, when Torres turns away to head back to her date, I lower my voice and add, "You look good, too."

She blushes, color working its way across her chest, but when she laces her fingers through mine, I don't let go.

The thing is we're not a couple either. Not as far as people know, anyway. Mostly, it's a balancing act, the careful art of giving her parents just enough information about where we're going and what we're doing to keep them satisfied while still finding moments alone. They can think whatever they want about us. They can have their suspicions, pray that their wayward daughter finds guidance, but I know for a fact neither of them will ever ask her directly. They won't risk getting an answer they don't want, and Julia will never tell them.

She'll get out of here next year, too. Maybe we'll leave together, find a place where no one cares who we are or where we come from, but for now there's this. Our clasped hands between our skirts, the occasional press of her shoulder against mine, and the overwhelming certainty that it won't always be this way.

There's a corsage on my wrist tonight, of course. There's one on Julia's, too, the two pieces just different enough that they don't look like a set. Dad helped me pick them out last week, and when Mrs. Young caught sight of the flowers on her daughter's wrist, she'd stopped midphoto and asked who her secret admirer was. My stomach dropped, momentarily worried we'd been too bold, but Julia had just looked her straight in the eye and said, very seriously, "Jesus Christ."

Her mother didn't ask again, and I had to duck behind Hannah so the others wouldn't see me laughing.

The adults are still standing on the porch, one eye on us, the other on the bottles of wine Mr. Torres keeps bringing out from the kitchen. They're all deep in conversation, my dad utterly immersed in something Mrs. Young is saying, and there's a minute where I think Mom almost laughs, too. Pastor Young is noticeably absent, and I have a feeling it's because Mrs. Torres told him, in no uncertain terms, that he was not welcome anywhere near her family's home.

Greer's dad had donated an obscene amount of money to Pleasant Hills the day after we walked out. I think Amanda's parents did, too, because no one on the board said a single thing

SAY A LITTLE PRAYER

about it to them. Delaney, Torres, and I, however, received a page-long document stating that due to "uncouth behavior," the three of us were no longer members of Pleasant Hills Baptist Church. The names of the eight board members were scrawled across the bottom with Pastor Young's signature inked in stark black and white.

Delaney had taken one look at the thick ivory envelope and cried, "I literally don't even go there!" before shredding it into the trash.

I'd tossed mine aside, too, but Torres had been quiet, reading the letter again and again. Guilt rose in my chest the longer I watched her. Her family had always attended Pleasant Hills. Maybe she wanted to stay. Then she looked up, paper stretched tight in her hands, and said "Who the hell says 'uncouth'?" with so much disdain Delaney and I had burst out laughing.

We burned the letters that night with a matchbox Julia stole from her father's personal collection, a fitting goodbye, and that's why we're here now, clustered in Torres's driveway instead of the Youngs' backyard.

I don't know if anything will ever really change at Pleasant Hills. In the month since we left, some people organized. They wrote letters to the board expressing concern on our behalf and questioned Pastor Young's role in it all, but no one orchestrated another walkout or boycotted his sermons. He still preaches every week. I'm sure he still says terrible things, but I know for a fact that he hasn't singled anyone out since. People are watching him now—the congregation, the town, the board. They're all locked behind closed doors, quietly wondering if he's a risk and monitoring their own public image.

That's where their cowardice comes in handy, I think. Because they don't care about anything enough to make a stand, not even their own pastor.

Julia and Ben spend most Sundays with us, watching bad Hallmark movies and eating brunch. They still get dragged to a service or two when their dad puts his foot down, but for the most part, there's a distance. I know that Julia's gone to Delaney's church in Franklin a few more times. Once, she even took Hannah with her, and when the two of them came back, they looked so genuinely happy it momentarily made me think I could try again, too.

Mostly, though, I've been thinking about Julia. Julia sitting cross-legged on my bed as we help Ben pack for art school. Julia handing me an ice-cream cone in the lobby of the DMV after I finally passed my driver's test. Julia running laps on the baseball diamond with her hair tucked in a cap.

Julia kissing me in her car at a red light, in the dark, in the privacy of my bedroom. Anywhere and everywhere we can.

It's not perfect. Most days, I feel like I'm walking a delicate, dangerous line, but it's mine. Ours. The first time Julia ditched class to meet me at the local Dairy Queen, I took one look at her in her pressed school uniform and thought I understood what Hannah had been trying to say about faith. I don't know how long we'll last. I don't know if this kind of feeling is forever, but I know I have her *now*.

SAY A LITTLE PRAYER

I only let go of Julia's hand when the limo pulls into the driveway. The driver steps out to open our door, and we all cram inside, waving goodbye to our parents and pretending not to notice them snapping more pictures as we do. I've never been in a limo before, but when I gaze up at the ceiling sparkling with fake starry lights, I decide I have no choice but to become rich and famous. I deserve to ride in something like this all the time.

"Hey, check it out!" Torres's date—whose name may or may not be Travis—pulls a bottle of bubbly liquid from a refrigerated compartment to his left. "Free booze."

Julia squints at the label. "That's apple juice."

"No." Maybe-Travis shakes his head and uncorks the bottle with an ease that makes me think he's done this plenty of times. He takes a long sip, then pulls a face. "Okay, yeah, that's pure sugar."

The ride across town isn't long. Last year's prom had been at the zoo, and it's clear the graduating seniors blew our entire events budget because this year, we're stuck at the banquet hall next to the high school. It's a nice space, the same venue the drama club uses to host cabaret shows every fall, but the idea of slow dancing next to the polar bear enclosure is too good to give up.

Maybe we'll upgrade next year. Maybe I'll rent out the zoo myself, just so I can kiss Julia in the flickering light of the aquarium. That's true romance, I think.

We pull up to the curb, and the driver rolls down the partition to tell us he'll be back at eleven. He hands Torres his business card, and the others clamber outside in a flurry of skirts

295

and wilting flowers. I'm about to follow when Julia's hand curls around my wrist.

"What?" I ask.

Her eyes flash, then she leans in and kisses me hard against the seat. I tug the door closed with my free hand, momentarily shielding us from the outside world, and we get exactly two seconds of privacy before someone raps on the window. I pull back. Julia's grinning, and when I press a hand to my mouth, I find that I am, too.

"We're coming!" I yell, and the knocking abruptly stops. Someone giggles, and there's a scurry of footsteps as the others head inside. I roll my eyes and slide across the seat. "We should go."

"Should we?" Julia's looking at me with one eyebrow raised. Usually when she does this, I know exactly what she's thinking, but now I'm completely lost.

"Yes?"

"Hmm." She leans forward and knocks on the partition. When it lowers, she sticks her head through the opening and asks, "Are you getting paid hourly? Or is this kind of an all-night thing?"

"I'm yours until eleven, ma'am," the driver says.

"Excellent. Can you take us to the Taco Bell on Juniper Street?"

I lurch forward. "What are you doing?"

She shrugs, like this is all completely normal. "Going to the Taco Bell on Juniper Street."

"Now? What about the dance? Those tickets were not cheap."

"Relax." She brushes a kiss to my cheek. "We'll be right back. If this was a real date, we'd get dinner first, right?"

SAY A LITTLE PRAYER

I try to point out that if this was a real date, we'd be borrowing my mom's minivan, not living it up in the back seat of a limo, but when I open my mouth, nothing comes out. I rarely see this version of Julia, the one who breaks the rules, who abandons our plans and sets off through town in a limo, just so she can kiss me again. I want to hold on to her as long as I can.

I take her hand, and this time, when she squeezes back, there's no reason to let go.

Maybe one day, we won't have to commandeer a limo for something like this. Maybe next year, things will have shifted enough for us to slow dance together in the middle of the Madison High School gymnasium. That future always felt imaginary, something that belonged to other people, not me. Now I'm not so sure. Maybe by the time we're ready, the predetermined boundaries of what we're allowed to be in this town will have slipped, just a little. Enough for us to get through.

I look over at Julia as we turn back into the street. The fake ceiling stars overhead catch in her eyes, glimmering off the sequins sewn into the bodice of her gown. *More*, I think, when she leans her head against the seat. *More, more, more.*

And this time, there's no lingering voice telling me it's wrong.

This time, when I kiss her, there's no one around to tell me to stop.

ACKNOWLEDGMENTS

This will come as a surprise to no one, but I did a lot of thinking about my own religious upbringing while writing this book. Pleasant Hills Baptist Church is by no means a replica of any of the churches I attended throughout my life, but rather an amalgamation of many experiences spread across many brutally formative years. I had cool youth pastors! I had youth pastors who wore faded jeans and played the guitar at us! I had youth pastors who looked me in the eye and told me people could stop being gay if only they prayed hard enough and maybe donated to the church a bit! The duality of man! The point is that this book—which started out as a silly, "haha, maybe one day" bullet point idea in my Notes app—ended up becoming an incredibly necessary, cathartic writing experience, and I'm so grateful for everyone who helped bring it to life.

To Claire Friedman, who's been the best, most surefire advocate I could ever ask for. Once when I was deep in the query trenches, a friend asked me what qualities I wanted in an agent, and I was like, "IDK, someone who can sell my books and who also likes me?" I feel very fortunate to have ended up with someone who checks those boxes and many, many more. And, of course, endless thanks to the rest of the incredibly talented Inkwell Management team.

To Maggie Rosenthal, who heard the "haha, maybe one day" bullet point idea from my Notes app and let me write a whole book about it. Thank you for always treating my work with such enthusiasm and care. Working with you is a complete joy, and I simply cannot believe we're on book three!

A huge thank-you to everyone at Viking and Penguin Young Readers for working tirelessly to get this book into readers' hands, and an extra special shout-out to Louisa Cannell and Kristie Radwilowicz for giving me the cover of my dreams for the second time in a row.

To all the booksellers and librarians who have stocked my books and recommended them to readers. I still have to pinch myself whenever I find my book in the wild, and I know a big reason why they're out there in the first place is because of your enthusiasm. Ten-year-old me, who read Animorphs in the back of her public library and secretly thumbed through romance novels in her hometown Barnes & Noble, is literally quaking.

To the friends who help make the publishing industry a little more bearable: Serena Kaylor, Sasha Smith, Sophia DeRise, Mary E. Roach, Brit Wanstrath, Morgan Spraker, Libby Kennedy, Emma Benshoff, Jenna Miller, and Brian D. Kennedy. It's so silly that some of my favorite writers also happen to be my friends. Who would have thought! Your talent speaks for itself, but your generosity and kindness are truly unmatched. You inspire me to be a better writer, a better person, and a better friend. And to my AMM group chat, which is still going strong all these years later. Watching you all thrive has been my very favorite part of this journey.

To my family, blood and chosen, who've never missed an opportunity to promote my books to random, mostly unwilling strangers. Thank you for the lifetime of love and support and for bearing with me through copious deadlines. To Maria (and Athena), who once again had to live with me while I sold, drafted, revised, and marketed another book. We could live together another four years and it still wouldn't be long enough for me to express how much your friendship has changed me as a person. To Sarina Anderson, who knows better than anyone that sometimes you have to laugh at your religious trauma or it swallows you whole. I'm endlessly proud of you and the life you've built for yourself on your own terms.

And to Emily, who's teaching me every day that love stories don't just exist in the pages of books. You're my Metaphorical Jesus Lighthouse in a storm.